MW01439740

CONVERGENCE

Convergence

Cat Austen

Cat Austen

This is a work of fiction. Names, characters, businesses, places, events, locales, and incidents are either the products of the author's imagination or used in a fictitious manner. Any resemblance to actual persons, living or dead, or actual events is purely coincidental.

Copyright © 2022 Cat Austen
All rights reserved. Quotes used for review purposes are cool, though.

ISBN: 979-8-9893873-1-1

Cover design by K.B. Barrett Designs

Self-published by the author because she's a control freak.

Other Titles by Cat Austen

Convergence- *August 2022*- a polyamorous, contemporary, romantic suspense.

Aisle 5- *November 2022*- a contemporary, erotic, romantic comedy.

Solace- *August 2023*- a dark romantic comedy, mafia, why choose (polyamorous). First in a trilogy.

Spite- *November 2023*- second book in Solace trilogy.

Check out catausten.com, and subscribe to my newsletter at catausten.com/subscribe to be the first to hear about ARC (advanced review copies) and new books!

This book is for all the “nerdies” who are building their own family and finding their voice.

And, *always,* for the stay at home moms.

Author's Note

This book is a work of fiction that contains the topics of bio-weapons and bacteria. It is largely inaccurate and highly fictional. I have to say this because my sister is a biologist and would literally murder me if she read what I've written. Again, this is fictional. For funsies.

Also, this book contains mature themes including sex, three-somes, and some male-on-male action. It is not suitable for readers under 18.

1

The late summer sun was bright on the sidewalk as I left the hotel. The walking directions on the navigation app on my phone told me to head left down the sidewalk. It was a ten-minute walk to the Truman College campus where my orientation into their prestigious Ph D. program for microbiology was being held.

I shouldered my black overnight bag and headed off down the mostly empty Cleveland city sidewalk. I placed a quick pick-up order for the Starbucks I had scoped out when I checked in yesterday, so I wouldn't have to talk to the barista.

I walked confidently and with reserved excitement for this opportunity ahead of me. I had been recommended by a graduate school professor for this program and my coursework from that class had single-handedly earned me an invitation to this program at Truman College. I had been selected specifically for this work, which had yet to be disclosed to me, but I knew it had something to do with bacteria, as that had been the concentration of my coursework with the professor who had recommended me. During my only interview for the program, completed over Zoom, Professor Hoffmann had explained that the nature of the experiment we would complete required confidentiality, but I would be compensated for my work and contribution. It wasn't unusual to have secrecy in the scientific community, but having to sign a non-disclosure agreement before even hearing what the experiment entailed seemed out of the norm. I had hesitated only a moment before accepting. Professor Hoffmann had quoted my coursework, so it felt like they needed me for this experiment.

After picking up my caramel macchiato and blueberry muffin, I walked and drank and checked my text messages. Caleb, my sort of ex- sort of friend with benefits, sent me a message.

Caleb: Good luck today! You'll do great!

I replied in thanks as a message from Dad came in.

Dad: *heart emoji. thumbs up emoji.*

I smiled and returned the heart. Pocketing my phone, I ate my blueberry muffin while I took in the new scenery and thought about my most recent date with Caleb. I wasn't sure if it could be called a date since we had stopped being exclusive after our first semester of undergrad away from each other, but we still met up for dinner, a movie, and sex when we were both in town. He knew about my opportunity at Truman, and while he was back in our hometown and single, he supported my achievements. For sure, he was not leaving my life completely. He was one of the two people in this world I could talk to, my dad being the other. He was also one of two people who knew the physical pain and emotional struggles I dealt with after my accident and my mom's death.

A little clench of my stomach went with every thought I had about my late mom, even now after twelve years. She and I had been in a terrible car accident that killed her on impact and left me in the hospital for months. I had to miss her funeral due to being in a coma.

I shook my head and finished my muffin as the navigation app alerted me to my arrival at Harold Hall at Truman College. With a pep in my step, I quickly ascended the stone stairs and pushed open the large wooden doors. The grand architecture suggested this was once a church and was now part of a college, priding itself on its contributions to the science community. I found that to be a bit tongue in cheek, but I appreciated the beauty of the building. A small receptionist desk was placed at the back of a marbled lobby, and I approached the young woman.

"Are you here for the PhD meeting?" she asked before I could even begin thinking about how I was going to ask her where to go.

I nodded with a small smile.

"It is back there in the 1948 room. Last door on the right," she said, pointing behind her.

I smiled again in thanks and headed down the hall. Taking a deep breath, I entered the open room to see a large ornate conference table with plush maroon office chairs. I felt like I was about to sit in on an important business meeting and not like I was starting the first day of school. In the room was Professor Hoffmann and another student, a girl with curly red hair.

"Hello, Miss Reid, it is good to see you," Professor Hoffmann said as I entered. He held out a hand for me to shake. I smiled brightly and gave a firm handshake. He was a large man, while maybe six feet tall, he had a barreled chest and torso like he was muscular under a thick layer of fat. His hair was gray and neatly cut short, only visible in contrast to his dark skin. His eyes were a dark brown and while not unkind, they were more serious in expression. Maybe this was a business meeting after all.

I sat in the chair he gestured to as the other student leaned over from the chair next to me. "Are you the one who can't talk?"

she asked curiously. No malice sounded in her tone, only blatant curiosity.

"I can talk. It's just difficult for me." I swallowed a gulp of air and said, my voice hoarse from disuse and therefore proving my point more.

"Oh, that's wild," she said, sitting back in her seat. She had shoulder length auburn hair with a tight curl, and bright blue eyes. Her skin was clear and had a lightly shimmery layer of foundation, thick black mascara, and a blood red lipstick. She was beautiful and had an atmosphere of excitement about her. As she moved, her hair circulated the bright scent of peonies and apples.

It was true when I said Caleb and my dad were the only people I could talk to. The accident that killed my mom had left me with a broken spine, among other injuries, which required a brace that extended up my neck to my chin. It was painful to speak around the brace, so I didn't speak for three months. After the brace was off, I needed surgery on my jaw, which was another painful few months without speaking. I had to do speech therapy to regain my ability to articulate. Overall, it was well into a year before I could speak clearly after the accident. The trauma of being a thirteen-year-old girl who had violently lost her mother, experienced extremely painful injuries, and endured multiple difficult surgeries further affected my willingness to speak to anyone. It is twelve years after the accident, and I am now physically able to speak and can hold conversations when necessary. If I know a person well, then I can talk to them more freely. I was mostly worried about saying the wrong thing, accidentally offending someone, or plainly not being listened to, which causes my current speech anxiety. I've done the therapy and taken the anxiety medication, but I always find something else to fear.

"My name is Francesca, but you can call me Daisy," she said and reached out a hand for me to shake. Her eyes were bright in color but also in expression. She was warm and confident, with a huge smile. As I shook her hand, I noticed she was wearing a low cut hot pink blouse. It showed more cleavage than I would typically show, but further showcased her confident personality.

"Evangeline, Eva," I mumbled. I swallowed a gulp of air down, feeling the air bubble go down my throat before I spoke again. "I'm a microbiology student. What do you study?"

"Oh, I'm an accounting student," she said with a dismissive wave. "But I'll be working with your team to compile data and make reports. I'll be your stats girl."

I nodded, not sure what to say next, and shifted in my seat nervously. I wanted to be a better conversationalist. Dad was not one for long conversations if he didn't have to, Caleb and I were typically looking for another type of activity these days, and I was academically focused in school and had no other friends to speak of, or to. Bacteria don't speak, so I chose a line of study that required little communication.

Daisy looked up through her black lashes as a guy that entered quietly walked past us to Professor Hoffmann.

"Mr. Monroe, hello, good to see you," Professor Hoffmann said as he shook the guy's hand.

"Good to see you too, Professor," the deep rumble of his voice made it seem more commanding than he had intoned. A slight twang of a Southern accent detectable in his words.

"Hi, I'm Daisy," she said, standing and leaning over the table to shake his hand. She was probably showing off her cleavage even more now. I honestly envied her level of confidence. Fighting a smile at her efforts, I decided I liked her.

I also couldn't blame her when I took a closer look at the newcomer. He was a tall, golden skinned, sun bleached blonde, blue eyed, strongly muscled man. He was wearing a light blue button-down shirt and neat khakis, but what looked like cowboy boots peeked out from under the crisp, new khakis. He looked like he had been shucking hay or harvesting corn or whatever cowboys did an hour before this meeting, threw on some brand-new clothes, and then came here. His blonde hair was streaked with lighter, honeyed locks from sun exposure, matching his tanned skin.

He gave a polite smile, but his eyes flickered to her rack. I could excuse him, as Daisy was clearly flaunting her large chest towards him. Even I was distracted by the view. He shook her hand. "Everett Monroe, pleased to meet you," he said in his rumbly southern accent.

"The pleasure is all mine," Daisy giggled as she sat back down and looked at me with wide "Can You Believe It?" eyes.

"I'm Evangeline, Eva, Reid," I introduced myself with a clearer voice than before and shook his hand. He gave a kind, closed-mouth smile and a nod as he shook my hand. He was quiet. I liked it.

"Now we are waiting on Mr. Nathaniel Gibson," Professor Hoffmann informed us. "We'll give him another few minutes before we-"

"I'm here, sorry," a guy said breathlessly as he practically ran into the conference room. He wasn't late by any means. In fact, he was two minutes early, but the receptionist must have told him he was the last to arrive. He came in with an outstretched hand to Professor Hoffmann, who shook it as cordially as with the rest of us. Nathaniel had brown hair with sun lightened streaks through it, though his was longer than Everett's and had a curl at the ends. It gave him a skater vibe, like he would look at home in a beanie hat. His eyes were a deep green that looked almost black until seen up close while shaking his hand. He wore thick Ray-Ban glasses and was wearing cargo khaki shorts and a short black sleeve button-down shirt, buttoned all the way to the neck. Where Everett was muscled, Nathaniel was rounder. He was not overweight, but it looked like weightlifting was not part of his routine. He had a boy next door aesthetic to him.

We all introduced ourselves quickly and looked to the Professor for the next instruction.

"Alright, now that we are all here," Professor Hoffmann began after clearing his throat. "Welcome to Truman College to the three newcomers."

"Woo!" Daisy gave a little cheer. "Tru Tigers!"

"Yes, Miss Rossi, has been a student here before this semester and can show you around," Professor Hoffmann said without giving more than a small smile at her cheer. He was more straight-laced than I thought.

"Truman College prides itself on its thriving scientific community and contributions to the field. I have selected you four for this new endeavor, as we have discussed in our interviews. Before we can continue, a non-disclosure agreement must be signed. After it is signed, we can continue our discussion on how your groundbreaking contributions to the scientific world will be compensated by financing your doctorate degrees and upon completion of the project each of you will earn your PhDs from Truman College," Professor Hoffmann said and began handing out paperwork to us with fancy new black pens.

Daisy let out an excited squeal and quickly signed her paper without reading it. I, at least, looked it over. I'd never seen an NDA before.

The document was full of legal jargon, and a general idea of "Do not speak to anyone about this ever in a million years, and also do not take your work out of the lab." Nothing about it was surprising for what I considered an NDA to be. I signed it carefully with my new pen and looked up. Nathaniel had already signed and was looking around at us with his openly friendly green eyes. Everett was the last to slowly sign the agreement, a stern look on his face.

A small crease played between his eyebrows, and I wondered if he was concerned with the terms.

Professor Hoffmann gathered the forms and checked our signatures before giving us a flat smile. "Now we can begin."

I quickly took my notepad out of the outer pocket of my overnight bag, leaving my plain Bic pen in the bag to use my fancy new pen from the school. This thing was legit. It wasn't some metal-colored plastic pen; it felt heavy enough to be real metal with a gold plated pocket hook.

"Your roles in this project have partially been assigned to you based on your areas of study and experiences. You will work closely on this project, so your roles will probably fluctuate. Daisy, your role will not change, as you are not a scientist," Professor Hoffmann said with a terse smile to Daisy before continuing. "There will be three major phases of the project. The first will cultivate a strong, antibiotic-resistant bacteria. The second phase will create a new treatment for it that will be effective in both humans and animals. This treatment might help model future treatments for other resistant bacteria. The third phase is studying the short-term effects of the treatment." Professor Hoffmann paused for a breath, not allowing us space for discussion. "Your contributions to the scientific field would be held in the highest of regards, and you would earn your complete PhD diplomas at the completion of your project upon publication. This is a monumental project for Truman College, and we are deeply honored to have three promising young scientists in our midst."

While he ended with another terse smile, I couldn't help the unease that crept up my spine. Well, I had already signed the paperwork. I guess I could at least let him finish the meeting and I could think about it later. Shifting in my seat, I looked around at the others. Daisy appeared in awe of the project, Nathaniel had a look of apprehensive acceptance, and Everett was unreadable but still had the creased brow.

"Ms. Evangeline Reid, your superior work in your graduate program qualifies you to be the person overseeing the development of the bacteria. Mr. Everett Monroe, your experience and graduate work has you overseeing the bacteria's effects on human and animal biology. Mr. Nathaniel Gibson, your knowledge and work qualifies you to oversee the development of the treatment for the bacteria. Ms. Daisy Rossi, you will be the one to compile the date for statistical analysis and publication," Professor Hoffmann announced with what I could consider warmth in his voice as he looked at each of us.

"Sir, with all due respect, this is a huge undertaking. Creating a new antibiotic?" Everett said, glancing at me and Nathaniel. He also had a notepad open on the table and was turning the pen over in his long fingers in what appeared to be a nervous habit.

"Indeed, it is," Professor Hoffmann confidently said. "And I have every faith you three will have the beginnings of some fantastic research at the end of this project."

"If I might add," Daisy spoke up in a soft, feminine voice. "If this bacteria is medicine resistant, then why are we messing with it? Like, why create it to begin with?"

"They will not be creating the bacteria in the sense that you are implying, Daisy," Professor Hoffmann explained. "The bacteria already exist. We will cultivate it and allow it to grow so we can create the cure for it. In terms you may understand, respectfully."

"Well, isn't that, like, a little bit dangerous?" Daisy asked, her outgoing nature faltering for a moment.

"It is. Which is why there will be some rather intense safety measures going forward," he explained and took a breath, as if this was exactly where he was going next with the orientation. "Because of the nature of this project, you three will have incredibly limited interaction with people outside of the experiment. Meaning, the three of you will live together in a college-owned home just off campus, commute to the research facility together, and will have no contact with other people outside of myself and Daisy on designated days based on the bacteria's status. While I know this sounds daunting to not have access to girlfriends or boyfriends, parties, shopping, and family, but not only is public safety of the utmost importance during this project but so is the secrecy of the research."

He took a moment to reach into the pocket of his navy-blue slacks and pulled out four credit cards. "These cards are a credit line sent up for the project for you to use for your food, clothing, toiletries, and other necessities as you see fit. We at Truman College know this will be an intense project with isolation from the world, and we want to help you feel as comfortable as possible. I have a handbook here with information about how to get food and other items delivered to your house, who to contact about home repairs if needed, who to contact about health concerns, and what to do if, God forbid, one of you gets sick." Professor Hoffmann handed us the credit cards and the one-inch-thick handbooks. "This handbook outlines the safety procedures that will be followed in the research facility."

I took a deep breath. It was a lot to take in. This research sounded more dangerous and difficult than I had expected. All the secrecy and isolation made sense, but accepting it as my job and life now was what I was struggling with.

"Do we get time to think about it?" Nathaniel spoke up.

Professor Hoffmann looked troubled by that question. "You may have until tomorrow afternoon to drop out of the program. Though I would have to ask for your credit card back, your tuition would not be paid, and you would need to sign a non-compete agreement and another non-disclosure agreement."

"Our tuition is paid?" Nathaniel asked, hesitantly.

"Yes, your tuition and room and board in the college's house, and a weekly stipend of $200," Professor Hoffmann informed us.

Okay, well, that kind of changed things, didn't it?

We went over some more basics about the college's science department, the staff who work there, and some of the other projects going on in the school. Afterwards, Professor Hoffmann gave us the access cards to get into the research facility that was entirely ours for this project.

The four of us were silent as he pointed out the address of our house on the handbook and directed Daisy to lead us to our temporary home. I stretched out my legs under the long table as we all started packing up our belongings. My right knee had been injured in the accident and had required a few screws to be placed. It rarely bothered me, but it required some warming up before walking or running.

Hoffmann watched as we packed up our stuff. Everett and Nathaniel were both quiet as they stood, though Nathaniel looked me and Daisy over. I blushed under his gaze and stood with everyone else.

2

I grabbed my overnight bag and followed everyone out of the room. We all said goodbye to Professor Hoffmann, who led us out of the building. Daisy gave the guys directions to keep their cars parked in the lot they were in for now, as we could walk to our house from here. They had parking passes in their handbooks to park in one of the nearby student lots.

"How will we get to and from the facility?" Everett asked her as we walked down the sidewalk in the opposite direction of where my hotel was last night.

"That is one question I do know the answer to!" Daisy said proudly. "A golf cart!"

"A golf cart?" Nathaniel questioned with a chuckle and looked at me incredulously. I smiled back and shrugged good-naturedly.

"Yeah! I totally got to pick it out and decorate it for you. Your lab is on the edge of campus and your house is pretty close. Like maybe two or three blocks from the facility and off campus. It's mostly college owned or student rented houses over there so it won't be too weird to see a golf cart. There's like a hundred on campus during the day. Before I was a student here, like back when my parents would have gone here, it became really popular to use golf carts so they ended up making little parking lots and widening the sidewalks,"

Daisy said as she walked a step in front of us with her hips swaying. "Everyone decorates them. It's part of our campus culture."

Our house was a ten-minute walk, and we looked up at a well-kept bungalow on a street of other, almost identically built, but varying in color and landscape, bungalows. Ours was a pale gray, recently painted, with dark gray shutters and trim, black metal address numbers, a black Edison style outdoor lamp, and perfectly trimmed green boxwood hedges. It looked like the cover of a magazine. A little matching shed was at the top of our short driveway, instead of a garage, and Daisy used a key Professor Hoffman had given her to open it. Inside was a golf cart, decked out with little battery-operated lights. They looked like Christmas lights in blue and white, but upon closer inspection they were little test tubes. A plush tiger head wearing a Truman College hat was dangling from the ceiling where a rearview mirror would go in a car. A fuzzy blue and sparkly steering wheel cover was in place and looked like something out of the early 2000s.

Despite not knowing how to drive, I smiled at Daisy while both guys groaned at the decked-out golf cart. "You better take care of her. Her name is Marie Curie, but you can call her MC for short," Daisy said and sat on the back bench in an effortlessly sultry way.

"We will honor her," Nathaniel said in a serious tone, with his hand on his chest and head bowed.

Daisy giggled and showed us into our home for the duration of the project. She explained she would not be living with us for the project, but based on our projections and isolation periods, we would let her know when she can come see us in person other than using Facetime. "I'll be your contact with the outside world while you're in isolation. Me and Professor Hoffmann will be your only other people you see, even during those less restricted times. But don't worry, I'll take care of you." She winked back at us as she led us up the side entrance stairs.

"So, if you look down there, it's a basement. There's a bunch of space down there, but it's basically one big room for storage and your laundry," she said, pointing down the dark stairs. "It's mostly finished, only empty in case you have a lot of stuff to store. Up this way is the kitchen slash dining room, through that doorway to the right is the stairs to upstairs, further is the living room and the front door, then there's a bedroom, an office, and a full bathroom. Oh, my gosh, I feel like I'm on HGTV! Anyway, upstairs there are two bedrooms and another full bathroom. Everything has been painted and updated for you three. You'll have to fight over who gets which room."

We looked around the place and Everett volunteered to take the first-floor bedroom. "I'm an early riser," he explained in his light Southern accent.

I was also an early riser; I had been jogging almost every morning since being in physical therapy for my knee and spine. Not only because excess weight put strain on my reconstructed joints, but because it was a good way to keep my muscles warmed up to avoid strain. I ended up loving the quiet morning runs and kept up with them.

When we were upstairs, Nathaniel volunteered to take the first bedroom to leave me the one with the most sunlight streaming in. It felt like a kind gesture, so I thanked him and smiled. Daisy helped the guys go get their cars parked in the right places and I sat my overnight bag on my new bed and looked around. The walls of the room were bright white, but the afternoon sunlight had them glowing yellow. My windows looked out the front and side of the house, so I saw the guys and Daisy coming back on the golf cart after I got started unpacking my overnight bag. I'd have to send for my other clothes and a few other things once I got more settled.

I went down to meet them when they came in. Daisy left us to go back to her dorm for the evening, though she gave us a little pout about leaving her new friends. Everett offered to have her stay for dinner, but she sighed and declined. She said she had a date to get ready for. I walked her out when she left and thanked her for all her help.

"It's no problem. It's actually part of my job, silly," she giggled. "Though I am sorry to have to go on a date with someone else. Had I known I'd be meeting three hot scientists, I'd have ghosted him last week."

I giggled with her but felt a creeping warmth climb up my chest and I broke eye contact. She waved as she headed off down the street back the way we came from the meeting.

"Did she just hit on you?" I heard Nathaniel's friendly voice behind me.

"I think maybe?" I said, my voice cracking from the nerves.

"Because I thought she was hitting on me earlier. She was definitely hitting on John Wayne over there, but you, too?" Nathaniel joke whined.

Everett sat at the kitchen island with his handbook and smirked at Nathaniel. "Do you not enjoy competition, Nathaniel?"

"You can call me Nate. And yes, I love competition, but it's not exactly an even playing field. I mean, you look like a fucking movie poster," Nate laughed.

"What about Eva?" Everett asked, his eyes smiling more than his minutely smirking mouth.

"Well, that's alright because then that just means she likes what I like. Now, who's down for ordering pizza from the top three yelp reviewed places in the area and comparing them?" Nate opened every drawer and cabinet looking in them. Each one was stocked with clean dishes, pots, pans, mugs, glasses, and silverware. He came across a mostly empty drawer that held only a few take-out menus and pizza flyers. He rifled through the pizza ones and slapped them on the kitchen island in front of me and Everett.

"Sure," I agreed. "I'm not a great cook."

"I am a good cook, but I still want pizza," Everett said and stood to open the new stainless fridge. It was stocked with beautiful, fresh ingredients I admittedly could do little with.

We agreed to order both a standard pepperoni pizza and the best-selling specialty pizza from each of the three places to decide who had the best slice. With a smile on my face, I took three slate blue plates out of the cabinet, found napkins, and sodas for us. It was nice to be around like-minded people. People who loved science and were as dedicated as I was to my education. Not to mention it didn't hurt they were both attractive, but I would not linger on that thought. It also didn't hurt they were stuck with me and had to talk to me.

We set up to eat at the kitchen island and Nate connected his phone to a Bluetooth speaker bar he set on the counter. His taste of music leaned more towards the emo rock bands of the 90s and 2000s. I wasn't surprised by his preferences one bit. Everett cast one disdainful look at the speaker but didn't make a comment about what was playing.

When the pizza came, we sat at the island together chatting about pizza in our hometowns and other good pizza we've had. It was small talk, but a necessary part of getting to know each other. Listening to small talk used to make my skin crawl with anxiety and secondhand embarrassment. Listening to these guys talk was entertaining. I was invested already.

"My mom makes her own dough and freezes it, so every Friday she thaws some and we all make our own personal pizzas. God, she and my dad had one of them margarita pizzas one time and you would have thought it had changed their damn lives, it has been the only pizza they've eaten in years," Everett said with a laugh.

"We had a chain pizza place near my house growing up and that's all we ever would order. But we took a family vacation to Chicago and tried deep dish and we've been chasing that high ever since. So, I get what your parents are feeling," Nate added, gesturing with a drooping slice of pizza.

"There was a nice place that did wood-fired pizzas near me," I said after gulping in a breath. The guys were patient with me as I formed my sentences. "They had one with peppers they pickled themselves and it was the best."

"Do you think Daisy is a deluxe pizza girl or a plain cheese pizza girl?" Nate asked suggestively. I didn't understand what his innuendo meant, but I knew he'd said one.

"Nate," Everett said in a warning tone like he was scolding a child.

Nate glanced at him with a grin.

"I can ask her," I said after a moment, fighting a grin. "She wrote her phone number on my handbook."

"Ohhhh!" Nate shouted excitedly. Everett gave me a smile that was mostly in his blue eyes.

They were so different in their natures. While Nate was louder and more animated, Everett was quiet and reserved in a calm and confident way. Nate seemed to be always making some sort of sound, whether it be talking or moving around.

"So, what do you guys think about this project?" Nate asked a little while later.

I shifted in my seat. I wanted their take on this as well.

Everett cleared his throat and threw his crumpled napkin on his plate. "I think it might be too good to be true."

"But what could be the catch? We stay inside, get our work done, and we come out as published Doctors. Doctors with their degrees fully paid up. We would walk out with less debt than we thought we'd be in, and we'd be getting paid this whole time with very few bills. I mean..." Nate trailed off to prove his point, his arms wide in gesture.

They looked to me. "What do you think, Eva?" Everett asked.

I thought for a moment, and they waited as I gathered my thoughts. "I think Professor Hoffmann quoted enough of my research from last year to make me think he was serious in selecting us as participants." I paused and swallowed a few gulps of air. "But it feels like maybe I'm waiting for the catch."

"What would the catch even be?" Nate asked. "What, we have to pay interest on what our education costs? Or do we have to work for the university for a year after we graduate? All the money earned from the publication goes back to the school?"

Everett made a face like he was considering what Nate was saying. "You make a good point. Do any of those things make you want to not do this?"

"No, I mean, it all makes sense. I would totally give up the potential earnings from the publication for the guaranteed free degree," Nate replied, writing "Winner" in big letters on the box for Maria's Pizzas.

I picked up the flier for the restaurant and used a Truman Tiger magnet to stick it to the side of the fridge. "I agree. The degree is more important than publication earnings. And if they want interest back, then I would work out a payment plan."

"I think I do, too," Everett said with a sigh. The crease was back between his brows.

My dad had always said if something was free, then you were the product someone was buying. I couldn't ask him if he felt that statement applied here since I was bound by the NDA. This was going to have to be my decision. And if the guys were all in, then I couldn't think of a reason for me to back out.

"Is it decided then?" Nate asked, raising his soda like he was waiting to knock his can against ours.

"It's decided," Everett nodded and raised his soda to Nate's.

"Decided," I echoed, and raised my own.

Nate knocked his can against ours and gave a merry "Go Tru Tigers!"

Everett and I chuckled.

We were quiet as we cleaned up the pizza, Maria's Pizzas a clear winner with her Greek lover's pizza with olives and a pepperoni pizza with crispy pepperoni.

"So, Eva," Nate started while he rinsed the plates. "Professor Hoffmann let us know you have a problem with talking. What's that about?"

He asked in a way that was, like Daisy that morning, without judgment and with genuine curiosity. I knew the difference as I had been the recipient of both many times.

Again, they were patient as I gathered the words to speak. "I was in a serious car accident when I was thirteen. It left me with some injuries that made it difficult to talk for a long time. I can talk now, but it is still difficult. I'm not mute or anything."

"Wow, I'm sorry that happened to you," Nate said, and Everett nodded.

I smiled. I still never knew what to say here.

"Then we will have to shut up sometimes and let you talk when you're ready," Nate said and put the dishes in the dishwasher.

"'We,'" Everett whispered to me with a deep chuckle.

"Yeah, yeah, yeah," Nate shot back. "But if one of you is a mute cowboy and one of you is the strong, silent type, I gotta fill the silence."

Everett warned, "No, you do not."

After we cleaned up, we went our separate ways to our rooms to check in with family and organize the bags we had brought. Each of us had only brought overnight bags, as had been directed by Hoffmann.

I texted dad and Caleb to let them know I was settled into my new place and that I had had a good day. Dad asked about the project, and I let him know I signed an NDA that prohibited me from talking to him about it. We coordinated how the rest of my bags would be shipped to me, as he could not take time off work before my project started and I had to isolate. I had grown up only a few hours away from Truman College, but I didn't mind dad not making the drive. I hadn't even wanted him to drop me off at the hotel- I had taken a bus. Ever since the accident, both he and I had dreaded time in cars and limited our traveling time. I went as far as to never learn how to drive. That level of responsibility for my safety and the safety of everyone around me seemed like too much only three years after my accident, and I never went back to learn as I got older. Caleb sent me flirty texts and a selfie at one of the local bars back home. He was alone at the bar, but we didn't have the type of relationship that held him back from picking someone up or dating. Our casual, friends first, relationship wasn't typical, but it worked for us. I wished him luck and was about to put my phone down when a text came through.

Unknown number (1): Hey nerdies, how was pizza? *Pizza emoji*

Unknown number (2): Maria's Pizzas is the winner.

Unknown number (2): Wait who is this and how'd you know we got pizza?

Unknown number (1): It's Daisy!

A pouting selfie loaded. It was indeed Daisy... and her cleavage.

Me: Hi Daisy! This is Eva, everyone.

Unknown number (2): I'm Nate.

Unknown number (3): Ev

Daisy: Okay nerdies, now I need selfies from you.

Nate: *low-res gif of a lawnmower flying through the air.*

Everett: No.

Daisy: Oh please! Come on, I'm on the worst date everrrr.

Me: *a quickly taken selfie of me at the window with the setting sun on my face.*

In quick succession, all three of them liked my selfie. I blushed, alone in my room.

Daisy: oh, girlll *heart eyes emoji* I'll see you three in the morning for your lab tour!

3

The sun was just peeking over the horizon and creating a soft glow over the neighborhood when I woke up for my run the next morning. I threw on a black, longline sports bra, a pair of black running shorts, and my hot pink shoes and tiptoed down the stairs. Once outside, I put in my earbuds and chose my music. I didn't know the area or any parks yet, so I did a jog around the neighborhood. Most of the houses on my route looked similar to ours, a few better taken care of than others, but otherwise similar in size and design. This neighborhood was right outside the city and most of the houses were old city bungalows with tiny yards. A coin op laundromat, a convenience store, a deli, a bar, and a church were within three blocks of our house. I wondered if I'd ever set foot in them or only jog past them before they were open most mornings. The birds in the area were active at this hour and the city was just waking up to start its day. Warm yellow sun unmarred by city pollution streaked through the trees and between houses.

After my jog, I returned to the house to find Everett in the kitchen. He was wearing low slung red plaid cotton pajama pants and a white t-shirt. He looked up sharply when I snuck up the three stairs from the side door into the kitchen.

"Good morning," I said, breathless from my run.

He looked me up and down, taking stock of my running attire. His eyes stuck for a moment on the scars on my right knee before continuing. "Good morning," he replied after a moment.

"I didn't mean to startle you," I said, getting a bottle of water from the fridge.

"No, it's alright," he said, turning back to the coffee pot. "I thought I was going to be the early riser in the house."

I smiled and sat at the island while he made a pot of coffee.

"Would you like some breakfast? I was going to make some eggs and bacon," he offered, and opened the fridge.

"Sure, thank you," I said after a moment.

"Of course," he mumbled, and we settled into a comfortable silence while he cooked. When the coffee finished, I poured two cups and got the cream from the fridge. I poured cream in my coffee, but Everett picked his up black and took a sip of the piping hot coffee.

I watched him stand at the stove cooking- barefoot and casual. His muscled back was more visible through this t-shirt than it was through his dress shirt yesterday. I admired him, almost hypnotized by his muscles as he moved.

"Do you run every day?" he asked, making me realize I'd been staring.

A sip of hot coffee warmed my throat before replying. "I try to. I have screws in my right knee from the accident. Years ago, I began jogging as part of my physical therapy and it stuck."

He turned and looked at my knee. "Do you mind?" he asked and gestured to my leg.

I turned sideways on the seat so he could see better.

He kneeled down on the kitchen floor on one knee and traced a light finger over the scars. They really weren't all that noticeable unless you were close to me, or you were looking directly at my legs. I wasn't self-conscious of them, and they didn't bother me.

Goosebumps rose on the rest of my leg at his attention. I breathed evenly, hoping he wouldn't see the bumps. He smelled of a fresh shower and clean soap.

"My dad has screws in his elbow from an accident with a horse probably thirty or so years ago and his scarring is much worse than yours. You had some skilled doctors. Does it bother you in different weather?"

I nodded and said, "When it's damp or cold, yeah. If I don't run, I'll use heating pads. It's not too bad, though."

"My dad's always hollerin' about it. Doesn't let it stop him from working though," he said and returned to his cooking.

Bounding footsteps on the stairs preceded Nate's appearance in the kitchen. He came in happily and hummed a tune. "Good morning, that bacon smells amazing!"

"Yeah, well, this bacon is for early risers," Everett said.

"Dude, it's literally seven in the morning. This is early," Nate argued and sat next to me at the island.

Everett got out a third plate from the cabinet and poured a mug of coffee despite his response of "Eva's already been out for a run, and I've cooked an entire breakfast. What have you done?"

"I took a shit, that's what," Nate shot back.

I snorted into my coffee.

"And I ordered a portable sound system for Marie Curie," Nate continued as he plopped two spoonfuls of sugar and a healthy pour of cream into his coffee. "So maybe suck a dick, bro."

Everett stared at Nate with that smirk and the smiling eyes he had perfected. He shook his head and handed us our plates of eggs and bacon. I thanked him and he winked at me.

Daisy met us at our house soon after breakfast and we all piled onto the golf cart. Marie Curie had a two-person bench facing forward and a bench on the back, which fit two more. Daisy perched proudly next to Everett, who was first in the driver's seat. Nate and I sat on the bench that faced backwards as we drove the five minutes to the lab.

The lab we'd be working in was a small, unmarked building right on the edge of campus. It was near the back of the large science building on campus and was likely easily overlooked as storage. They marked one little parking spot for our golf cart that a wide sidewalk led to from the road. We parked, and I hopped down from the bench and was the first to use my access card to open the metal and glass door. The building was unassuming, but the technology used to secure it was new. The lock on the door beeped and I opened it.

We all filed into the vestibule, and Daisy explained the layout. "It's pretty small, but it has everything you need. There's a locker room though there," she pointed to a door on the right. "The center room is your super important lab, and the one on the left is like a lounge area with some computers."

Everett opened the lab door with his access card, and we hurried inside. The lab and equipment were ultramodern and so clean and new. I ran my fingers over the cool metal table and looked around in awe. My eyes met Nate's and we exchanged excited stares.

"This is all for our use?" Everett asked.

"Yup, just you nerdies," Daisy said and looked around like she was bored.

"Nobody else has access?" Everett asked, that crease in his brow again.

"You three, me, and Professor Hoffmann, as far as I know," she replied with a shrug. "But I'm only allowed in today to show you around."

Nate, Everett, and I walked around the lab to check out all the fantastic equipment we were given to use. Some of it was brand new and still had the protective plastic covering on it.

"I know Truman College has a great reputation in the scientific and medical communities, but this shit is... insane," Nate said, with wary awe in his voice.

Daisy laughed. "Um yeah. Seeing as most of the people who graduate with any honors here are picked up by huge pharmaceutical companies. Even us business students get scouted. They want to make sure you all know what you're doing with the best equipment."

I felt mildly uncomfortable knowing the proverbial Big Pharma gave the college the money for all this equipment. Was my education and participation in this program paid for by Big Pharma, too? Would it be a pharmaceutical company that comes for some sort of payment after I graduate? Unease grew in my belly as I considered if this was the start of The Catch we had discussed.

"Anyway, there's a gigantic party happening off campus tonight. We're totally going before you guys start your research," Daisy said, upbeat and confident. Her brightness and enthusiasm distracted me from my thoughts.

I wrinkled my nose and caught Nate's look of apprehension.

"I'm not one for college parties," Everett told her dismissively.

"Oh, please Ev, please?" Daisy begged him with an impressive combination of cleavage and pouty lips.

"I guess I could go to one party while I'm here," Nate said, clearly convinced by her display.

Honestly, so was I. She was good.

Everett huffed out an agreement.

"Eva?" she turned her pouty lips and cleavage to me.

"Sure, yeah. One party," I said with a smile.

Daisy squealed in delight and said, "I'm doing your makeup!"

We left the lab not long after with Daisy babbling about how she was going to do my makeup and hair and now let me borrow an outfit. I didn't mind her attention. It had been a long time since

I had a friend other than Caleb and a few people I talked to in my dorms and study groups through college. Caleb was an old friend and a friend I slept with, and the people at college were cool but not the kind to offer to do my makeup. I had gone to a few parties through my years of school, but it wasn't my scene. I couldn't help the almost childlike desperation for Daisy to become my friend. She was so beautiful and confident that I wanted her to teach me how she did it. I could use some of it.

Daisy left us back at our house so she could run back to her dorm and gather "supplies" for my makeover. I showered, shaved, and moisturized in preparation. I felt nervous and giddy. It felt like the first day of school. When she came back later that afternoon, she had Everett help her carry in armfuls of dresses and outfits on hangers, and two pink toolboxes of what I assumed to be hair and makeup supplies.

We set up shop in the upstairs bathroom, Daisy chatting mostly one sided at me as we set everything up on the long bathroom counter. At one point Nate came in with intentions to shower and stopped short, seeing an entire beauty parlor where it previously had not been.

"Oh, I was going to shower. I guess I'll go use the one downstairs," he said, eyeing the makeup on the counter.

"Or you could pretend we're not here and go on with your shower," Daisy said huskily, looking up from beneath her lashes.

Nate smirked at us. I blushed. He leaned back against the doorframe and said nothing for a second. "Hmm, while that sounds like a great idea, I'm going to pass."

"Too bad," Daisy said airily and turned back to pulling makeup pallets out of her containers.

Nate shot me a grin before grabbing his soap out of the shower and leaving.

I looked up at Daisy and we both burst into giggles at the same time.

"Those boys are too much fun," Daisy said as she plugged in a hair straightener.

"They're really nice," I said and settled into the seat we had Everett bring up from the kitchen.

"To look at," Daisy giggled. "So, tell me what your normal beauty routine is."

I looked at my reflection in the mirror. I had dark brown eyes and mousy brown, shoulder length hair. My hair was thin and tangled easily, so I typically kept it in a low bun or ponytail. My lashes were nowhere near the length of Daisy's, and I was suddenly self-conscious over their shortness. I curled them and applied mascara every day, as well as my favorite deep pink tinted lip balm. I wasn't against make-up and had followed many YouTube tutorials to varying degrees of success, but I felt most comfortable with a minimal amount on my face. Covering the occasional zit didn't count.

She chatted about boys while she worked, and I felt more and more comfortable with her. I was able to tell her about Caleb, much to her surprise.

"No way! You had a casual hookup situation? Let me see him!" Daisy demanded and handed me my phone, which was playing some pop music playlist Daisy had recommended. I pulled up a picture of me and Caleb we had taken at the fourth of July fireworks this summer. "Oh, my gosh, he's delicious!"

I giggled and swiped to a picture of us from high school. "We dated in high school. He and I agreed we'd see other people in college and if we didn't find a serious relationship when it was over, then we could come back to each other. I think we just didn't want to lose each other permanently; you know?"

"And you two hook up over every break?" She asked incredulously.

"Yeah, pretty much. He sleeps with girls at school and comes back to show me what he has learned," I said with a laugh. I realized how odd that probably sounded to someone who didn't know me and Caleb. It felt like a logical plan to us.

Daisy practically screamed with laughter. It was infectious, and I joined her laughing. "And has his education been worth the tuition?!" she said between cackles while wiping tears from her eyes.

"Ivy League," I said, wiping my own eyes. She high-fived me.

"I bet Everett is good," Daisy said a few minutes later as she straightened my hair.

"Why?" I asked, unsure of her criteria.

"He's a cowboy, right? I bet he rides real good," she said dreamily.

"He mentioned a horse to me once, but I don't know if he's actually a cowboy," I teased after a moment of gathering my words. I felt uncomfortable discussing the guys like that with her and I didn't know why. It was harmless girl talk.

"Oh, his family has a real, actual farm. Like they're really farmers that raise cows for milk and beef," she explained.

"How do you know?" I asked, a little jealous.

"I read his application. Actually, I read all of your applications. I wasn't supposed to, but I was in Professor Hoffmann's office and saw them. I'm nosey," she said simply and with a little shrug.

Daisy straightened my hair to smooth it and put a slight wave in with a curling iron. It was casual and pretty and swished when I turned my head. She kept with the minimal makeup look and applied a foundation, some glittery bronzer, a subtle smokey eye and a shimmery nude eyeshadow.

Clothing options were laid out on my bed, and she rifled through them before turning to me. "I honestly don't know what to dress you in because I can't see your body shape."

I looked down at my jeans and pink t-shirt. My body was slim to minimize pain in my reconstructed joints, but I had a healthy hourglass shape. I was a jeans and t-shirt girl when I wasn't in my running gear, and I didn't flaunt my shape. It occasionally invited conversation if I wore a flattering outfit. I shrugged and took off my shirt to stand in front of her in my bra. I wasn't self-conscious of my body, and I technically wore more revealing clothes when I ran than this simple bra.

She whistled. "Oh girl, you are beautiful!"

I blushed and looked at the clothes on my bed. "Um, I like that black top."

She held out a black, backless halter top that tied around the neck and mid-back. It's not a top I would have bought myself, but I knew it would look cute on me. She looked thoughtful as I put it on and then removed my bra.

"I was going to say a pair of lighter jeans would look cute, but your dark ones look great," she said and had me spin around. "You have a great ass. I'm jealous."

I laughed and blushed again.

"Shoes!" she shouted and dug through her bags to pull out a pair of black stilettos.

I hesitated before taking them. Walking would be easy in a pair of wedge heels or traditional pumps, but I had not tried stilettos. I was worried about my balance and coordination with my injuries. I would at least try. Worst comes to worst, I could take them off and go barefoot.

Daisy changed her mind on my hair and put it up in a loose and delicate bun on top of my head as I stepped into the stilettos. Even wearing the heels that were a little too big on me, she was tall enough to reach the top of my head. I was only five feet tall and in these heels I was five feet four inches.

Daisy stepped back to admire her work. "Absolutely fuckable," she moaned, and I laughed. "But I think I'm going after Ev tonight."

"Oh?" I said, my voice hoarse.

"Yeah, I have to test my theory about the cowboy thing," she said and picked out a short red dress and a pair of black stilettos for herself.

We arrived at the party at nearly ten after Everett forced us all to eat a heavy pasta dinner and the party was in full swing. Music blared from inside the large home that had Greek lettering on the front door.

"Okay nerdies, we meet at the kitchen sink at midnight and decide what we're doing next. Can you set alarms on your phones?" Daisy said as we parked Marie Curie next to the dozen other golf carts.

The three of us all showed her our wrists where we all wore watches.

"Nerdies!" she tipped her head back and laughed. "Who even wears watches that aren't Rolex anymore?!"

"It's a G shock," Nate informed her like she was missing some vital information.

"Whatever. Ev, you're coming with me and we are dancing," she said and pulled him after her. She gave a naughty expression back at me, and my stomach clenched. Why did I feel jealous? It honestly made no sense.

I turned to Nate, who was looking down at me. "I guess it's only us tonight. Let's go get a drink," he said and grabbed my hand as we pushed into the crowded house.

His hand was warm and strong around mine as we weaved through people towards the kitchen. I made note of where the sink was as Nate and I grabbed drinks. Nate filled me a plastic cup with beer from a keg and then one for himself. We headed towards the living room where the music was blaring. I wasn't much of a dancer, but I would do it if he wanted to. We stopped inside where the music was loudest and looked around, sipping our drinks. I tried to find Ev and Daisy but couldn't see over the other dancers. Nate was at least a foot taller than me, so he had no difficulty.

"Oh, there they are," Nate shouted over the music as if he had just spotted them and pointed to the other side of the room.

I looked up at him and shook my head with a little smile.

"You can't see?" he chuckled. I nodded, and he set our drinks down on the tv stand behind him. Before I knew what was happening, he was lifting me under the arms like baby Simba in The Lion King. Oh, yup, Ev and Daisy were grinding on the other side of the room. Cool.

He set me down and asked, "Did you see them?" like it was any other day he lifted his new roommate and colleague like a child out of a crib after naptime. It seemed like zero effort to him, so I made a questioning look and squeezed his bicep.

He laughed and handed me back my drink. "During the summers I work in inventory for a grocery store."

I looked him over as his eyes scanned the people in the room. He was wearing a fitted black t-shirt under a blue and white plaid flannel shirt and jeans. He wasn't wearing a beanie hat like I had predicted would be part of his wardrobe, but a backwards baseball hat with a faded logo I couldn't read from a foot below him. Nate was handsome in a way that suggested he had no clue about his own appeal. His thick framed glasses reflected the lights of the party and his deep green eyes shone with a shy happiness as he looked around the room. From this angle I could see his long brunette lashes were interspersed with blonde. His evening stubble along his strong jaw was dark and added to his handsomeness.

He looked down at me staring at him, and I startled a bit, realizing I was being awkward. He leaned down and said, "Do you want to grab another drink and go outside?" His breath was hot on my neck as he practically shouted into my ear. I shivered despite myself.

I nodded, and we headed back to the kitchen. Outside in the backyard, we sat at a patio table that had seen better days. I looked up at the stars and sipped my fresh beer. Few were visible this close to downtown Cleveland, and a spotlight was shining into the sky on a rotation.

"I didn't go to many parties like this earlier in college. I did a few to check them out, but I made some good friends and we partied together, mostly. Video games, pizza, and beer was our typical weekend," Nate said and sipped his drink.

"Me neither. I went to a few with friends from study groups," I added.

"Was your idea of a party a late night in the library then?" he teased.

"No," I giggled. "I had a few acquaintances who were willing to spend time with me outside of the library. They liked when I drank because I could talk more."

"Do you like talking more when you drink?" he asked, and it felt like he honestly wanted to know my feelings.

I exhaled and considered the question. "I mean, I like feeling more uninhibited with my words. I wish I felt like that all the time. But... when I was in therapy after the accident, they warned me it could be a slippery slope. So, I am careful," I said and looked away from his gaze.

"That makes sense. And I imagine you feel better in smaller settings?" he asked.

"I would think most people do," I said in answer. I felt awkward telling him I was a severe introvert and unable to talk.

"Not Daisy," Nate said good-naturedly.

I smiled. "No, not Daisy. Though I am sorry you didn't get to dance with her tonight. We could go in and find them again."

"Nah," Nate said and shook his head. He finished his drink and leaned back in his chair. "I had wanted to dance and party once while I was here for this project, but now I'd rather chill with you."

Our eyes met, and I blushed and looked down. "Thank you."

"It's going to be an interesting year with her around though, that's for sure," he said and smiled. Behind his thick-framed glasses, his eyes were focused on me and seemed to dance when he smiled.

"I dare you to send a selfie the next time she asks," I said with a grin.

"Ew, like a dick pic in the group chat?" He barked a laugh, his posture still open and relaxed in his chair.

"No! I said selfie! You're the one with the rotten mind!" I laughed with him.

"I'll send a dramatic GPOY," he said, knocking his leg against mine under the table. "Do you remember GPOY? Gratuitous Picture Of Yourself? Like from earlier internet days?"

"I do. I remember it from my time on Tumblr," I admitted.

"Yes! And LiveJournal. I spent a lot of time on Dungeons and Dragons pages. And Star Wars," he confessed.

"I cycled through too many fandoms to name any," I said and finished my drink.

Nate opened his mouth to say something, but his eyes shot up to the sliding door behind me. He tensed, then jumped out of his seat and pulled me up from mine as the sliding door flew open and yelling voices boomed out. It was a fight and one guy in basketball shorts and a tank top, holding a t-shirt and his shoes, was thrown out of the door and smashed into the table and the chair I had been in. Nate stepped us off of the cement patio as a guy screaming obscenities came barreling out towards the guy on the ground. More people poured out after them, shouting and watching the fight.

Nate put me down gently but pushed me mostly behind him as we edged around the fight to get back inside. We went to the kitchen sink and checked the time. It was eleven thirty- thirty minutes before Ev and Daisy would meet us here.

"What do you think? Do you want to call it?" Nate asked and pulled me against his side as a group of people pushed through the kitchen to find the fight.

"Yes, please," I said and pulled out my phone.

Me: Me and Nate are ready to go, are you two ready? There's a big fight in the back yard and I think the cops are probably going to come.

Daisy: The cops are definitely not coming for a little frat fight. Me and Ev are staying. You two can go ahead and take MC, we'll Uber home. Don't wait up *kiss emoji*

Nate: *eggplant emoji*

Ev: Nathaniel. *Rolling eyes emoji*

"Well, that answers that," Nate said with an exhale. "Good thing I have the key, I guess."

The way to the front door was mostly clear, since most people were outside to watch the fight. I wondered where Ev and Daisy were since I didn't see them outside.

"I feel kind of weird about Ev and Daisy," Nate said, reading my mind as we drove home.

"Same. I think I was really looking to hang out with Daisy and have a friend to talk to tonight," I said, watching the houses we passed.

"Well, you have me," Nate said cheerfully and clapped a hand on my knee.

"That, I do," I said and relaxed into my seat.

4

I woke up early the next morning to go for a run and I tiptoed down in my pink running shorts and matching sports bra, holding my shoes. The kitchen light was on, and Ev was leaning against the island in a pair of black basketball shorts and a red fitted t-shirt. He had running shoes on his feet and was clearly waiting for me. He smiled at my shocked face as I came around the corner.

"You're home. I figured you'd be in Daisy's dorm," I said with not a single drop of distaste.

"She's asleep in my room," he said casually and pushed away from the island. "Do you mind if I join you on your run?"

"No, I don't mind. I was going to check out a park I saw on google nearby. We could take Marie Curie there," I said and stooped to put on my shoes. I had planned on walking there since I didn't drive, but if Ev was going, he could drive us.

Stumbling footsteps on the stairs sounded behind me and I turned around to see a sleepy Nate in blue basketball shorts and a black t-shirt. He was wearing what looked like Vans instead of running shoes, but they were tied tight like he had intentionally put them in sport mode. A baseball hat, different from the one he wore to the party, was in his hand.

"I'm coming," he mumbled and glared at us with half-closed eyes, his glasses over his hair and around his ears, askew on his nose.

I grabbed three bottles of water and three bananas from the kitchen and Ev grabbed the key to MC. He shot a quick text and I heard Daisy's phone chime in his room. I shoved down the strange feeling rising in my stomach.

We quietly headed out to Marie Curie, and I navigated Ev to the park while making sure Nate didn't fall back asleep and consequently off of MC's bench. The park had a little parking lot at the entrance and we got out to do our stretches. Nate pushed his wild hair into his hat and fixed his glasses before stretching.

"Do we get breakfast when we're done?" Nate asked as he yawned through a calf stretch.

"Yes, and lots of coffee," I smiled and bent to touch my toes, and then hugged my arms around my knees. I heard crunching gravel as Nate struggled to keep his footing during his stretching behind me. It sounded like Ev had caught him.

"Get ahold of yourself," Ev said to Nate, his voice deep and raspy.

I stood and turned to them. "Are you guys good?"

"Yup," Nate said, looking more awake after his stretching. Pink stained his cheeks, and he turned away from me and looked around the parking lot.

We looked at the trail map near the start of the gravel path. It was about three miles and boasted some wonderful scenery. It surprised me this much green space existed so close to the city, and I appreciated the work that went into keeping it.

"Three miles?" Nate groaned.

"You'll be fine," I said encouragingly. "I'm a slow runner, anyway."

We set off on a jog through the little forest. It was dark in some spaces, and I tucked my phone into the top of my bra with the flashlight on and peeking out and led the way. We came up to a small clearing that had a small sign discussing the foliage in the area and a bench. Nate crashed down onto the bench.

"For someone who doesn't run, you jogged with us for about three quarters of a mile on hilly terrain, man. That's not bad at all," Ev praised Nate, his own chest heaving.

"I played rugby in high school, so I'm not that out of shape. It's just been a while," Nate panted.

I remembered the way he lifted me with no effort at the party last night, and I knew he was strong. Warmth seeped through my body and I lifted my ponytail off the back of my neck and fanned myself.

"It's probably harder on little thing, Eva. Seein' as she's about half of our size," Ev said with a smirk aimed at me. Everett was also six feet tall minimum, but was maybe two or three inches taller than Nate.

"I've done this almost every day since I was fourteen. It's nothing.... No offense, Nate," I rushed the apology after I realized how I may have sounded.

He flipped me off with both hands anyway and sat back up. "Okay, we can go. I'm fully awake now."

We jogged for another mile before the sun was visible enough to not need my flashlight. A faded signpost and a less maintained path headed off to the right and I was about to jog past it when Ev whistled for us to follow him down the path.

At the end of the path, there was a wooden lookout platform next to a little brick building. It wasn't as well maintained as the bathrooms at the front of the park, but not entirely abandoned either. Ev peered in the windows.

"Is there a water fountain?" Nate asked breathlessly behind me.

I handed him my unfinished water bottle, and he thanked me before taking a swig. I could hear water and went to look off the platform. It was a small river, low in autumn compared to its likely height in spring.

"I think it's locked," Ev said and pushed on the door. The lock had been engaged, but as he pushed the handle it slid, and the door opened freely with a metallic *click.*

"Oops," Nate said for him. "Guess we have to go check it out."

"You only want another break," Ev said, but still carefully entered the building.

He called out a greeting in case, but there was no answer in the darkness. He felt around for a light switch and flipped it on. Lights blinked on in the little building and I could hear the hum of a water fountain.

"Not abandoned," Everett said as he looked around. A little reception desk stood to the left, and he looked at the papers on it. "It's an education field house used for summer school camps and field trips."

"Well, if someone comes and sees us, Eva can pretend she was desperate for the toilet," Nate said and approached the large picture windows along the back wall. "Oh, cool view."

Ev and I followed him to the windows. It was a fantastic view of the gorge below. Fall colors were making an early appearance on the trees and birds were swooping across in their morning paths.

Nate stepped away first and laid down on the floor with a groan. "We're walking the rest of the way."

"Fine by me," I said, turning to join him.

Everett refilled our water bottles and came back to us. "Get up or you'll both end up sleeping until the summer camp kiddos arrive."

"They're all in school, Ev," Nate said sleepily, like he was actually about to fall asleep on the linoleum.

"Let's go," I sighed and got up. I reached out a hand to help Nate up, and he gave me a lazy smile and grasped my hand.

Once Nate was up, Ev wordlessly handed us our water bottles and we followed him out of the building.

"Let's run here every day," Nate said. "And let's see if anyone else comes by since we're leaving it unlocked."

He put some grass on the ground inside the door. Presumably to see if anyone has moved it aside when they walked in.

We walked the rest of the loop pointing out different birds and wildlife as we went, chatting quietly about parks in our hometowns.

Everett's phone chimed to signal an incoming message as we were getting into Marie Curie. He checked it and put it away.

"Did Daisy go home?" I asked him from the bench seat, peeling my banana.

"Wait, did Daisy spend the night?" Nate asked, shocked.

"She did, and yes, she has gone home," Ev responded, not looking at Nate next to him.

I felt weird, feeling Nate's jealousy over Daisy, knowing Everett had spent the night with her, and because I didn't get to spend any time with my new friend that I wanted to impress. I stayed quiet and so did the guys until we got home. We went our separate ways for showers and ended up eating breakfast alone in our rooms. I didn't mind. I needed some space from them already to put my uncomfortable feelings to rest.

Monday came and we spent the day in the office at the lab planning out our estimated timeline for the first phase of the project. We grossly estimated much of it because of the nature of the research, but we had a plan of action. Our experiment began on Tuesday morning with the materials provided by the college. We donned our safety suits and began work. We worked almost wordlessly until it was dark, went home to eat cereal for dinner, and crashed into our beds.

Our days became rather monotonous now that we were in official quarantine status and were well into our research. We woke up early and ran at the park, visiting our so far undisturbed field house, had breakfast together where Everett would make us eggs and toast and coffee, went to the lab until late, came home to blearily eat breakfast cereal for dinner, and fall into bed. All until Everett decided our work life balance was off, and it was making us all grumpy. He was correct; we had determined, when I almost fist fought Nate for finishing the last of the coffee one morning.

So, we left the lab as close to five in the evening as we could. When one of us had to stay late, we always would come back to the lab in MC when they finished. We started playing video games on the Xbox that came when Nate had his belongings delivered. Everett would sometimes join in on a racing game, but would watch us play anything else. Everett and I both loved watching Nate play his intense fantasy games and often chimed in on the dialogue choices as he played. The couch in the living room was comfortable and was often where we spent most of our time when not in the lab, running, or sleeping. We ended up eating dinner on the couch while binge watching shows on Netflix. We still mostly ate cereal or had take out delivered, seeing as neither of us had the energy to cook in the evenings.

My boxes had also arrived a few days after moving in, and it was beginning to feel like home. I talked to Dad, mostly through quick texts, every day to check in. Caleb had started seeing a girl we had graduated with back home, so he stopped texting me. It wasn't unusual for us to stop talking when he was seeing someone. It didn't feel like a rejection. The guys and Daisy were the only people I talked to regularly. Professor Hoffmann communicated with us mostly through email while we were in quarantine, and we had weekly Zoom meetings to check in.

We had a week of only restricted contact, not full quarantine, after a few weeks of work. Nate and I enjoyed walking on campus and seeing the different sports that picked up on the grass lawns.

Truman College had official teams for many sports, but we couldn't be that close to other people. We could watch some recreational games on campus, though. Mostly, we wanted to be out of the house while Everett and Daisy were locked in his room. They were respectful, but me and Nate would always rather be elsewhere for as long as possible.

One of the good things about Daisy being around, other than having another girl to talk to, was that she was an excellent cook. It was a surprising talent she had, but she could make an amazing meal. She cooked for us every night of our restricted contact, and afterwards would sit with me in my room and gossip about the girls in her dorm and drink wine before going down to Everett's room for the night. I pretended in my mind she was actually leaving to go back to her dorm, otherwise I stayed up all night thinking about them together downstairs.

I was relieved when our full quarantine began again, and I felt guilty for it.

5

Daisy reminded us it was Halloween through a texted selfie of her in a sexy, revealing costume made to look like a scientist. A porn star scientist with a fitted body suit that looked vaguely like a white lab coat, thick framed black glasses (similar to Nate's Ray Bans), bare legs, and her hair up in a high ponytail.

"Oh, right, it's Halloween," Nate said, putting his phone back in his pocket as Ev drove us back to the house after our day in the lab. "I can't believe I forgot."

Ev scratched at the slight beard he was growing. His beard grew in red despite his blonde hair. Nate and I had taken to calling him the Ginger Beard Man, much to his annoyance.

"Too bad we can't hand out candy or anything," Nate continued. "We can watch some horror movies tonight to keep with the Halloween spirit."

I shrugged and agreed.

"Fine, but nothing too gory. Blood and guts aren't scary, it's nasty," Everett said as we pulled into our driveway.

We ended up ordering Chinese takeout and watching a classic horror movie that each of us had seen before and a new one neither of us had seen. Curled up in fleece blankets I had bought for the house as the weather got cooler, we all sat close on the couch. The newer movie ended up being more terrifying than I had thought, but I played it cool and said nothing to the guys. I didn't want them to think I was acting like a child. Our phones chimed near the end, and I almost jumped out of my skin.

Daisy: Hey nerdies, you all okay? I haven't heard from you. *Sad face emoji.*

Nate: We're good. Bummed we're not out partying with you.

"Really?" Ev asked Nate wryly.

"Eh, it would beat being cooped up at home," Nate said with a shrug.

It had been a few weeks since we had contact with people outside of our program. It was starting to wear on us all differently, but seemed to bother Nate the most.

Daisy: What are you babes doing instead? I want selfiessss!

Ev: Watching movies.

I held up my phone to take a selfie of the three of us, the guys on either side of me on the couch. They leaned in close and we gave relaxed smiles for the camera. The picture came out sweet, despite it being dark in the room and the reflection of the movie was shown in one of Nate's glasses' frames rather than his green eyes.

Daisy: Ugh, OMG you three are too smokin hot for your own good! You need to frame this pic. For real.

I stared at my phone for another minute after the guys chuckled and put their phones back in their pockets.

"What's wrong, Eva?" Everett asked, peering over at my phone which was still open to the group chat. Nate paused the movie.

"Why do you think she does that?" I asked after a moment of gathering my words. The guys had waited patiently for me to answer.

"Ask for selfies, you mean?" Nate asked as he ran a hand through his hair that now almost touched his shoulders.

"No, I mean... call us hot?" I clarified, not looking at the guys. I set my phone on the oversized ottoman we used more like a kitchen table.

"Perhaps she finds us attractive," Ev suggested in his deep voice.

"But like... doesn't she include me in a patronizing way? Is she making fun of me?" I asked quietly, now ashamed of my question.

The guys were quiet for a moment, and I felt them share a glance over my head. This was exactly why I didn't talk- it opened me up to ridicule.

"Is that a fucking joke?" Nate asked, incredulously.

Everett reached over me to smack Nate in the chest. When he settled back in his seat he said, "No, baby girl, it's not a joke. Now, can we finish this movie? I'm beat and want to get to bed."

A blush settled on my face and chest, and I curled up further in my blanket as Nate pressed play on the movie. My heart thumped louder in my chest at being called "baby girl" by Everett and at Nate's disbelief that I thought I was unattractive. I wasn't the type of girl to fish for compliments, but part of me wished I did it more often because it felt pretty damn good.

I could have lived the rest of my life not seeing the terrifying end of that movie. When the movie ended, I was wide awake and sure I wouldn't sleep well. Nate rambled on happily about a haunted house he went to last Halloween while we cleaned up. I brought the takeout containers to the kitchen and Ev packed up the leftovers for our lunch tomorrow at the lab. Nate folded our blankets on the couch and picked up a few things I missed.

Everett yawned and said goodnight as Nate and I headed up to our rooms. The evening was chilly and my knee was aching, so I ran a warm bath with some lavender Epsom salts. I hoped it would relax me and get that dumb movie out of my head as well. Settling into the bath, I closed my eyes and leaned back against the tub.

A few minutes into my bath, the door opened, and someone came in. I had drawn the curtain closed to soften the overhead bathroom light, and I was glad for that fact. I didn't think to lock the door because it had never been an issue knowing someone was in the bathroom before now. It was always clear that water was running when Nate or I were showering. I hadn't taken a bath in this house before today.

I gulped and held still. I saw a corner of Nate's reflection in the bathroom mirror as he brushed his teeth. He was shirtless, and I hoped very hard he was not planning to take a shower. I didn't move a single muscle and practically held my breath.

Nate finished his teeth and I heard the toilet seat lift. No. Oh no. I was not about to listen to a guy I sort of had a crush on poop. No. I cringed. But instead, I heard him pee, and it was clear from the sound he was standing.

As Nate finished and I heard the snap of a waistband, the water that was gathered around the tub faucet dripped and it landed in the full bath. I whipped my head towards the faucet as it had startled me and sloshed a bit of water with the movement of my shoulders.

I was sure Nate heard it and expected an awkward conversation. But what I didn't expect was for him to whip the shower curtain back so fast the hooks holding it on the curtain rod came off the track.

I screamed and Nate yelled in shock. I hugged my knees to my chest to cover my body.

"I'm so sorry!" he yelled as soon as he realized it was me in the bath. "I'm so glad I didn't fart!"

"I should have locked the door! Oh, my god!" I yelled at the same time he yelled.

Bounding footsteps on the stairs gave a split-second warning that Everett was coming in. His bright blue eyes assessed me in the bath hugging my knees, my horrified expression, the shower curtain hanging off the rod, and Nate standing over the tub in his gray boxer briefs. In a flash, Everett, who was also only in a pair of black boxer briefs, slammed Nate against the bathroom wall by the door by his neck. Nate gaped for a moment before his arms came up, over Ev's arm, and dropped his elbows on Ev's arm to break the choke.

"What in the *hell* do you think you are doing?" Ev was bellowing in Nate's face.

"I thought she was a demon!" Nate yelled back as Everett shoved him by the chest back against the wall.

"It was a mistake!" I shouted from the bath. My voice broke on the shout as I was not used to raising my voice.

Ev looked back at me, his palm still pressing into Nate's chest to hold him still. "You're alright?"

"Yes," I said in a hoarse voice. "I didn't lock the door."

Nate shoved Everett's hand off his chest. "I'm sorry, Eva," Nate apologized.

"It's okay. I'm- I'm sorry for not saying anything when you came in," I returned the apology.

"You're going to fix that curtain," Everett demanded coolly, shoving Nate one last time as he left the room.

Nate stepped towards the bath, looking at the curtain.

"Not right now," I said, my eyes still wide.

"Right, not right now. Got it," Nate said, shaking his head like he was embarrassed and quickly left the bathroom, closing the door behind him. A semi-hysterical laugh bubbled out of my lips and I swore I heard at least one other male voice laughing in the house.

I was very much finished with my bath after he left and I got out, brushed my teeth, and hurried to my room. My pajamas were a pair of boy short panties and a perfectly baggy science club t-shirt from high school. My knee felt better after the soak, but I was no more relaxed than when I got in the tub. I sighed as I laid in bed, staring out my window. A car drove by blaring music, a girl screamed in the distance, and people laughing down the street filtered in.

Maybe if I watched a happy show on tv, I would relax enough to sleep. I tiptoed downstairs and pushed the oversized ottoman up to the couch to create a sort of bed. I curled up under the blankets and turned on The Office, letting the safety and humor of that show relax me.

I was about to doze off when Nate came down the stairs, now wearing a pair of black pajama pants decorated with the green Xbox logo. He found me on the couch and brushed back my hair from my face. "Are you okay?"

I nodded, too drowsy to speak.

"Are you mad at me?"

I shook my head.

"Can I join you? That movie was fucking dumb," he asked and ran his hand through his own hair and looked away.

I gave a little smile and patted the space next to me. He lifted the blanket, and a rush of cool air met my skin before he slid in next to me.

"Did that movie weirdly scare the crap out of you, too?" he asked as he settled with his bare arms behind his head as a pillow.

"A little," I said sleepily with a yawn.

"Well, let's sleep down here where we know big bad Everett will come save us in his undies," Nate said through his own yawn.

I giggled quietly and fell asleep almost at once.

When I woke up, Everett was shaking Nate awake behind me. Nate was curled around me, and my backside was tucked securely against him.

"Wake up if you want to go running," Everett said flatly and left the room. I heard him in the kitchen filling his water bottle.

I sat up with a stretch and looked at the clock on the wall above the tv. It was close to six in the morning and my alarm must have been chiming for thirty minutes upstairs.

Nate and I rushed to our rooms to get changed into our running gear and met Everett out at Marie Curie. He was silent and stoic the entire drive to the park. Nate and I shrugged at each other behind his back.

"Did you sleep well, Ev?" I asked him, thinking about how Nate and I were scared after the movie.

"Not as good as it seemed like the rest of us did," Ev said with a hint of malice.

I didn't understand. Was he mad about me and Nate sleeping on the couch? Or was he grumpy because he actually hadn't slept well?

Nate exhaled hard and leaned back in the seat, knocking his shoulder against mine where I was leaning over the seat to talk to Ev. I dropped the effort to hold a conversation and sat on the bench, facing the back of the cart. Nate ran his hands through his hair and the evergreen scent of his shampoo washed over me.

We stretched and started our run-in relative silence, only pointing out the doe that was grazing in the woods. We made it to our field house that we now deduced was checked in on and maintained once every two weeks, and the lock had not been repaired. Every time a park maintenance person had locked it after their rounds, it slid open again when we pushed it.

Ever since that first trip where Nate laid down on the linoleum, we've all started doing it. The floor was clean and cool against our heated skin from the run there and it helped me relax. We would listen to the water outside and talk. The place was so quiet and calm that we felt safe talking about anything when we were there. Therefore, it was no surprise when Nate sighed and said, "I really hate isolation," with frustration in his voice. "I didn't think I was a very social person until I wasn't able to speak to anyone other than you two. No offense."

"I know what you mean," Everett said. "Sometimes I feel like the quarantine is a bit severe, considering we follow all appropriate safety measures."

"You won't believe it, seeing as I don't speak to anyone, but I feel the same," I said.

"No, I believe it. Even if you weren't actually *saying* anything, I always knew what you were thinking," Nate said nonchalantly.

I smiled at him.

We were quiet for a few more minutes before Everett spoke. "Being isolated makes me think of my brother."

Nate and I turned our heads to him, and Nate went up on an elbow to see Ev over me. "You have a brother?"

"Yeah, he's my only sibling. His name is Easton. He's older than me by about six years," Everett didn't look at us and cleared his throat before continuing. "Man, I looked up to that guy more than I looked up to my dad. He joined the Army right out of high school. My parents were so proud of him. *So* proud. I was too. It was a big deal in our family to defend our country and enlist in the armed forces. A few years in, he was on a mission and got hurt. Nothing too serious, but he had to take some time off and he ended up kind of going AWOL." Everett stopped to clear his throat again. I recognized it as a nervous habit and waited quietly for him to continue.

"When he came home, they discharged him from the Army and they told us he likely had PTSD from what happened. He did the therapy, he did the work, but he claims to have seen something... knows something that no therapy would erase. He got big into different conspiracy theories and alcohol, stuff got combative, and my parents ended up kicking him out of the house."

"Where is he now?" Nate asked quietly.

"Somewhere in the Smoky Mountains in Tennessee. He lives off the grid in a cabin. I haven't seen him in years," Everett finished, looking at us again. His blue eyes were distant and stormy.

"I'm sorry to hear that," Nate said sincerely. I nodded and reached out to give Ev's hand a quick squeeze.

We were quiet again for a few minutes before I spoke. "I feel like if I don't talk to my dad, we're going to lose contact."

"How would that happen?" Ev asked, not understanding.

"My dad is kind of different. Ever since my mom died in the accident, he's been reclusive and shut off. He's not... unkind or unloving. He's just a quiet person. When I'm home we can go many days on end without speaking to each other. Not because we're angry, but we just... don't talk," I said quietly. "I know, ha ha, Eva doesn't talk to anyone, but I could talk to my dad. I just... don't."

"So, isolation like this is normal life for you?" Nate asked with disbelief in his voice.

I smiled. "Not quite. Well... maybe, but it wasn't forced on me, so it didn't feel quite so stifling."

"Stubborn," Ev chuckled.

"Very," I conceded with a giggle.

We had an office work heavy morning ahead of us, so we finished our run and went back home for showers and breakfast. As we were headed out to Marie Curie, a delivery driver was dropping a package off at our front door. Ev waved at him in thanks as he ran back to his delivery van.

"Ooh! Our cereal dispenser!" Nate exclaimed and went to pick up the package.

"Our what now?" Ev asked him, looking suspicious.

"It dispenses breakfast cereal when you turn the dial on the front like a gumball machine. It has three different containers so we each can have a type. Isn't that so cool?" Nate explained excitedly.

I grinned at him. It was pretty cool, to be honest. His excitement was cute and even Ev was grinning as Nate went to put it in the house.

"That man is something else," Ev chuckled as we settled in the two seats of Marie Curie.

Nate came out and gave a small pout when he saw me in the passenger seat. "Ugh, scoot over. You're small enough to fit between us."

I didn't have time to form a response before Nate was pushing into the seat and sliding me down towards Ev. I fit between them fine. It was tight between their muscular torsos and their splayed legs, but considerably warmer in the autumn wind. I was wedged close enough to feel Ev's phone vibrate in his pocket against my thigh.

Nate pulled out his own phone and showed me the text from Daisy.

Daisy: Did you guys really put in a grocery order for six different types of breakfast cereal, milk, coffee, and beef jerky?!
Nate: Yes. We keep a very balanced diet.
Daisy: You're ridiculous! *Crying laughing emoji.*

Nate had read the texts out loud for Ev. "How does she know?" was Ev's response.

Nate: How'd you know, anyway?
Daisy: A selfie for a secret.

Nate snapped a quick, rather unflattering picture of the three of us smashed into Marie Curie.

Daisy: Cuties! I set up the email address for your grocery and delivery accounts. Did you see what it was? It's nerdiebabes3@trumanc.edu

Ev had his signature smirk on as we pulled into the lab for a long day of work.

6

I had to work late one evening, and the guys left me to finish with the promise Nate would stay up to come get me. I was finishing a batch of information that was to be sent to Daisy for her processing. It was a long process, but I worked better on it without the distraction of the guys. It was a satisfying feeling hitting send on the email after hours and days and weeks of work.

Leaning back in my desk chair, I shot a text to Nate to let him know I finished. It was nearing one in the morning, and I let out a jaw cracking yawn and stretched. I tidied up my desk and filed away the notepad I had been annotating in with bits and pieces of research. No reply had come.

Me: All done!

Me: Hey Nate, can you come get me?

Me: *gif of a man yodeling on a mountain*

Me: okay it's been twenty minutes and you're not reading these texts or answering my calls. Cool.

I sent a text to Everett to see if he was awake and could come get me. I called him, too. No response ten minutes later. Awesome.

I put on the sweatshirt I had left in the office a few days ago and layered my jacket over it. It was chilly when we drove in this morning, but now it was cold and raining. Sighing, I shut the lights off behind me and started on my way home. I could have stayed in the lab and slept on the couch in our office, but I was exhausted and wanted my bed and my coziest pajamas. The rain was freezing cold in the November air, and it seeped into my jacket and clothes quickly. I was mad. Then I was enraged. Then I was Throw The Whole Man Into The Bowels Of Hell angry.

There was a small side street I was pretty sure went between two buildings and would get me to our house faster. We had never driven any way other than our usual path, but I was certain this way would be shorter while walking. That side street turned out to be an alleyway between a cute café that had what looked like French style patisserie in the windows, and a shop that sold teas. I made a mental note of them being a few blocks away and wondered if they did delivery. I rushed down the alleyway at a sloshing jog in my Ked sneakers. My feet were numb in my shoes and my nose was streaming.

I came out of the other side of the alleyway and heard an engine barreling toward me. On reflex, I jumped back thinking it was a car and panicked. I fell back onto the sidewalk as the tires came to a skidding halt near me.

"Eva!" a man's voice shouted through the rain.

I looked up to see Everett, in a raincoat, pajama pants, Nate's baseball hat, and his running shoes. He rushed to me and grabbed me up by the shoulders. "Are you alright?" he shouted over the thundering rain, water dripping down his nose and onto me despite his hat brim and raincoat.

I tried to answer verbally, but I couldn't find the words. I nodded stiffly and gave a large sniff. He said nothing, but had to practically carry me to Marie Curie. Ev set me on the passenger seat and got in the driver's seat. He wrapped an arm around me and held me to him, but it did not help for sharing warmth. Though, heat did bloom in my belly from being smashed against him, banded in with his powerful arm. I breathed in his clean soap and beeswax beard balm scent and held on as we skidded through the turns.

"I'm going to fucking kill that kid," Everett grunted as he drove as fast as Marie Curie could take us in the rain. MC had no windshield, so water drenched us as we drove, the drops feeling like pin pricks on my cheeks.

"I f-finished the report and sent it to Daisy," I said through shivering teeth.

"That's great," Ev said, a bit flat.

"And I saw these t-two shops I w-want to check out. A p-place that l-looked like a French p-p-pastry shop and a c-cool tea shop," I told him, if only to keep part of my body moving against the cold.

"You were supposed to be coming home, not sight seein'," Everett lightly scolded me with a squeeze.

"I was t-taking a shortcut through that al-alley. It connects to Chestnut Street b-before the turn we make," I informed him.

He hummed in response and concentrated on his fast driving.

We flew into the driveway as Nate was running out the side door, pulling his pants up as he ran. Crocs on his feet and an open raincoat over his bare chest. He whipped around to see us pulling in and I saw the look of both regret and relief cover his features.

"Oh, thank god. Eva, I'm so sorry-" he started desperately.

"How could you?! You promised!" I practically shrieked at him. The cold and emotions were limiting my vocal abilities, and I didn't mean to sound so shrill. "I had to walk in the rain and it's so fucking cold!"

I realized I was shivering so hard I could barely stand, but I forced my legs to walk up to Nate and push him in the chest. My hands slapped against his now wet skin.

"I'm sorry," Nate said regretfully, as Everett again half carried me into the house with his arm around my shoulders.

"Go upstairs, throw your wet clothes in the tub, and wrap up in towels and get into bed. I'll warm some pajamas in the dryer," Everett said quietly as he helped me up the stairs. He said louder, "And Nate will make you some lemon and ginger tea."

I followed his directions and huddled in my bed, naked but wrapped in towels and blankets. Everett returned to my room a few moments later with a pair of gray lounge shorts and a red Hanes zip up hoodie I had seen him wear. "Here, these were in the dryer already, so they're warm and dry for you." He handed warm and soft clothes to me.

"Thank you, Ev," I said, my voice hoarse from yelling.

He gave me a soft smile instead of his usual smirk. "Thank me after I beat that kid to a pulp," he said before leaving the room.

I hurried and put the clothes on while they were still warm, inhaling deeply the smell of him where it clung permanently to the cotton fibers. I could hear his voice rumbling downstairs as he spoke to Nate. The kettle we had yet to use clunked down on the stove. I felt nervous, wondering if Ev was going to beat Nate up. Nate's voice rumbled back, though I couldn't hear what they were saying.

I tiptoed to the top of the stairs and listened more carefully.

"I don't care if you had something personal going on. You gotta hold to your word. Especially with women," Everett was saying in a scolding tone.

"It wasn't intentional, man. I didn't-" Nate started back angrily.

"It doesn't fucking matter because it happened. It did. And she could have frozen to death out there. Did you see the state of her?"

"I did and I feel so fucking bad about it," Nate snapped back.

"You gotta understand that women are always thinking about way more than we are, okay? While I saw her and thought 'Oh shit, she's going to freeze,' she was thinking about her safety, the cold, the project, *and* the two new places she saw for takeout when she took a wrong turn. She didn't know it was a wrong turn, but I'm not going to tell her that," Everett said, and I heard Nate rummaging through the tea that was in the cupboard when we moved in. "But what I'm saying is, you put that woman in a situation where she could have gotten hurt or- or kidnapped or somethin' and she didn't need to be there. She put her trust in you, and you dropped it."

"Is that all women? Or only Eva?" Nate asked with a sigh.

"It's all women, but right now Eva is the woman you just pissed the hell off, so you better make it right. Shit, son, how old are you?"

"I'm the same fucking age as you, but not all of us are fucking ripped cowboys from the covers of romance novels, with tons of romantic experience," Nate snapped at Everett as the kettle whistled.

Everett chuckled despite Nate's tone. "Nathaniel, are you a virgin?" He asked in a deep, smooth voice.

"No, but shut up," Nate said, and I heard him coming towards the stairs. I hurried back to my bed, feeling guilty like I was a little girl eavesdropping on her parents' private conversations.

I pulled the piles of blankets up over me and shoved the damp towels onto the floor as Nate stepped into the room with a steaming mug of a spicy smelling tea.

"Here's some tea," he said hesitantly and sat it on my nightstand.

I barely looked at him, still shirtless but in low slung gray sweatpants now. He had a visible Adonis belt, despite having less defined abs than Everett, and I could do little to keep my eyes from straying to his body. He had hair on his chest and a little on his belly before getting darker and leading from his belly button to beneath his sweatpants. My mouth watered, and I mentally scolded myself. I was supposed to be mad at him.

"Can I sit?" He asked, shyly.

I nodded and reached for the hot mug of tea. I let the spicy steam wash over my face and breathed it in before I took a tiny burning sip. A few sips and I was sure to be thawed and warmed from the inside out.

"It's no excuse, but I feel like you're the kind of person who wants to know *why* things happen," he started, the uncertainty audible in his voice.

"It might have something to do with me being a scientist," I joked hoarsely.

He shot me a quick grin before continuing. "This evening I basically talked to my parents for the first time since coming here. They were trying to arrange their holiday plans and had bought a plane ticket for me to come home for winter break. I had to tell them I was not coming home for winter break because I do not get a break this year. They were beside themselves with anger. It was absolutely ridiculous coming from them," he said, running his hands through his hair in aggravation. "They don't give a single shit about me any other day except for my dad's business holiday party and the family picture for Christmas cards. They didn't even buy my ticket to get here from Connecticut. Not that I care, but it's so ridiculous- the dramatics they employ when they need me for something. I fought with my parents for a while and then ended up crashing into bed. I had meant to stay awake but fell asleep by accident."

I drank my tea and thought about what he had told me.

"Are you still cold?" he asked softly after a moment.

When I shook my head, the towel I had on top of my head wrapped around my hair came loose. I tossed the towel onto the floor with the other ones. "Well, my feet are still cold," I whispered. Probably because I had been standing barefoot at the top of the stairs eavesdropping, but I'd never tell.

Nate lifted the blankets and got into my bed to sit next to me against the headboard. The clean, crisp smell of his soap curled around me as he took my cold feet into his hands on his lap under the blanket. He hissed at the chilled contact at first and shot me another apologetic glance. He let out a sigh and relaxed against my pillows and headboard. I felt slightly giddy at him being in my bed, but I played it cool.

"I'm... not so mad at you anymore," I said quietly and set my empty mug on my nightstand.

He knocked his head back against the headboard with a soft thud and a smile. "Can't stay mad at a guy with a villain origin story?"

I laughed. "Are you serious? I'm practically a bionic woman. And outside of my close people, I'm practically mute. You know nothing about villain origin stories."

"Am I one of your close people now?" he asked, looking down at me.

"If the vibes are right," I said with a shrug, but I was joking to deflect.

We were silent for a few minutes, listening to the persistent rain outside. The sound of water in the gutter near my window was like a water feature in a spa, and I closed my eyes to relax as I gathered my own story. Nate had shared so much with me, I felt comfortable but also compelled to share something personal with him in return. I wrapped my arms around me and held my shoulders, sort of hunched over and not looking at Nate.

"My dad cares about me, but... I think he cares about his routine and the safety in predictability more. He... wears the same clothes every day, eats the same food, does the same things the same way every day. My mom died like fourteen years ago and her closet is still full of her clothes." My voice lost its strength near the end, and I was whispering. I couldn't remember the last time I had done this much talking. I swallowed. "I think if I made talking to me or seeing me too far out of his daily routine, then he would never reach out to me and I would lose him, too."

Nate was quiet, but he began absently stroking my calf. I hyper focused on the touch and goosebumps formed. He bundled the blankets further up my legs and held his warm hand around my leg as if to warm it up. I focused on how large his hand was to be almost fully wrapped around my calf.

"Dude, are we both in this program to earn the recognition that we are lacking with our parents?" Nate said with a groan, but a smile on his lips.

"Dude, that's too deep for after two in the morning," I copied his inflection though in my hoarse whisper.

"Yeah, you're right," he said with resignation.

"For what it's worth... I see you," I whispered, looking down at my hands.

"I see you, too," he said, his voice soft and deep. He pauses a moment before sliding out of my bed. "Goodnight, Eva. I hope we can all agree that we are *not* going running in a few hours."

I smiled as he left and shifted down to lie in the warm spot on the bed he had left. I inhaled the pine and leather soap scent of him on my pillow and it blended in with the scent of Everett on my clothes, creating a wonderful and relaxing aroma I would burn in a candle any day of the week.

7

We were still in isolation and working for Thanksgiving Day. We had the Macy's parade playing on Nate's laptop in the morning while we worked in the lab, and at lunch, Ev and I called our families. It was kind of sad to be away from home for the holiday, but Everett promised to make us dinner so we could still celebrate. Nate drove him home at noon so he could spend the afternoon preparing our Thanksgiving dinner.

My stomach was rumbling as Nate drove us home as the sun was setting. "He better make it right. No southern bullshit like... like, I don't know, but it better be right," Nate said as we pulled in the driveway.

"As long as there are no marshmallows in the sweet potatoes, I'll be fine," I agreed.

"Ew, fuck that. Brown sugar and honey or it's fucking garbage," Nate said, opening the door for me. The smells of Thanksgiving enveloped us, and it carried us into the kitchen with our noses up like cartoon characters.

Everett was setting a small roasted turkey on a full table of food and wine.

"Where's your apron, Mama Monroe?" Nate teased with a grin, picking up a dinner roll.

Everett smacked it out of his hand and scolded him. "Wash your hands and come be thankful someone takes care of your ass."

Nate looked at me with his eyebrows raised and whispered sarcastically and loud enough for stressed Everett to hear, "Do you think that's a promise?"

I threw my head back and laughed and led the way out of the kitchen to wash my hands.

We sat and stared at each other over the food and glasses. "Um, do we say a prayer or something?" I asked.

"Do you typically pray before you eat?" Ev asked me, curiously.

"No," I said. "Do you?"

"No," Ev replied.

"Soooo, can I eat then?" Nate asked, his hand hovering over the spoon sticking out of the mashed potatoes.

"Yes, you can eat," Everett said, fighting back his smirk but his twinkling eyes gave away his amusement.

We filled our plates while marveling at how the food looked. Everett anxiously watched us take our first bites of everything. I took a bite of mashed potatoes- it was perfect. I moaned out loud to show it was tasty, and Nate dropped his fork that was loaded with turkey. Everett's signature smirk made an appearance, but featured a little pink blush peeking out over his red beard. "So good," I said after I swallowed my bite.

"Okay, I need some of hers," Nate said and reached over with his fork and scooped up some of my mashed potatoes. He ate it then let out an over dramatic, high pitched porno moan. Then paused and said in his normal deep voice, "Yeah, man, it's pretty good."

Everett and I burst out laughing, and the rest of our dinner and two bottles of red wine continued with jokes and jabs at each other and stories about previous holidays.

"We should go around and say what we're thankful for," Nate suggested after we ate large slices of pecan pie and were stuffed.

"Well, I'm thankful for my country, my education, my family, good food, and good company," Everett said and raised his wine glass.

"I'm thankful for you guys, and great food," I added.

"Oh, shit. Now I have to say something nice," Nate said, his cheeks rosy from the wine.

"What were you going to say?" I asked him.

"That I was thankful nobody has talked to us about my quarantine induced browser history, and for big booty bitches. But I guess I can say I'm thankful for the grumpy asshole who made us dinner and the pretty girl who picks out good wine."

I raised my wine glass, and the guys followed suit "To big booty bitches and Nate's horrifying Pornhub search history," I said cheerfully.

"Jesus," Ev muttered but smiled, eyes twinkling around his glass as he drank.

Nate laughed and drained his wine. "Ugh, I could sleep for days after that."

"Absolutely not, we're running at 6," I demanded, and cleared the plates. "Now help me clean up. Ev, you go lay on the couch like every other suburban mom in America right now."

Our phones chimed.

Daisy: Hey nerdies I got you an Instant pot on a black Friday sale. And a recipe book so you have no excuses to not eat real food. I need you all healthy! *Kiss emoji*

"I'm still eating cereal," Nate said and helped me clear the dishes and put away leftovers.

After we finished cleaning up, we piled on the couch on either side of Everett and attempted to drunkenly play a few rounds of a racing game on the Xbox. We were laughing at Everett looking at the wrong car the entire time and driving his car into a guardrail for four minutes of a race when our phones chimed again.

It was a picture of Daisy in a huge bubble bath, her boobs barely covered with bubbles. I stared at the picture for a moment, admiring the confidence it took to send. The guys both put their phones down before I did after seeing the picture. It struck me as odd they didn't linger on the sexy picture- especially Everett. An irrational and unfair feeling of victory swept through me when I realized they were happily spending time with me and not her. Feeling guilty now, I was about to put my phone down when another message came through.

Daisy: um are you three okay? I sure hope you're not working! Can you send me a selfie?

I held out my phone and leaned into the guys to take a picture. They knew Daisy well enough to know what I was doing and why. Nate leaned into Everett while I did the same on his other side and snapped the picture. All three of us had rosy cheeks, hooded eyes, and an easy smile- clearly drunk. Everett looked comfortable and confident between us, and I couldn't remember if I'd ever seen him that relaxed.

I sent the picture and picked up the Xbox controller. We played another round of the racing game with only slightly more success before our phones chimed again.

Everett let out an exhale through his nose as he reached for his phone like he did not want to see what Daisy had to say. I thought maybe he was feeling sad he couldn't see her for the holiday.

Daisy: You guys look like you're too cozy and having too much fun without me *mad face emoji.* I think you need to really sober up and go to bed. Ugh. *Green sick face emoji.*

I didn't know what to reply, but I felt bad for making her upset. Was she upset I was with her boyfriend? We looked cozy in the picture- she was not wrong. But it wasn't exactly a picture of us in a bubble bath sent to the group chat. What was I supposed to say? I paused. What would I want said to me in this situation?

"Don't even reply to that," Everett said grumpily, looking at me with my thumbs hovering over the keyboard before he slid the phone out of my hands. "We should get to bed if we're going to run before work tomorrow."

"You both know how I feel about that," Nate said and stood and put away the controllers.

I tidied up the blankets on the couch before I went up to bed. I still felt bad about upsetting Daisy, despite Everett being dismissive about it. I couldn't help but think maybe I was missing something, and I was about to lose my only female friend.

Over the weekend, Nate worked late to send information to Daisy after our last day of isolation for another week. He was slower to compile the data, so he drove me and Ev home and went back to the lab. He had been working on it most of the day, so it wasn't likely he'd be there all night like I had.

I made dinner in our new Instant Pot while Everett read through our plans for the approaching phase of our research at the kitchen island. We shared some red wine together, and Everett played some country music on Nate's speaker. I was making a beef pot roast with potatoes and carrots and a rich gravy if the recipe and my ability to follow basic directions treated us well. Nate had said he was coming back soon because he had finished earlier than he expected, so I poured the wine for dinner and set the table.

"I ordered the best beef I could get delivered. It's grass fed and there's no growth hormones or antibiotics used, like the cows we had at home," Everett said as I carefully unlatched the lid after it was done depressurizing.

"Oh, your farm was organic?" I asked.

"Free range, pesticide free, organic, you name it," he said proudly. "We sold mostly local and to quite a few restaurants. Only the best quality we could produce. That's what I want to do with my degree; work with a team to develop safer pesticides, safer antibiotics, safer ways to produce quality food."

"That's a wonderful way to use your upbringing in a career and a career to support your upbringing," I said conversationally as I poked at the roast.

"Thank you, baby girl," he said warmly. "Mm, that smells wonderful."

I practically glowed at his words and sipped my wine. There was something about the deep, honeyed timbre of his voice calling me "baby girl" that turned my insides to liquid. I needed to get myself together before I dropped something and took a longer gulp of wine.

A new song came on and it was a slow, crooning country love song I had never heard. I swayed a little to the music as I started plating dinner. The half of a glass of wine was warm in my empty belly and helped me feel loosened up.

"Do you like country music, Eva?" Everett asked, his voice rasping and quiet, and I startled when I realized he was watching me dance.

"I think I like this song at least," I replied. I wasn't familiar with the genre, but this music was almost sensual and romantic.

"What music do you like?" he asked.

"Well, I liked typical pop music as a kid and teen. But I've been into classic rock the last few years," I said with a shrug.

"Have you been to any concerts?" he asked as he brought the plates to the table for me.

"I've been to some local orchestra performances with my dad, and a few clubs had famous DJs come in when I was an undergrad, but not much else," I said and set out water glasses on the table.

"What?" Nate exclaimed as he came bounding up the stairs from the side entrance. He was tugging his hair out of the bun he now typically wore in the lab. "You've never been to a concert?"

I shook my head, suddenly shy.

"I'm taking you. Tonight. Who's playing?" he pulled out his phone as he toed off his shoes by the landing.

"We can't go to a concert," I reminded him and shook my head.

"Ugh, I'm sick of isolation. We're in restricted contact officially as of an hour ago and I want to use up all of my contact at a concert," Nate said, his eyes glued to his phone as he searched for a concert. "I need to rage."

"That's not how restricted contact works, and you know it," Everett warned.

"Just don't tell Professor Hoffmann and we're golden," Nate said nonchalantly, giving Ev a quick wink.

Everett rolled his eyes and sat at the dinner table. I followed suit and Nate followed me, still on his phone.

"What do you mean by rage?" I asked as I cut into my roast. It fell apart as I cut into it, and I was thankful it turned out great.

"Like a metal concert," Nate explained.

"And you think you're going to find one for tonight?" I asked, and took a bite of the perfectly prepared meat.

"Uh yeah, this is Cleveland. There's always someone ready to go berserk," Nate said like it was obvious. "Aha, found one. It's not far from here and it starts in an hour. We're going."

"I'll pass," Everett said and tucked into his dinner.

"Me and Eva will go rage. She needs it, I think," Nate said with another wink now aimed at me.

I wasn't sure what that meant but I didn't question it out loud.

After our quickly eaten but thoroughly enjoyed dinner, Nate ushered me upstairs to get ready. He threw a black t-shirt at me from his room. I was pretty sure he had been wearing it under his sweatshirt all day because of the soft warmth and the male scent clinging to it. "Here, I don't know if you have anything not cute and girly, so wear this."

I put it on over my bra and it fell to almost my knees, so I decided it could work as a dress. I wore it with my white Ked sneakers, put on some dark pink lipstick and thick black mascara, and met the guys back downstairs.

Nate was wearing a black and white plaid flannel, dark jeans, his Vans, and his long hair loose and wavy around his shoulders. Everett wore sweatpants and a frown as he looked me over.

"She's going to catch her death... again," Everett said with a warning tone to Nate.

"She'll be fine. She'll be sweating by the time we leave," Nate said dismissively.

I blushed from my head to my toes at the idea, and Everett watched me with discerning eyes.

8

Nate picked up his car in the student lot and came back to get me. Everett voiced his unease about us going out in public and to a part of the city neither of us had been. Before we hopped into his warmed-up car, Nate snapped at Ev to call Daisy. Nate's car was a red Honda Civic, and the inside felt older than it was because it was all manual. I had seen the outside when we walked and checked on the cars, but had not been inside of it.

I went to move my seat back as Nate maneuvered out of the driveway and he glanced at me out of the corner of his eye. "It's a bar under the seat," he said, with the corners of his mouth turned down slightly.

We had taken Everett's truck to the park when it started being too cold in the mornings for Marie Curie, so I knew his silver Toyota Tacoma well. Everett had always offered to drive, so we never took Nate's car.

"The windows and transmission are manual, too," he said in a slightly grim tone.

I hadn't moved any seats in Ev's truck since my legs fit fine in his back seat, but I had opened his windows with a button, and I was pretty sure his truck was automatic. I didn't see how the windows or the transmission of either vehicle mattered.

"So?" I asked and adjusted my seat.

"My parents bought me this car when I graduated from high school. I'm thankful for it, don't get me wrong, but basically my dad's a dick," Nate replied and pulled his lips in like he was self-conscious.

"What happened?" I asked. "I mean, um, if you want to talk about it."

"Well, my dad owns a chain of grocery stores in the area back home and he thinks he's hot shit. I've been working for him at one of his stores since I was twelve years old. At twelve, I was sweeping up and tidying. Then, as I got older, I started working in different areas of the store. This summer I worked in the warehouse doing some deliveries to the stores while some of the guys took vacations or whatever. Anyway, he has always stressed the need to work hard to earn success. Not a bad lesson, but working every day after school and over the weekend, on holidays, not having many friends or a girlfriend, only participating in rugby, was *not enough.* He would always say I needed to work harder, work longer, to earn what I had. Acted like I was some lazy kid because I liked to listen to music while I worked or because I would rather get my homework done. I had great grades and was in love with science, but it was not *working* like my dad did. So even now, with his adult son, he has to exert this control over me. He got me this car as a *gift,* without me asking for it, and made sure it had everything manual and not automatic or electric, so even my comfort in my seat had to be worked for," Nate explained. He tapped his fingers against the steering wheel and the foot that wasn't on the pedals bounced.

I listened, absorbed in his story. It was the most I had heard Nate talk about something serious or about his family. I had little to say, so I reached over his hand on the gearshift to pat his thigh affectionately. "Thank you for telling me. It means a lot. Truly, I was not judging you for your car."

He gave me a glancing shy smile before his GPS said our destination was on the right. It was previously a warehouse in this industrial area but was now a concert venue. Nate hummed curiously as he looked around and followed a few other cars to a parking lot probably four or five blocks away from the venue.

"I fucked up, I'm sorry, we have to walk," he said entirely genuinely as he turned his body to face me.

It was nearly December and close to twenty degrees outside. I shivered in anticipation. We had not brought coats thinking we would not want to carry them around all evening. Nate blasted the heat so we might carry the heat with us on the walk to the concert. It did not work for more than a few seconds into the bitter cold wind coming off Lake Erie.

"This is the s-econd t-time you've almost had me d-die from exposure," I shivered in a warning tone as we hurried down the sidewalk with a few other concert goers.

"I know I'm s-sorry," he groaned back as we stood in a short line.

"Now you have to buy me a drink," I taunted with a grin.

"Deal," Nate grinned back as we stepped up to the bouncer and Nate handed him both of our IDs since I didn't have pockets.

Once inside, we headed straight to the bar. Loud music was playing, but the band was not on the stage yet. At the bar, many other girls wearing short dresses, shorts, or tank tops were shivering, waiting for drinks.

The heavily pierced and tattooed bartender cast smiling eyes up and down my body. "Another cold bitch looking for something to warm her up! I'm making all you fuckers coffees with baileys or hot toddies."

Nate wrapped his arm around my shoulders as everyone turned to look at us. I smiled at the bartender. "She'll take a coffee with Baileys," Nate ordered for me as we both leaned against the bar. Then he looked down at me, his eyebrows raised like he was nervous he was wrong. "Right?" I nodded with a grateful smile.

I looked around at the people piling into the venue while we waited for our drinks. It was mostly men, but some women, and many of the fans were wearing masks that looked like goat heads or devil masks. I couldn't tell if it was one or both without staring too intently. Many people wore face paint as well, and I saw a lot of repeated designs in the masks and paint, so I assumed it was symbolic of the band. I had heard the name of the band, but it escaped my memory, and the font on the t-shirts looked more like blood smears than legible English.

I was out of my element, and this was more people than I had seen in months. It was a bit jarring to the senses to suddenly be surrounded by other people after months of being so isolated. I stuck close to Nate and didn't make eye contact with anyone as more and more people crowded in to get drink orders.

When Nate and I had our drinks, we stepped aside, and he grabbed my hand to keep me near him in the crowd. "Are you good?" he asked over the din of people around us.

I nodded up at him. "There's a lot of people here," I said and finished my drink in a long gulp.

"I know. We can go if you're freaking out," he offered, his hand warm and strong in mine.

I made a face and gesture to say I was fine and wanted to stay. We set our empty drinks on the bar and headed into the crowd by the stage.

We stopped near an open area where a few people were standing. I knew enough about metal shows to assume that was the mosh pit, if that was still what it was called. Maybe my first metal show was not the time to join a mosh pit, so I clung to Nate's warm hand. His thumb absently stroked up and down on my hand as he looked around at the crowd.

It wasn't long before an opening act came on and I learned all the bands performing were local bands. People were decked out in t-shirts and masks and hats and other merch as if they were a major label band, and I understood then how enthusiastic the metal community in the area was.

The music was blaring loud this close, I could feel the hammering of the drums in my body. It wasn't my normal taste in music, but I could appreciate their talent and admire the hold they had on their fans. The opening band wore various scary looking face paints and ripped up clothes. It reminded me of what I'd seen in advertisements for haunted houses around Halloween. I looked at Nate next to me to see him smiling and looking down at me. I mouthed "What?" to him and he shook his head as if to say, "Never mind" and looked back at the band.

The opening band played maybe five songs before the main act came on stage. Some of the band members wore the goat-devil masks and some didn't. As they took the stage, more people were crushing in towards the front and into the mosh pit. My five-foot self drifted away in the current of people, but Nate grabbed me and held me to him, laughing. I gripped his flannel shirt, dreading being separated from him. As the crowd settled a little, I couldn't see the stage other than a few glimpses under people's arms as they moved and cheered. Nate shifted to stand behind me, his hands on my shoulders and his body warm against my back.

I was watching a guy next to us who was rocking his body to the first song and bobbing his head so that his hair flipped in front of his face and back over. Nate squeezed my shoulders and I looked up to him and he jutted his chin at our neighbor and raised an eyebrow at me, silently asking if I wanted to do that. I nodded in response. When in Rome, I figured. Nate moved one leg to be in front of mine so he had more secure footing, banded a strong arm around my ribcage, and did a slow bend to show me the movement.

His front pressed against my back, his body almost curled around mine, and I could barely breathe from it. His chest pulled back, and I went with him back to standing. Then, as the music took on a deeper, slower, more bass filled tone, Nate rocked our bodies with the music, his slightly curled brown hair flipping over and tangling with mine. He stopped and ran his hands through his long hair with the curl at the bottom and marveled at how long it was now. I laughed as he experimented with banging his head and having his hair flip like the guys on stage and around us. His eyes were alight with joy over his hair.

The next song was heavy on the drums and the screaming from the singer brought up feelings of anger in me even though I didn't understand what he was belting out. People around us were screaming along with the song and I looked up to Nate when I felt his chest rumbling like he was screaming as well. He was screaming, not to the lyrics, but as loud as he could. I couldn't hear him over the deafening sound of the band and crowd, but I knew he was screaming based on the bulging veins in his neck and puffed-up chest. He looked down at me and made a face to suggest I follow suit. Again, when in Rome? I couldn't remember the last time I screamed. Like screamed, screamed.

I took a deep breath, tilted my head back, and let out the loudest sound I could. I wasn't even sure if an actual sound was coming out of me because of the level of sound around us. But it felt amazing to scream. To scream out my grief over my mom, my anger with my dad, my confusing feelings about Nate and Ev, and my frustration at being so isolated. I also screamed out what I now realized to be a blinding rage at my own anxieties over speaking to people. I balled my hands into fists so tight I was sure to have nail marks in my palms. When I screamed three chest cracking- lung bursting times, I looked up to Nate with unexpected tears streaming down my face. He smiled down at me, a smile I had not seen from him before, touched with warmth and almost devotion. I gasped as he leaned down and pressed his sweaty forehead against my equally sweaty one. He grabbed my face and rather forcefully wiped my tears from my cheeks with his thumbs.

"See? You needed to rage!" Nate mouthed to me with that same smile. "Drink?"

I nodded vigorously, my throat burning from the screaming, and we navigated to the bar. For the rest of the concert, we stayed near the bar to avoid having to push through the sea of people near the stage and drank some more.

By the time the band was saying their goodbyes and bowing, we were ready to leave. Nate and I ran back to his car, laughing at each other as we slipped and almost fell on the poorly salted sidewalk. At one point I fell, scraped my knee, and ungracefully flashed Nate my underwear under the black t-shirt I was wearing as a dress. He laughed, scooped me up, and ran with me in his arms while shouting about saving the princess. We were both out of breath, laughing, and shouting about being chased by various video game and fantasy villains as Nate jogged us back to the car. It was not lost on me he was literally carrying me and jogging. While I was not a large person, I still found it incredibly sexy he could do that. He unlocked the passenger side with his key and shoved me into the seat and slammed the door. While running around to his side he slipped on the ice, disappeared below the front of the car, but resurfaced near his door. I was laughing so hard at his fall that I could barely breathe and tears were streaming again.

"Shut the fuck up!" he laughed breathlessly as he climbed into his seat, brushing ice and salt off his dark jeans. He started the car and cranked the heat.

I curled my knees up to my chest and stretched the shirt over them to cover my legs. "Here, give me your legs. I think the heat works better on this side anyway," Nate suggested with his arms outstretched.

I uncurled my legs and placed them on his lap. I couldn't tell if the heating was better over on his side, but I certainly warmed up. He cupped his hands around his mouth and blew into them to warm them up before placing his hands on my calves and rubbing them up to my knee and back down to my ankle over and over. I swallowed hard, my core clenching and unclenching like a pulse. I couldn't speak as he warmed my legs. He stared at my bare skin attentively, watching his hands move over the scars on my knees.

My ears were ringing from the concert, but I could hear our still elevated breathing, the slushy snow melting and falling off of our shoes as the heating worked, and my racing heartbeat. I watched his hands slide up and down my skin and my goosebumps were no longer from the cold but from his touch. I was so attuned to his skin on mine that I swore I could pinpoint the individual skin cells and blood cells he touched. His fingers brushed over my scars and moved to the backs of my knees, and I shivered. I bit my bottom lip as he looked up at my face. His deep green eyes looked almost black from his dilated pupils as he looked at my bit lip. I released it and he practically lunged at me.

His mouth met mine, and my breath caught in my throat. I paused in shock for only a second before I kissed him back. My hand came up to his face and tangled in his hair. When I returned the kiss, he tipped my chin back and gave me little kisses that felt like sips of what he was holding back. His tongue teased my lips. My heart beat so fast and hard, but I didn't care if he could hear it. Butterflies erupted in my stomach… and south of my stomach. We kissed like that for a few minutes, with my legs still in his lap, and Nate leaning over and propping himself up with an elbow on the center console and his other hand on the nape of my neck.

I broke away for a breath. My heart was beating so hard in my chest it felt like my lungs couldn't get enough air. He smiled lazily down at me, his eyes hooded and his cheeks flushed.

"Holy shit," he whispered, awe in his voice. His eyes darted around my face like he was carefully taking in my reaction to him.

"Yeah," I so eloquently whispered back. Ever the wordsmith, I was.

He smiled again, more devilishly now at whatever he saw on my face, and reached across the console to grab me. He pulled me by my waist until I was over him and I moved my legs so I could straddle him in the driver's seat. The seatbelt buckle dug into my left knee, but I ignored it. I put most of my weight on my right knee- my metal implants would have to take one for the team.

This time, my lips crashed to his as I sat on his thighs and gripped his hair at the back of his neck. I felt out of control- this was not how I saw this evening going. I swiped my tongue against his in a playful, teasing movement. He groaned and pulled me closer to him with one large hand on the small of my back and the other in the middle of my back. Those *kitty butterflies* needed attention. As I shifted towards him, I rolled my hips against his and sighed at the friction. Instead of reducing my need, the move amplified it. I felt crazed with the need for him *right now.* He made a deep noise in the back of his throat and pulled me even harder to him with two hands gripping my ass almost too hard. He adjusted his legs as he braced his feet against the floor and ground his hips against me. I could feel his arousal pressing against my own, and I rolled my hips again. The want for him felt all consuming, and I whimpered.

"You feel that?" he whispered huskily, breaking our heated kiss.

I nodded, swallowing nervously as I caught my breath again.

"That's because you've been wearing my t-shirt all night. And you had your perfect ass pressed against me so tight when we danced this shirt rode up and I could see your little purple panties. Fuck, Eva," he sighed and pressed his hips up against me again and I moaned at his words and movement. He gripped my ass so tight I was sure I'd have marks in the morning. I didn't care even the slightest bit.

"All those metal heads were staring at you and your beautiful legs all night, but you were there with *me* hanging on *my* arm," he said in a low voice unlike anything I'd ever heard from him before. It rumbled through my chest where it pressed against his.

My body felt like it was about to burn up at his touch and his words. I desperately wanted more from him. He kissed along my neck and collarbone where the large t-shirt hung off of me and he lifted it over my hips, so I was straddling him in my panties.

"Mm, you feel warm now, baby," he said with a smile. He gripped my ass again and this time his ring fingers and pinkies spanned to the edges of my rather damp panties. I gasped at the contact, and he groaned into my mouth. "You're so wet. I fucking love it."

I reached down and undid his belt with shaking, desperate fingers. He grabbed my hands away and held both of my wrists in one of his hands. He looked up at me with an easy-going smile. "There's no rush, baby. When I make you come and when I come for you, I want us to take our time. Not rushed in my car," he said, his voice deep and rasping but soft. "Is that okay?"

I nodded enthusiastically.

"No, I wanna hear it. Tell me you want us to take our time when I fuck you," he demanded, holding my wrists tighter in his hand.

I swallowed and took a breath. He waited patiently. "I want us to take our time when you fuck me," I whispered, still sounding desperate and needy.

He rolled his hips up to me at my words.

"That's a good girl. Now, get back in your seat and buckle up. We should get home," he said and let go of my wrists.

I did as he said. He smiled over at me as I pulled the t-shirt back down and buckled with still shaking fingers.

Nate turned on the radio and began the drive home.

"So, uh, that was different," I said hoarsely from screaming at the concert.

"What, the concert?" Nate asked, his voice and demeanor back to his normal happy, golden retriever self.

"No… you and how you talk when you're… you know," I elaborated clearly.

"Oh, ha. Well, yeah, is that alright?" he said nervously and rubbed a hand over the back of his neck. "I get a little… possessive and rough sometimes."

"It is… absolutely alright," I said. The butterflies in my stomach and south of my stomach had barely let up in the ten-minute drive. My thighs were still firmly clenched together and slightly damp.

"Good," he said brightly, more confidently now.

"We might want to keep this from Ev for now," Nate suggested, his tone and expression saying he was still debating on that choice. "I get the feeling he would get weird about it even though he's with Daisy."

I nodded, not really caring what Ev would say since I had to deal with him sleeping with Daisy in our house. My butterflies turned to a swirl of jealousy at thinking of them together and then guilt because it didn't matter- I was with Nate. I was feeling dizzyingly confused and needed to process on my own later.

We pulled up to our dark house and Nate said he'd move the car in the morning as we parked in the driveway. I unlocked the front door quickly as it was freezing and I wanted to get in bed with Nate. The house was quiet, and I assumed Everett was sleeping or in his room with Daisy. We both grabbed water bottles and headed upstairs. Nate spun me and pressed me against the wall outside my room and kissed me until I was breathless again. I reached up on my tiptoes and wrapped my arms around his neck and deepened the kiss.

He pulled away and smiled warmly down at me. "Good night, Eva."

"G-good night?" I stuttered as the butterflies angrily demanded his attention. I pouted, having thought I was going to be in bed with him by now.

He stepped back and went into the bathroom with a smirk in response to my angry pout. I didn't move until I heard the shower turn on. I went into my bedroom and changed into a short nightgown in a silky light pink fabric, forgoing panties or a bra in case Nate came back. My nipples were visible beneath the light fabric, and my navel and the small patch of trimmed pubic hair. I knew my butt crack was also clearly visible. I'd bought this nightgown over the summer for spending time with Caleb and I vaguely wondered at my subconscious for having packed it.

A soft knock sounded at the door, and my stomach jumped in anticipation. I quickly put my hair up in a messy bun with pieces hanging down casually. Pinching my cheeks to give them a rosy color, I opened the door.

"Oh, Everett," I said breathlessly, shock clear on my face.

He looked me over, assessing me, and reached out to my shoulders and turned me around as though he was checking me for damage. Like a dad who had let his son take his project car out for a date and was now checking for scratches in the paint. I frowned at his intrusion and worried if he could see my nipples or my butt crack outline through the pale nightgown as he spun me back around.

"You're okay?" he asked, worry etched in his brow.

"Yes, I'm fine," I said in my still hoarse voice.

"Are you sick?" he asked urgently and felt my forehead.

"No, it's from screaming," Nate answered him, standing in the bathroom's doorway, only a towel slung low around his waist. His broad chest was on display and his wet hair slicked back. The butterflies in my stomach and my core started a parade with banners and bells. I bit my lip as my mouth watered.

Everett removed his large hands from my bare shoulders and looked at Nate. "Screaming?" he asked like he was perfectly aware of the naughty undertones of Nate's words.

"Yeah, at the concert. Nate taught me how to scream," I whispered to preserve my voice, furthering the innuendo. As Everett's eyes swung back to me, Nate's eyes darkened to a smolder. I struggled to move my eyes away from Nate's towel to Everett's face. But when I did, I saw Everett's hurt expression for a millisecond before he blinked it away.

What the hell?

"She'll be better after something hot in her throat," Nate said, keeping the innuendo going.

Everett swallowed hard, and I watched his Adam's apple bob.

"A couple good swallows of something hot and she'll be good as new." Nate pushed it a bit too far. If I wasn't blushing before, I was positively crimson after that. Honestly, it was kind of hot, so I clenched my thighs together.

"I'll help you," Everett said, seemingly innocently. Like he was going to fix me a tea or get a lozenge. But neither Nate nor I heard it that way, I was sure.

I felt a million emotions all at once in an explosion dominated by panic in my stomach. "NOPE!" I coughed at the awkward strain in my voice. "Nope, I'm good. Good night, guys!"

I twirled quickly into my room, feeling my short nightgown lift with the movement and effectively flashing the guys my ass before I slammed my door shut. That was the second time I had flashed someone tonight. I heard Nate's booming laugh as he walked down the hall to his room and Everett said "Oh, um okay, goodnight," to my closed door before going back downstairs. My phone chimed a few moments later.

Nate: Nice ass *peach emoji*

Me: OMG stop I didn't mean to do that. *Face palm emoji*

Nate: I appreciated the show.

Me: Bet Everett didn't haha

Nate: Sure.

Me: Thank you for taking me to the concert tonight.

Nate: My pleasure. I had a great time with you.

Me: *kiss emoji*

Nate: Yeah that was the best part. See you in the morning.

Me: Goodnight

Nate: *eggplant emoji*

I laughed and put my phone on the charger and settled into bed.

9

I woke to my alarm the next morning and sat up with renewed energy, remembering the concert and kiss with Nate. I dressed in a black sports bra, black running leggings, and a white zip up hoodie. Downstairs, Everett was already tying his shoes and dressed in his gray sweatpants and blue college sweatshirt. "Good morning," he greeted me with his rumbly sleepy voice.

I smiled in return and grabbed us waters and bananas, listening as Nate's alarm blared loudly. Everett slid my pink knit headband that covers my ears, the matching scarf, and a pair of black gloves to me on the kitchen island. "One man in his house won't let you freeze to death," he said with a smirk.

"She warmed up pretty quickly last night," Nate said casually as he bounded down the last of the steps and rounded into the kitchen. He was wearing black sweatpants and a gray hoodie, his hair looking wild and sleep tousled.

I blushed and Ev clenched his jaw and grabbed his keys off the counter before leading us out to his truck.

We did our normal run, but the cold air was especially painful in our lungs now. We entered the fieldhouse where maintenance had yet to notice the lock on the door was broken but had been in and replaced a few lightbulbs. I sat on the floor in front of the big windows and watched the stillness of a winter morning. Nobody spoke, the only sounds being the slight hum of the heating, and our combined heavy breathing. The guys sat on either side of me and looked outside.

Nate, of course, was the first to break the silence. "How is Daisy doing?"

Everett shrugged. "I don't know."

"Oh, I thought you were with her last night," Nate explained and drank from his water.

"I wasn't."

Silence.

"Is she your girlfriend?" Nate asked.

"No." Was Ev's curt, deep voiced reply.

"Do you have another girlfriend? Back home, maybe?" Nate asked.

"I do not," Everett replied, and took a deep drink of his water.

"A boyfriend then?" Nate pushed.

Ev sighed through his nose. "No, there isn't someone back home. Not in... awhile."

"But, like, was there someone?" Nate asked, leaning around me to look at Ev. I elbowed Nate in his side. Nate wasn't being rude intentionally; it was his genuine curiosity and enthusiasm for other people.

"I had a girlfriend of five years until a year ago," Everett answered in his quiet, deep voice.

"Did she leave you for a more rootin' tootin' cowboy?" Nate asked, his voice serious, but his mouth curling up into a smile.

Ev shot him a sardonic look and shook his head. "No, her parents wanted her and I to get married and take over their farm so they could retire. She was in law school and I was still in school and the pressure got to us, so we ended it."

"Were your parents on board with hers?" Nate asked.

"They liked her and her family well enough, but they thought two farms would be too much for us to handle when I eventually take over my family's farm," Everett explained, his tone lighter now as he realized we were listening to him attentively. "They weren't heartbroken when we broke it off. I still see her sometimes when we're both back home. There are no hard feelings."

"Huh, no fighting with your ex? I wouldn't know that life," Nate laughed.

"I don't fight with my ex," I added with a shrug.

"What's your ex like? And how 'ex' are we talking?" Nate asked eagerly.

I smirked at his ardent tone and expression. "Well, his name is Caleb, and he was my boyfriend throughout high school. We broke up to go to college and be with other people."

Ev cleared his throat. "Daisy may have mentioned that you and he are still involved."

"Not really. We hook up casually when we're both home," I said with a shrug.

"Like friends with benefits?" Nate asked, incredulously.

"Sure," I said. "That's probably the closest way to describe it." I grew uncomfortable talking about my previous relationship, so I changed the topic. "What about you, Nate?"

"I had a girlfriend maybe six months before moving here," he replied. "She and I were… not compatible, to say the least."

"Anybody else? Or only her?" Everett asked, focused on Nate and eyebrows raised.

"Nope, just Sidney," Nate said and leaned back on his hands.

"Wait, you mean you've only had one girlfriend?" Everett asked in a nonjudgmental way.

Nate nodded with a "Mhm" of confirmation.

"Were you a virgin until her?" Everett asked almost at once after Nate's response. Everett was still focused on him and his eyes were scanning Nate's face intently.

My head snapped to Nate, remembering last night and the way he spoke to me.

He blushed. "Yeah, I was. Okay, ha-ha, you can make fun of me now."

"I don't think we're making fun of you," Everett said with a shake of his head.

"We're not," I clarified with another shrug. "I've only been with Caleb, too."

"What's your body count, Ev?" Nate asked him, clearly trying to get the attention off himself.

"I'm not answering that," Everett said, then stood from the floor and stretched his arms over his head. Nate rolled his eyes, and we followed suit. Conversation about our past relationships ended as we headed out to finish our run.

We had an office heavy day, and Everett went home to bring us lunch. I wanted to go to Nate and kiss him again, but he was clearly involved in his work and music, so I opted not to derail him. I worked at my desk quietly as he typed away at his, tapping his foot to the beat of the music in his headphones. Ev came back with our lunches and set us up at our desks. He had, like always, put so much thought into our lunches. I would have probably thrown together some peanut butter and jelly sandwiches with some salads and called it a day, but not Everett. He had made each of us grilled cheese sandwiches, still warm in their containers, and some piping hot tomato soup. A little container of sliced vegetables and hummus, and a small piece of chocolate, were all carefully packed into an insulated lunch box. He unboxed it on the space on my desk next to me and I watched him with a smile on my face. He did this most days when we didn't shovel cereal in our mouths during a quick break. I loved the care he took of us, regardless of Nate's attitude or my silence. He truly enjoyed taking care of others. I thanked him and squeezed his hand before he stepped away.

He moved to Nate's desk and unboxed Nate's identical lunch for him. He set the spoon down on Nate's left side, knowing he was left-handed. Nate lowered one headphone. "Did you make the soup?"

"No, Mrs. Campbell did," Ev said with his signature smirk. "I made the sandwich, though."

"Thanks, baby," Nate said brightly and blew him a kiss. It was silly and total Nate to talk and act like that, even to Everett. It always caught Ev off guard before he would respond, and I loved watching their banter. I watched them today while I ate my soup as Ev walked to his desk with a pink blush staining his cheeks above his beard. My chest swelled with affection for both of them.

Everett unpacked his own lunch, the same as ours, and we ate in comfortable silence. Only the sound of Nate loudly slurping his soup and occasionally humming to his music met my ears. Everything Nate did was loud. He had no mute button. But strangely, I liked his noise. As a person who lived life on mute, it was refreshing to be around someone who came with their own soundtrack. Even if that soundtrack was often stomach sounds and random parts of songs or viral videos shouted out. I always knew when Nate was in the room.

Later that evening, Nate and I were playing video games on the couch while Everett did a few chores around the house. Nate called it "putzing" around, but we both knew Everett needed to keep busy.

"If I win, I get a kiss," Nate murmured to me, his eyes on the screen intently.

"You're already winning, that's not fair," I laughed. He was literally two seconds away from winning the round of our game.

"Fair and square," he said as he won and turned to me and quickly pushed me back on the couch, so I was lying beneath him.

I lifted my head enough to kiss him and he sighed as he pressed his weight down on me. Kissing him here, with no alcohol, in our home after a day of work, was no less exciting than last night. My stomach fluttered as his tongue slid against mine and his thigh notched against my core. I gasped into his mouth and gripped his considerable biceps.

"I've been thinking about this mouth all day," he said in that deep, commanding voice again.

"Oh, yeah?" I questioned breathlessly.

"You have no idea," he replied and removed this thigh to grind his hips down on mine. I felt his arousal against mine and I gasped again.

The door to the house by the kitchen opened and Everett came in, knocking snow off of his boots against the door frame. Nate jumped up and we arranged ourselves to not look like we'd been kissing just before he came through to get to his bedroom. My heart pounded with the adrenaline of almost getting caught, warring with the dampness of my panties.

"I took out the trash, but if one of you could bring down the bin tomorrow, it would be a great help," Everett said casually before looking at us sitting on the couch and the paused game.

"Yeah, sure," Nate said and pressed play on the game again. He ran a hand through his hair and adjusted how he was sitting with the blanket on his lap.

Everett narrowed his eyes at him, then looked at me. I sucked my bottom lip into my mouth and swallowed nervously. He looked between me and Nate a few times again.

"You wanna play?" Nate offered.

"No, I'm headed to bed," Everett replied, and went to his room, shutting the door behind him.

"That was close," I said nervously.

"Nah," Nate dismissed. "Besides, we're only not telling him to keep the house from getting awkward. So, if he found out, it wouldn't be the end of the world."

That was true. I still felt worried about how Everett would react and wondered if he would be upset. Shaking my head, I tried to dismiss the thought. I was with Nate. I didn't need to worry about how Everett would feel about the relationship.

"We should get to bed," Nate sighed and turned off the Xbox. "As much as I want to spend all night with you, we have a lot of work in the morning."

"Right, and you want to take your time," I taunted.

"Absolutely, I do," he said in that deep tone with a look that sent shivers down my spine.

We tidied up and went upstairs to our rooms. Nate kissed me goodnight outside my bedroom door. He had me pinned between his arms against the wall and kissed me until I was breathless and shaky. He pulled away with a smile and rested his forehead against mine, though because of our height difference, he had to bend down.

I smiled back at him. "Goodnight, Nate," I whispered.

"Goodnight, Eva," he whispered back before pushing back from the wall and walking into his room and shutting the door.

I let out a shaky exhale and gathered my things for a shower. In the bathroom, I looked at my reflection. My brown hair was longer than I typically kept it and was now halfway down my back. My cheeks were pink from kissing Nate, and my lips were red and swollen. His scruffy beard had worn my skin around my mouth and my body tingled at the thought of what it would feel like on my thighs. I shook my head and took a rather cold shower.

Back in my room, I checked my phone to see if Dad had texted me back after I had checked in with him. But instead of a text from him, I saw one from Daisy.

Daisy: Girl are you really sleeping with Nate?!

I panicked but I wasn't sure why.

Me: No...
Daisy: Good.

Daisy was my friend, so why wouldn't she be supportive? She was sleeping with Everett, why couldn't I be with Nate?

Me: Why is that good? Nate's a great guy.

My fingers trembled as I typed. It felt like confrontation, and I loathed confrontation more than most things.

Daisy: He is a really great guy.
Me: I know. So what's wrong?
Daisy: Then you ARE sleeping with him! *Mad face emoji*

Tears stung my eyes. It felt dumb to be so affected by her anger, but she was my only female friend since childhood.

Me: I have not slept with him. Why would it be so bad?
Daisy: Did you make out with him?
Me: I'm not sure why you're so upset. I would love to understand what is wrong so that maybe I can fix it.

Daisy: Ugh only bad friends sleep with guys their friends like.
Me: Wait, you're with Everett though.

I sat up in my bed, tears streaming now.

Daisy: Stop, you're being a bitch.

What? I read back over everything I said to her and tried to see how she was taking it as me being a bitch to her. I couldn't find the fault in anything I'd said.

Me: I think we should maybe talk in person. We may be misunderstanding each other.
Daisy: You? Talk? *Laughing face emoji*

I gasped as I read that. It was like being in high school again. I was way past this level of meanness from girls I was trying to be friends with. It was so mean and so childish my tears stopped. I wasn't sad or worried about my friendship with Daisy anymore, in fact I felt sad for her for feeling like insulting my anxiety around talking was a valid point in an argument.

Nate needed to hear about this, it was so wild. My clean hair was up in a tight bun and a long shirt from my undergrad school covered my cotton shorts. I quietly walked down to his room. I knocked softly, not wanting to wake up Everett.

"Come in," Nate replied.

I opened the door and stepped into his room. It was decorated the same as mine in white and oak furniture. His clothes were strewn everywhere on the floor and the overwhelming scent of him enveloped me as I shut the door behind me. His leather and pine soap scent was comforting as I looked at him lounging on his bed. He was on his belly on the bed, only wearing his navy boxer briefs and was looking at his phone.

"What's up?" he asked, noting the tears still on my face.

"Daisy was texting me and I don't understand," I explained in a whisper and held out my phone to him.

Something flickered over his face as he sat up and took my phone from me. I didn't know what his expression meant; it had happened so fast. "Let's look," he said and scrolled back to the beginning of tonight's conversation.

He read it while I perched on the edge of his bed. The only guy's room I had ever been in was Caleb's. A few dorm rooms of study partners in college, but not a guy I had made out with an hour before. The only sound was the quiet tinkling of snow hitting the window outside and the occasional howl of wind. We were supposed to get a steady layering of snow tonight. I felt chilled thinking about the weather and looked at Nate's bed.

His bedspread was black cotton and his sheets looked like they were also black or a dark navy. Only the bedside light was on, like he had been scrolling on his phone before going to bed for the night. His phone was attached to his charger and laying on his pillow now, and I saw he had a few unread text notifications pop up. I didn't look to see who they were from.

The ticket stubs from the concert we had gone to were on his nightstand and I felt a soft affection over the fact he had kept them. After lab today I had thrown in a load of laundry but had not thrown in the black t-shirt I had borrowed for the concert. I had kept it, smelling of him, under my pillow. If he asked for it, I would pretend to find it and offer to wash it. But for now, it was mine.

"What a fucking bitch," Nate snarled as he handed back my phone. "Why would she make fun of you like that? That's a fucking garbage thing to do."

I was quiet for a moment and looked down at my dark phone. I felt my lower lip tremble and I bit it.

"Hey," he said softly, sliding toward me on the bed. He reached up and thumbed my lip. I let it go. "Talk to me."

I shook my head, feeling anxious about telling Nate that I had been feeling worried about losing a friend and now she had insulted me, and I didn't know how to feel.

"Would it help if I said I didn't have any interest in Daisy? She keeps sending me these pictures. And at first, they were pretty hot, and I didn't exactly discourage them. But when she started hooking up with Ev, it was weird. Like... he's my friend and his girlfriend is sending me nudes. I asked her to stop one time when she was over here, and she just giggled." Nate reached over to unhook his phone from the charger and opened up his messages. "I've always deleted them. I mean, that shit is what Snapchat is for. But she sent this one to me tonight, maybe five minutes ago."

He showed me his phone and sure enough; it was Daisy, in her bed with her white sheet up to her boobs but showing them seductively. Her eyes were hooded, and her tongue was curled up over her top lip like a cartoon character seeing a slice of cake, but in a porn star way. My stomach soured. I felt sad for Everett and mad for Nate and grossed out all at the same time.

I shot to my feet in an almost blinding wave of emotion. I paced his room, stomping on his clothes littered all over the floor. As I spoke, I felt hotter and hotter despite the chill of the house, my hands clenching and unclenching. "Does she think she can have you both?! She seduced Everett right away. Like day one, as soon as he walked into the room, she zeroed in on him like 'Yummy, yummy cowboy.' And then all the group texts and the flirty comments. She was kind of flirty with me too, but I guess maybe I friend-zoned her? Then she's sending you nudes even after you said not to. And she tells me she wants you too? You guys are mine, and she can't have you. It's- ugh, it's so unfair because I thought finally, *finally*, I had a female friend. Someone to talk to about girl stuff and go shopping and do make up. But no. She has to go and insult my anxiety and steal my guys! I mean… guy."

Nate had leaned back on the bed on his elbows and watched me pace and rant with a smirk on his face. When I turned to him, panting, he raised his eyebrows at me. "You done?"

I took a deep breath and considered. "Yes."

"There's a lot to unpack in that monologue for a man stealing bitch who doesn't talk," Nate teased, his eyes warm and focused on me.

I rolled my eyes and crossed my arms over my chest, inadvertently pushing my breasts up.

"Are you not wearing a bra?" Nate asked, his eyes bugging out at my chest. He sat up straight.

"No, I'm in my pajamas," I muttered.

"Gimme," he said, reaching towards me with grabby hands.

"No," I giggled and uncrossed my arms, but went to stand in front of him anyway.

His hands stroked my sides from my hips to my breasts, his thumbs hooking under them before stroking back down to my hips. My nipples didn't get the memo that I was in emotional distress and pressed against my old t-shirt. I licked my lips.

He hummed and bit down on one of them through the shirt. "You said 'your guys.'"

"I- I meant guy," I breathed. Butterflies swarmed in my stomach and core again at his touch.

"You said it more than once," he said quietly and licked over my cotton covered nipple.

My breath hitched in my throat, and I couldn't think straight. "What?"

"You said that me and Ev were your guys. Both of us. More than once," he clarified, licking over the other nipple.

"I meant- I-" I stopped to sigh as the licking turned to sucking.

"It's okay. That's hot that you liked both of us," Nate said and looked up to my face from where he was sitting with hooded eyes. "You picked me over the yummy, yummy cowboy."

I blushed at his teasing and ran my hands through his long hair.

"But you are right. The way Daisy has been with all three of us has been odd, to say the least," Nate said and let go of my body to slide up to sit against the headboard, leaving room for me. I crawled in and sat next to him. "I'm not sure what she thought she was going to achieve by going after all three of us."

"I don't know. I mean, she's with Everett, right? Why would she need you too?" I asked with a slight pout, resting my hand on his shoulder. I needed to touch him to know for sure he was with me and not her.

"I could think of a few reasons," Nate chuckled. "In all seriousness, there's something messed up about it."

We were both silent, thinking, for a few moments. "How'd she think to text you about that today? When we only started kissing yesterday?"

"Do you think Ev saw us?" I asked, feeling uneasy again.

"No, he would have said something, for sure," Nate said, considering.

"You think? He doesn't talk much more than I do," I said.

"I guess you're probably right. He either saw us or suspected something. I mean, I was hard as a rock after we made out on the couch. He might have seen it," Nate laughed.

"Oh my god," I groaned, embarrassed at the thought of Ev seeing us. Embarrassed but also... excited.

"You're thinking about it, aren't you?" Nate asked in that deep and rasping voice.

"About what?" I asked innocently.

"About us getting hot and heavy on the couch and Everett coming in and seeing us?" Nate asked, sliding a hand up my bare leg and stopping below my cotton shorts.

I nodded with a deeper blush.

"Does he join us?" Nate rasps and his mouth latches to my neck. I don't answer because I don't know what the correct response is. "Or does he stroke himself through his tight cowboy jeans while he watches us?"

I gasp as he pushes my shorts up.

His phone chimed. We both looked at it and saw Daisy's name. It chimed again.

"Wait, you should look at it," I said, sobering after the lust high. "What if it's about what she said to me?"

Nate sighed and sat up and opened his phone. He gasped, almost dropped it, and scrambled like he was deleting something. I caught only the smallest glimpse, and it was very flesh toned. He jumped out of the bed as he deleted it and slammed his phone on the dresser. He picked up his deodorant and tried to smash his phone with it, but the case on his phone held.

"What?!" I asked, not sure if I should laugh or not.

"It was- holy shit! What the fuck? It was a picture of her- I'm not even going to tell you. But the second text was the title of her... art-work. It was titled after me and Ev and a certain part of her body," Nate said, a flush crept over his chest.

I tried to hold my laughter. It was really not funny. It was basically assault. But I didn't know what to do with the information and emotions attached, so I just laughed. Laughed at her audacity.

Laughed at her effort. Laughed at the absolute failure of her attempt.

Nate calmed down and then laughed with me. He brought his phone back to the bed and opened up TikTok. "I think that killed the mood; don't you think?" I nodded in response as he reclaimed his spot next to me. Nate pulled the blanket over us, and we settled against his pillows and watched videos on his phone until we were both heavy with sleep. I was aware of him setting his phone down on the nightstand, the warm comfort of his body next to mine, the scent of him surrounding me, and then I was aware of nothing else until morning.

10

I awoke feeling warm. In fact, I was sweating. For a moment I worried I had gotten sick, maybe contracted an illness in the lab, but when Nate sighed in his sleep next to me, I understood the warmth. He was like a furnace, even though he was only wearing his boxer briefs. I felt his forehead, but he was at a normal temperature. He opened his eyes at my touch and smiled.

"I'm a sweater," he said in a sleepy, gruff voice. "Hence the underwear."

I giggled. "Just checking."

"I think we missed our run," he said and stretched.

"Yeah, I hope Ev didn't come looking," I yawned. I looked at his phone on the nightstand and the clock read eight fifteen.

"Oh shit, yeah," Nate said and sat up and pulled on a pair of sweatpants that had been in a pile of clothes on his floor.

I followed him out of bed and stretched. He crowded my space and dropped a kiss onto my lips. "Good morning," he said in his sleepy voice.

"Good morning," I replied and smiled up at him.

"It'll be hard to keep my hands off of you today," he said quietly and ran his hands lightly over my arms, causing goosebumps to surface. I shivered.

"Ditto," I whispered, running my hands over his broad chest, feeling the coarse hair under my fingers.

He groaned. "Let's stay in bed."

I giggled again. "We've got work to do. Now, let's go eat some breakfast and find Ev."

Downstairs was quiet and dark. Ev was nowhere to be seen in the kitchen or living room. "Is he still sleeping?" Nate asked as he pressed start on the coffee maker.

I shrugged and went to Everett's bedroom. I knocked lightly and didn't hear a response. Opening the door, I had a moment of panic in case Daisy was in his room. We were still in a limited contact phase, so she could be around. What if she had also sent that picture to Everett and he invited her over? But as the door opened further, I saw he was alone in his bed. I smiled at the sight of a soundly sleeping and sleep rumpled Everett. I had only ever seen him put together and groomed, so seeing him this way felt like a treat. The beard he had grown since beginning the project was becoming a full ginger beard with a few little spots of blonde throughout. His blonde hair had grown out too and was curling around his ears. We had regularly made fun of him for having a ginger beard and blonde hair, but as his hair grew out, I could see the tones of auburn through it. His face was relaxed in sleep, without either his worried, wrinkled brow or his sly smirk.

I tiptoed into his room. Even if we weren't running, we needed to get to the lab. "Hey, Ev," I whispered.

He didn't budge, so I tiptoed further into the room. He was curled up on his side, facing the door, with his blankets to his chin. I kneeled on the bed to gently shake him. "Ev, we need to get to work. Are you alright?"

He inhaled deeply and opened his eyes. His bright blue eyes blinked a few times before focusing on me. He sat up, his blankets falling to his lap, exposing his bare and sculpted torso. I swallowed, taking in his defined muscles. “Hey, what are you doing in here?” He asked in a hoarse whisper and reached out for my hand. He hadn’t sounded upset at seeing me in his room. In fact, he sounded pleasantly surprised. My mouth watered and my hand tightened on his.

“You’re still in bed,” I said for an explanation. “It’s almost eight thirty.”

“They closed the campus because of the storm. I figured we wouldn’t go running,” he informed me and rubbed a hand over his jaw.

“We have to get to the lab. Strain thirty-seven is ready to be tested,” I said, pulling my hand back from his grasp.

“Sure, yeah,” he said then smiled. “We’ve got time. We can stay in for a bit.”

He held up the covers as if to invite me into his bed. I hesitated a moment after sliding into the sheets- I thought of both Nate and Daisy. I looked around his room and saw it was the same as mine and Nate’s, though his was tidy compared to Nate’s messy room. A stack of books sat on his nightstand with bookmarks sticking out of each of them. His bed was warm from his body and his clean soap scent surrounded me. The door remained open, and I heard Nate shuffling around, getting coffee and breakfast.

“Maybe he’ll bring us breakfast in bed,” Ev suggested warmly.

“I bet we can get a bowl of cereal at least,” I said with a little giggle.

Nate appeared in the doorway. He grinned when he saw us sitting in the bed. “Well, this looks cozy.”

I felt guilty for a moment, like I wasn’t supposed to be in Everett’s bed when I was with Nate, but it hadn’t occurred to me before getting in. I guessed it was a weird thing to do, but there was no going back now. And it wasn’t like I was doing anything to be unfaithful to Nate.

“Bring us coffee and cereal,” I demanded in a silly, posh voice.

Nate bowed. "Yes, my queen," he said and left the doorway.

"You could ask that man for anything," Everett said with a shake of his head and handed me a book from his nightstand.

"What do you mean?" I asked and looked down at the book. It was a nonfiction book about the history of cooking over a campfire. Not a book I would have typically picked up but was vaguely interested in enough to open it.

Ev smiled down at me. "He's obsessed with you."

"I don't know about that," I said and felt my cheeks flame up. I stared down at the book on my lap. Ev made a noise as if he didn't believe me and he and I settled back against the headboard, each with a book, and waited for our breakfast. There was room on Ev's other side to fit Nate when he came back, and I hoped we could all sit and read and eat breakfast together.

Nate came back with three bowls filled with our favorite cereals and a jug of milk before he returned to the kitchen for three travel mugs of coffee prepared for our different tastes. He looked at Everett as if he was waiting for approval for his caring actions. I smiled as I took a careful sip from my coffee. Ev thanked him and pulled the blankets back for Nate. It was nice to see Nate and Everett learning from each other. Nate was learning from Ev's caring nature and Ev was learning from Nate's playful personality.

Nate climbed into the bed next to Ev and looked at Ev under the blankets. "That's not fair. How do you look like that?"

"I've worked on a farm my whole life," Ev said, his accent thick. He smirked with a tinge of pink in his cheeks. "These muscles don't come from a gym."

"No, but you totally hit the gym," Nate snorted. And poured milk into our cereal bowls.

Ev shifted towards me to make more room for Nate, and his leg brushed against mine. He was also wearing only a pair of boxer briefs. Did neither of them wear pajamas? I'd seen them both wearing them around the house, but I guessed it to be more for lounge than sleep.

"Says the man with a dump truck for an ass," Ev said in his quiet and calm way that I envied.

I coughed and almost spit my coffee onto Everett's comforter. Ev thumped me on the back while I gathered myself. Ev was not wrong; Nate did have a defined ass.

Nate had a pink blush over his own brown beard. "While it's not a farm, I worked in warehouses. Gotta lift with your ass cheeks."

"I'll have to try that," Everett said, and took a sip of his coffee. He hummed in pleasure. "Thank you for the coffee and breakfast, Nate."

"Yes, thank you," I agreed.

Nate smiled.

We ate our breakfast and lounged in Everett's bed for a few hours before hauling ourselves out to Ev's truck. It had snowed probably eight inches since last night and it was still dropping. Ev and Nate made quick work at clearing off the truck as I cranked the heat inside. The streets were covered in snow and brown slush, but plows were out and working as quickly as they could to make the roads safe. Everett had to switch the truck to four-wheel drive with a dial on his dash before we could make it out of the student parking lot. Our single parking space was cleared, and salt had been thrown down to melt the ice. The little path to the door wasn't shoveled, so we had to tromp through it. I followed behind, hopping into the guys' larger footsteps.

We worked until mid afternoon, when the snow was falling even harder. A thick covering of snow had fallen on Ev's truck since morning, and we thought it to be a good idea to head home. The rest of our work today could wait a day or two, thankfully. We bundled up, cleared off the truck, and headed home in the blizzard. The streets were completely covered again; the snow was falling too hard and fast for the plows to keep up. Nate drove us home in Ev's truck as he had more experience with driving in the snow from living in Connecticut.

The snow didn't stop falling for the rest of the afternoon. It was well over a foot deep by the time it was early evening. The guys and I had spent the afternoon playing video games and watching movies. I baked a batch of sugar cookies to snack on and the guys worked together to make chicken thighs by following a recipe they found online. It was a quiet day, more peaceful than we'd had in a while. Daisy didn't contact me and I didn't reach out to her. It didn't seem like she had tried to reach the guys today, either. Whenever I thought about my lost friendship with her, I felt a sort of twinge in my gut. Not so much at losing her as a person, but more so for myself for losing the first girl that had seemed interested in being my friend in a very long time.

I listened to the guys laughing and talking as they cooked dinner and when the wonderful smells reached me in the living room; I joined them in the kitchen. I didn't join them in conversation, though. It was more enjoyable listening to their conversations and opinions on things. They were two fascinating men and seemed like opposites that genuinely liked and respected each other. When I entered the kitchen, they both turned to look at me. Nate's forest green eyes seemed to eat me up whenever he saw me, and today, he looked ravenous. Everett's bright blue eyes looked me over with what looked like interest. I didn't understand what that look meant, so I pretended as though I didn't see it. They both went back to their conversation when I sat at the island. They worked side by side, their elbows and shoulders brushing, cutting vegetables to go with the chicken.

Dinner was being set on the table when the power went out. We looked at each other in silence for a moment while we waited for it to come back on. Everett rummaged in a kitchen drawer and found a pillar candle and matches. He lit it and set it on the table.

"Cozy," Nate said with a wink to me, and sat in his chair.

We ate by candlelight and set all of the dishes in the sink after. "I guess we should call it an early night. If you guys need a book to read, let me know," Ev said as he headed to his room.

With no power, we also had no internet access, so reading was all we had to do. Or so I thought until I looked at Nate. He was grinning wolfishly at me and I smiled back. He held out a hand to me and led me upstairs and to his bedroom. "We've finally got all night," he said as he shut his door behind me.

I shivered at his deep voice. "Seems like it. And someone has to keep me warm," I said in a whisper.

He didn't respond, only lifted me up to wrap my legs around him and kissed me. His tongue swept into my mouth as he laid me on his bed, his body hovering over mine. *Finally.* We kissed for a few moments before he pulled away and pressed his forehead against mine. "I told you I wanted to take my time when I fucked you. Are you ready for me?"

I nodded and swallowed.

"I want to hear it," he insisted and kissed a line down my neck.

"I'm ready f- for you to fuck me," I stuttered breathlessly. My core throbbed and I felt a rush of moisture.

Nate slid his hands under my t-shirt and pushed it up and over my head. I did the same to him before he resumed kissing down my chest to my bra. It was a plain cotton bra, nothing sexy or exciting. I felt nervous for a moment, thinking he might change his mind because I wasn't wearing sexy lingerie. But it didn't hinder him as he ripped it over my head to avoid the clasps. He sat back to look at me with my bare breasts and I sat up and propped myself on my hands.

"Beautiful," he breathed before taking a nipple into his mouth. I moaned and my head fell back. He did the same to the other before he kissed his way slowly down to the top of my sweatpants as he climbed off the bed to kneel before me. My breath caught as he swirled his tongue around my navel. He dragged down my pants, kissing over my pink cotton brief underwear. He closed his mouth over my sex, pulling at me with his lips through my briefs. I panted under him and laid back against the mattress. It felt like the best type of teasing and my pulse soared.

He stripped off my pants the rest of the way and slid his hands up my legs to my underwear in a slow and tantalizing movement. His fingertips were teasing and light on my body. Goosebumps surfaced on my skin and my breathing was ragged. I closed my eyes and tried to steady my racing heart. He chuckled deeply. "I know, I'm excited too. I'm going to take care of this pussy, okay beautiful?"

I nodded. My core clenched and butterflies took flight.

"What was that? I didn't hear you."

"I want you to take care of this pussy, Nate," I said, a hint of frustration at the anticipation mingled with my lust.

He hummed. "Are you wet for me?" He started to slowly remove my briefs.

I nodded and remembered he wanted me to talk. "Y-yes, I'm wet for you."

When my briefs were off, he kissed a wet trail up my legs, alternating which one he was kissing, all the way to my core. I felt his hot breath over me, and I was glad I kept myself trimmed neatly. The anticipation of waiting for him got to me and I sat up to look down at him kneeling before me, but a large hand pressed me back down at my stomach. I groaned in protest as his breath felt closer. He blew cold air on me, and I whimpered, fisting the surrounding sheets. He brushed his lips over me so lightly that if I wasn't hyper focused on my sex, I might not have felt it. I bit my lip to avoid crying out. I felt more wetness rush out of me. He groaned in response to seeing it trickle down.

"Nate… please," I begged.

My pleading was what he was waiting for. He closed the minimal distance and ran his tongue flat and firm over me and I cried out at the contact. My back arched off the bed and the hand he had used to push me down returned and pressed me back against the bed. He ran his tongue over my slit a few more times before going to the top and finding my clit. He swirled it with his tongue, causing me to cry out again, before closing his lips around it and sucking. My hips bucked against him on the bed and the hand on my stomach pushed harder, holding me in place. His other hand came up and a finger slowly pushed in at my entrance. I was gasping and panting at his touch and almost ready to climax. He slid his finger in and went back to lapping his tongue against my folds. I could barely stand it already and he was adding in the second finger. I was spasming around his fingers, almost about to climax, when he pulled away, leaving me untouched.

"Relax, beautiful," he coaxed. "I'm not ready for you to come yet."

"Please," I begged him, now knowing he liked it. "Please Nate, I need it."

"I know," he said in that deep voice that sounded both commanding and soothing at the same time. "I want you to wait a little longer."

I moaned and tried to bring my hand down to finish the job, but he caught my wrists with a chuckle. "No, I'm going to make you come."

He let go of my wrists and then ran his hands over my body again, stopping to pinch and pull at my nipples before moving back to my pussy. I clenched with anticipation and felt the trickle of wetness.

"That's so fucking hot," he groaned. "You're so ready for me."

"I'm so ready for you," I affirmed, harsher than I had intended.

He chuckled. "Okay, I'll take care of you."

And his mouth was on me again, wetly sucking at my clit as two fingers shoved back into me. I let out a cry that went hoarse as I bucked against him again. He pressed his free hand down on my pelvis to hold me and keep control. But my movements were out of my control as I got closer and closer to my release. He curled his fingers inside me, and after a couple of pumps, found the right spot. He sucked harder on my clit as he quickly tapped at that soft spot within me that had me seeing stars. I gripped his long hair in my hands as I pulled his face closer to me. I took one last gasping breath before I came harder than I had ever come with Caleb or on my own. He removed his fingers and lapped at me as I came with a cry, drinking me in.

"Good girl, come for me," he said between sucking and licking me.

I looked down at him as he climbed back up onto the bed. The lower part of his face was dripping with my release. He came up to kiss me and I gripped him hard as I kissed him, tasting myself on his lips. Aftershocks coursed through me as I breathlessly reached a hand down into his tented sweatpants. He gasped as my hand wrapped around him and stroked. I got three strokes in before he backed away from me and pulled off his sweatpants. He kneeled before me, completely bare. He was long and thick, his cock bobbing as he moved towards me. My mouth watered at the sight.

"Do you want to suck me, beautiful?" he asked, his voice rumbling between us.

I nodded and remembered to speak again. "I want to suck you."

This was something Caleb had said I was particularly skilled at, and I wondered if those skills transferred to Nate. He smirked and sat against the headboard between the pillows. I crawled to him and kneeled between his legs. When I bent down to take him into my mouth, my ass was sticking up in the air. Before I could wrap my lips around him, he groaned and smacked my ass. I was sure it would be pink as it stung.

I licked from the base of his cock to the head with a swirl at the top. He shuddered out a breath and hissed out a "Good girl." My pussy clenched at the sound.

I took him into my mouth as far as I could and relaxed my tongue to get even further. I bobbed up and down a few times before I took him as far as I could again, then undulated my tongue against the underside of his cock. He gave a loud moan, and the muscles of his stomach clenched. I knew I could only do that a few times before gagging, so I pulled off of him. I pumped him with my fist a few times to catch my breath before I did it again. This time he caught me by surprise when he reached out from his sitting position with both hands and grabbed my ass cheeks. He pulled me towards him as he thrust up into my mouth. I felt wetness trailing down my thighs at this. Nate smacked my ass a few times as he fucked my mouth, and I ended up gagging. He let go of me and I sat up, my eyes streaming from gagging, and continued to pump him with my hand as I caught my breath. He stilled my hand, and I let go. The muscles in his stomach were clenching, and he was breathing hard.

"I was so close," he panted with a grin.

"I have an IUD," I said in a commanding voice so unlike myself. "I want you to come in me."

His eyes sparked, and he gave me a solid push so I was falling back towards the end of the bed with him following on top of me. "You think you can call the shots, beautiful?"

I smiled slyly up at him. "Absolutely."

He forcefully knocked my legs apart with his knees, then he sank down into me quickly. I was surely wet enough that it wasn't painful. The stretch to accommodate him felt like a burning inside of me, but as he thrust in and out with an upward tilt, I forgot all about it. He kissed me hard as he thrust into me without mercy. I wrapped my legs around his waist and clung to his sweaty back. I felt the muscles in his back bunching and moving and his hot breath on my neck as he kissed me. We were hot, sweaty, and frantic as we moved.

His thrusts slowed. He kissed my mouth, and we both panted and moaned together. He pushed up and looked down at me as he fucked me. His expression was dark and sexy, and I squeezed his cock inside me.

"You looked so good sucking my dick, beautiful. Mmm and your pussy was so sweet and juicy, like a peach. I could fuck you like this all night," he breathed. "Every time I look at you getting fucked, I almost blow."

"Do it," I moaned back at him. "Come for me."

"Did you not hear that I wanted to fuck you all night?" he growled at me and wrapped a hand around my throat just tight enough.

I moaned as I got closer to my second release. "We have all night; we can do it again. And again," I panted as my voice got tighter, both from my impending release and his hand around my neck.

"I like the way you think, beautiful," he said, and started pounding an unforgiving rhythm. He continued with the upward tilt that hit that amazing spot inside of me.

My eyes rolled back as he gripped my throat and fucked me, and I came with a silent scream. I felt my release wet between us as he continued the same pace towards his own release. When he came with a roar, he pushed as far as he could into me with stuttering thrusts as his eyes closed and his head tipped towards me. He stayed inside me as he came and then crashed down on top of me, heavy and sweaty.

"Holy shit, that was so fucking good," he said breathlessly into my neck.

"So good," I echoed and petted at his damp hair.

"I can't wait to do it again," he said with a chuckle.

We spent the entire evening and much of the night in bed. When the power came back on at three in the morning, we took turns showering before sleeping in my bed to avoid changing the sheets on Nate's bed. He would have joined me in the shower, but we were both spent and ready to sleep. Being in there together would have been too tempting. I fell asleep with my head on his chest and his arms around me, feeling considerably more sated and exhausted than I had in a long time.

The next morning, we headed downstairs an hour after our normal time, though not clad in running gear. It had snowed so much I was sure we'd be spending our normal running time digging out Everett's truck before going to the lab. Halfway down the stairs, I smelled coffee and bounded the rest of the way into the kitchen, Nate not far behind me. We had been awake until almost four in the morning and slept for only three hours, but I felt great.

Everett was standing at the sink as he put his cereal bowl in the dishwasher. I smiled at him in greeting. He raised one eyebrow at me. "Good morning," I said as I brushed past him to get a mug of coffee.

"Mornin'," Nate greeted Everett and sat at the kitchen island. Nate yawned and stretched his arms and back muscles cat-like. Everett stared at him, still with one eyebrow raised. "What? Like what you see?" Nate teased.

Everett remained silent and poured a mug of coffee for Nate after I finished. He set it in front of Nate and leaned across the island between where Nate and I sat with his elbows on the cool surface and his hands clasped together. He looked from me to Nate, almost expressionless, but his slightly tightened brow told me he was expecting something. An explanation? Did I do some-

Oh.

"Remember when you were mute?" Everett asked me in his calm voice. I would have thought he was being mean if it weren't for the glint of humor in his eyes.

I knew my cheeks were heated as Nate snorted a laugh. "I know, right? Fucking wild." Nate sipped his coffee, his eyes far away like he was reliving the night. He squeezed my thigh with the hand not wrapped around his coffee mug.

Everett pushed himself back to standing and stood with his hands on his hips, his bright blue eyes laser focused on me. His head tipped to the side like he was studying me.

"Sorry," I murmured to Everett, not making eye contact.

Nate snorted another laugh. "Don't be. He jerked to it all night, I bet."

I looked at Everett, my eyes wide. He gave me his signature smirk with what I could only describe as a smoldering look in his striking blue eyes. Then he turned that same gaze to Nate. "You were just as loud as she was, so don't get so haughty."

Everett left with his mug of coffee and went to the living room.

"Did he just call me a 'hottie?'" Nate asked me, turning to me.

"No, but I think he said he jerked off to the sound of your moans as much as he did to mine," I said with a quiet sip of my coffee, trying to emulate the way Ev delivers his jokes.

"Hmm," Nate said, considering. "I can't tell if I want to laugh or feel desired. Either way, I have a boner."

I laughed, almost spitting out my coffee.

11

The snow was as high as my waist when we went outside, armed with the shovels they had left us in the little garage that housed Marie Curie. It hadn't snowed all morning, so we felt confident in being able to make it to the lab. I waited on the doorstep while the guys dug out the shovels, seeing as they could tromp through the snow much easier than I would have waded. We had two shovels, and we rotated who was shoveling and who was taking a coffee break. The snow was heavy and difficult to shovel out of the driveway, and it took close to an hour. The three of us were sweating in our snow gear and panting by the time we climbed into Ev's truck.

"Yeah, I do not like the snow," Everett said and turned up the heating despite sweating under our winter gear. His accent was thick in his irritation, despite his calm tone of voice.

"No snow in Tennessee?" Nate asked from his place in the driver's seat as he switched the truck into four-wheel drive.

"Not where I grew up. We would get a dusting, maybe an inch or two, every couple of years or so. Nothing like this," he said and rolled his head to stretch out the sore muscles in his neck.

"I'm moving in with you." Nate said as he maneuvered us out of the driveway "I could be a cowboy."

I giggled at his exaggerated Southern accent with his cowboy comment.

"Could you now?" Everett asked, a smirk curling at his lip.

"Yeah, I'd look fucking fantastic in some cowboy boots and jeans. And a good hat," Nate continued as he carefully drove us to the lab.

"I concur," Everett said, and the smirk remained in place.

I cackled in the back seat.

We worked all day in the lab and headed home for a frozen pizza and salad dinner. After dinner, I went to my room to call my dad and check in, but he hadn't answered. I sent him a text to say that I had called to say hello and got a waving emoji in response. I didn't want the guys to know I had been all but ignored by my dad, so I remained in my room while they decided if they wanted to play a game or watch tv. Hearing the rumble of their voices up the stairs, I relaxed in my room with Everett's history of campfire cooking book for a while. Since we had not run in two days, my muscles around my implants and surgery sites had got sore. Shoveling that morning hadn't helped since it didn't use the same muscles. I knew I needed to stretch them out.

I put on some running shorts and a t-shirt and headed downstairs to hang out with the guys who had decided on a movie. It was a comedy I had seen before, so I didn't mind coming in part of the way through it. They were both on the couch with their feet up on the oversized ottoman. One scoot and they could have been cuddling. Everett had one of our soft blankets over his legs, and Nate was scrolling on his phone while the movie played. Nate looked up at me as I walked in and his eyes smoldered.

I stretched out my sore shoulders and watched the movie. I wasn't standing directly in front of them, but I was within their line of sight if they looked over to the right of the tv.

Everett did a double take at me. "Are you going running?"

"No, I only wanted to stretch. My, um, my implant and surgery sites get sore if I don't work the surrounding muscles," I said shyly. We didn't talk much about my accident or injuries.

"Do you need a hot bath?" Everett asked, concern etching over his features.

"Maybe when I'm done. I like to soak in Epsom salt baths," I said, and my eyes flicked to Nate, remembering the time he walked in on me in the bath a few weeks ago.

"Okay, let me know and I'll run you one," Ev said casually and turned back to the movie.

His sentiment touched me, and I smiled as I resumed my stretching. I watched the movie as I went through some of my stretches, giggling at funny parts. When they didn't laugh at a funny part, I looked back, expecting them to be asleep, but caught their eyes on me. When they realized I was looking, they snapped their heads back to the tv. Were they watching me stretch? I wasn't doing anything particularly entertaining. I bent over to touch my bare toes to stretch out my hamstrings. There was a sharp intake of breath and when I stood and looked at them, I saw Nate blatantly staring at me with hooded eyes and I saw Everett's gaze snap back to the tv. They *were* watching me. Feeling powerful, I slid to the floor and did some bridging exercises to work out my transabdominal muscles and glutes. Nate groaned quietly and another funny part of the movie came and went with no laughter. This was fun. I got on all fours and did cat-cow stretches to relax some muscles in my back and to further tease the guys. I knew that my running shorts were giving me quite a bit of a wedgie at this point from all the stretching, but I didn't fix it.

"Why is nobody laughing at this movie?" I asked quietly. "I thought it was hilarious."

"Nobody is watching the movie, beautiful," Nate said in his deep voice.

Everett cleared his throat. "I'm watching it. I've seen the jokes before." His voice was husky and rasping.

I smirked at him like he usually smirked at me. He looked back at the movie as if it had absorbed him the whole time.

Nate didn't bother hiding his lust. He cupped himself through his lounge pants and bit his bottom lip. I smiled and nodded my head to the stairs, and he jumped off the couch and headed upstairs.

"Please keep the volume down," Everett said in his calm voice.

I didn't respond to him as I followed Nate up the stairs.

The next morning, I woke up to the sound of the guys arguing. I heard raised voices, but couldn't make out their words until I was on the stairs. I yawned as I entered the kitchen wearing nothing but one of Nate's t-shirts, as I had woken up naked and in his bed.

"You left the towels in the washing machine, and they molded! There was nothing in the dryer and you could have moved them over at any time," Everett was shouting at Nate. They were on either side of the kitchen island, both with their palms pressed against the granite, and shouting into each other's faces.

"I forgot, dude. It's no big deal. I'll just rewash them," Nate shouted back.

"Don't 'dude' me, boy. We all contribute to this house-" Everett argued, but Nate cut him off.

"'Boy?!' Is that a joke? I can't call you 'dude' because it's insulting, but you can call me 'boy' and that's perfectly fine?!" Nate bellowed.

I poured myself a cup of coffee. Thinking back, Nate had put a load of laundry in the washing machine, but he then had gotten distracted by putting a load in *me*, so I stayed out of this argument. I remained close in case I needed to break up a fist fight or mediate.

"Consider it even, then," Everett rolled his eyes. It seemed like Nate won that round. "Nate, we all contribute to this house and count on each other. This morning we have no towels for our showers because you didn't finish the laundry!"

"Well, I'll get right on fixing it, daddy," Nate said in a condescending tone and started to walk away.

Everett startled and spilled the coffee he was bringing up to his lips. A blush stained his cheeks. He looked away from Nate and mopped up his coffee.

"Wait, did you like it when I called you 'daddy?'" Nate asked incredulously.

"No."

"You totally fucking did."

"No, I didn't."

"You popped a boner at me calling you 'daddy.'"

"Stop it, Nathaniel."

"Oh my god. This is too good. Is it like library time boner or sexy time boner?"

"What?! What does that even mean?"

"When I was a kid, I loved going to the library and checking out video games and those *Eyewitness* books so much I would get a boner because I was so excited. And a sexy time boner is self-explanatory," Nate said casually and sipped his coffee like everything he had told us was perfectly normal to talk about. I watched, silent and eyes wide, but fighting down a laugh.

Everett huffed a laugh and shook his head before getting a paper towel to finish cleaning up the coffee he had spilled. He said nothing in response to Nate and I almost forgot there was even a question.

"So, which is it? Library boner or sexy boner when I call you 'daddy?'" Nate's voice dipped to his demanding voice he uses during sex.

Everett stared at him for a long moment, his expression unreadable. My heart raced in my chest as I anticipated his answer. They locked their eyes across the kitchen island while nobody moved for an extended moment. My breath hitched.

"Neither," Everett said finally, and pushed away from the island. His voice was quiet and calm, like usual. "Please fix the towels."

He left me and Nate in the kitchen, where we stared at each other for another moment.

"If you had gotten a library boner, what would it have been for?" Nate asked me as he started fixing his breakfast cereal.

"Hmm, science class in elementary school when we got to copy a Bill Nye experiment," I replied with a giggle.

"Fucking freak," Nate chuckled.

Later that day, while we were in the lab, the streets had been plowed and salted, so Everett offered to go grab us lunch from the house. Nate and I were removing our protective gear to be ready for a break and lunch when he grabbed my hand and led me out of the lab, leaving the music on, and down the hall to the locker room.

"Why are we going in the locker room?" I asked curiously, still in work mode.

Nate grinned mischievously back at me as he pushed the door open. "I'm hungry."

I didn't have time to respond before he picked me up and his lips crushed against mine. I squealed in shock and delight at the quick movement. "So hungry," he said in his deep, sexy voice as he walked us further into the locker room. The locker room had two toilet stalls and a shower in the back, separated from the front of the room by a line of lockers and a wooden bench.

Nate set me on the first sink and quickly kneeled before me. I worried for a second I was going to break the sink off the wall, but quickly abandoned that thought as Nate yanked my black leggings over my ass so fast and hard that I had to grasp the sink to not go flying. He winked up at me in apology before more carefully pulling down my black bikini panties. "I've been wanting a taste of this pussy all morning," he said in a tone not unlike a growl before descending to lick up the length of my slit.

I cried out and my head tilted back, thumping against the mirror behind me. I rolled my hips and tried to open my legs wider for him, but my panties and leggings near my ankles stopped me. "Fuck," I moaned.

"Tell me about it, beautiful, I've had to think about being deep inside of you again since last night," he rumbled against my pussy.

"Please," I whimpered, trying to move my hips against his mouth.

"Hmm," Nate said thoughtfully. "I think I want to play a little more."

I couldn't respond in English more than a few moaned syllables after that. He teased and sucked my clit between his lips, alternating between that and blowing cool air over my skin until I was trembling and moaning. I felt moisture dripping between my ass cheeks and my grip on the sink tightened.

Nate stood suddenly and unzipped his jeans and I watched as he shoved them and his boxer briefs down over his thighs. I hadn't come yet, so I bit my bottom lip and glared up at him.

He smirked. "Hold on, beautiful. I want to feel you clench and come around my cock," he said, and lifted me forcefully by my hips. With his pants around his knees, he carried me the few steps to the bench in front of the lockers and set me down on my feet. I assumed he was going to have me on my back on the bench, so I started to sit down, but he grabbed me by the shoulders and spun me around. I bent over, almost falling, but caught myself on the bench so I was in a sort of standing doggy style position. Nate slid his hands in the waistband of my black panties and through to the leg holes and twisted the fabric around his hands to create handles at my thighs, pulling my ass to where he wanted it. He pulled me to my tiptoes and towards him. My pussy clenched in excitement and anticipation before he slammed home. I cried out and would have gone flying forward at the impact if it wasn't for Nate's hold on my panties. I gripped the bench hard to keep from falling as he slammed into me a few more times. He pulled out abruptly and kneeled one knee on the cold tile, the other knee bent and still covered by his jeans. I almost screamed in shock at how far he went after licking from my clit to my ass. He licked me one more time before standing back up and slamming back into me with a groan. Nate did this two more times before I was spasming around him while he used my panties as a handle to fuck me almost senseless. He was speaking to me, but I couldn't hear him through my pleasure and the sound of our sweat slick skin slapping together.

A chill blew over my skin and I assumed it was an exhale from Nate as he came with a rumbling groan. His thrusts stuttered, and I felt him swell inside of me. He leaned over and pressed a kiss to my shoulder blade as I looked up to where I caught movement out of the corner of my eye. I gasped and froze.

Everett stood at the end of the locker bay, his expression full of shock and rage, and locked on where Nate and I were still joined. I opened my mouth to talk to Nate, but my voice was caught in my throat. I managed to reach a hand up and back over my shoulder to smack Nate on the head as he rested his forehead against my shoulder.

"Get out, Ev!" Nate shouted in shock, next to my ear, when he looked up.

Everett blinked at us once and ran out of the locker room. My heart pounded in my chest from both the exertion with Nate and the anxiety of Everett seeing us. Nate pulled out of me, and I felt his release slide down my thighs, but Nate handed me a paper towel quickly to clean up. With shaking hands, I cleaned up and pulled my panties and leggings back into place, the former having a considerably looser waistband. Once my clothes were back in place, I looked at Nate with panicked eyes.

"This could be so bad," Nate said, reading my mind. "He could blow this whole project up."

I turned and ran out the locker room door. I didn't know why, but I feared this could have caused me to lose Everett. While I should have been worried that he would cause our experiment to falter by ending our communication, I was more worried he would be mad at me. I couldn't make sense of it in the two minutes it took me to grab my coat and follow him out to where he was standing in the snowy driveway in front of the lab.

12

Everett was standing next to his truck, his hand on the handle like he was debating getting in and driving off. "Wait!" I shouted, my voice catching at the misuse.

He turned and glowered at me. He gripped the truck handle even tighter and clenched his jaw.

"I- I'm sorry," I sputtered, not totally sure what I was apologizing for, but knowing I felt upset.

"Why?" Everett barked.

"F-for upsetting y-you," I stammered nervously as I clutched my coat to my chest.

Everett laughed a sharp, non-humorous laugh and pushed away from the truck.

"But I don't understand." I swallowed. "I don't understand why you're so mad. It was awkward and I'm sorry, but I don't understand why you're mad."

Everett looked down at his boots for a moment before he turned to me with a sigh. "You being with him made me furious," he said in his calm voice, though this time I heard a slight tremor in his words. His shoulders were tight, and he pressed his lips into a firm line.

I did not understand why my being with Nate was so insulting when he had been with Daisy. Did he think we were going to ruin the experiment? Did he think Nate and I were going to jeopardize our work? He and Daisy could have just as easily done the same. None of his rage made sense. "We see you with Daisy-" I started to say, taking a step towards him.

"Daisy?" Everett interrupted, his accent thick and voice harsh. He took a halting step towards me. "I haven't seen her like that in weeks. Months, even."

We were facing off in front of the truck now, barely out of arm's reach. I clutched my coat to my chest still to fight the cold air. I didn't want to think about putting it on and taking away from our argument, but my teeth chattered.

"Regardless of that, it's- it's not fair for you to be mad at me and Nate for being together," I shouted at him, my face scrunched in anger. "So, why are you mad?"

My communication skills in a time of conflict needed work. I knew this. Hell, my communication skills in general were considerably lacking, but it didn't mean I felt emotions any differently than other people. I just couldn't *tell* someone about them as effectively.

"Because-" Everett shouted back at me. "Because I have feelings for you too, Eva!"

I froze. *What?!* Tears sprung to my eyes, and my chest tightened with emotion.

"That's not fair," I whispered, my lower lip trembling. I bit it to keep some of my emotions in check. It wouldn't help anything if I started blubbering.

"No, what's not fair is listening to you moan his name," Everett said in a hoarse, straining voice. His shoulders curled in and his hands clenched in front of him.

"Everett, I-" I started to speak but didn't know what I was going to say.

"Kiss her," came Nate's voice from behind me. I spun around to see him approach us. I hadn't heard him come out of the lab. He stood a few feet behind me, his hands in his pockets.

"What?" Everett and I said simultaneously.

Nate smiled at us. "She came running out here after you. I know how she feels about me, and she feels the same for you."

"But-" I blurted but said nothing else. I stared at Nate, looking for any sign of negative feelings.

Nothing about his relaxed posture and smiling face showed any signs of anger or jealousy. He stood with slightly open arms and gestured with a shrug and opened palms. "I don't know about you two, but I think this isolation shit has me all fucked up. Sometimes I can barely think straight and other times it's so clear to me. I have a feeling that what me and Eva have is rock solid and I think adding you to the mix would only strengthen it. It's so weird because I've never been so chill and sure about something like this before."

Nate's speech struck home. Maybe it was the isolation of our experiment. Maybe it *was* getting to our heads and messing us up. But, as long as they were feeling the same, maybe we could give it a shot. I felt the same about me and Nate. While we had only been romantic together for a short time, I knew we were great as friends and coworkers and roommates first. I felt connected to Nate and when I allowed myself to consider Everett; I knew I also felt connected to him in those same ways.

I turned around to Everett to see him looking at Nate with a look of care and understanding. When he looked down at me, his expression changed to one of longing. I smiled shyly and shrugged as if to say *okay, let's try this.* And before my shoulder dropped from its shrug, Everett was barreling the three steps towards me. I didn't have time to gasp before his lips crashed down to mine, so I gasped as his lips pressed against me and his arms wrapped around my chest. I dropped my coat, and it fell into the salty, slushy snow below us. With my mouth open in my gasp, Everett slid his tongue into my mouth.

My heart was leaping and pounding in my chest as I reached up and wrapped my arms around his neck, standing on tiptoe to reach him. His beard brushed against my chin. He sighed into our kiss when he realized I was holding him as tightly as he was holding me. I was breathless and wanting more when he pulled away from me. I grasped his hands as he stepped back, not ready for our physical contact to end. He smirked down at me, his signature smirk but with swollen lips.

"See? Feelings. Any who, what did you bring for lunch today?" Nate asked, as if he hadn't watched his girlfriend make out with his friend.

"Uh, I brought hot ham and cheese sandwiches," Everett said, his voice a quiet rumble as he looked at me still. "It's all in the office."

I pulled my bottom lip into my mouth shyly, not sure what to do now. Everett tucked a lock of my hair behind my ear and then bent to pick up my dirty coat. He tried to brush off the slush from it but was unsuccessful.

"Excuse me, but I have grown used to having my lunch set out for me," Nate said from the door to the lab. There was humor in his voice, so I knew he was trying to break the awkward tension between us. I gave a small smile as Everett rolled his eyes, and we both followed Nate into the building.

Ev had made ham and cheese sandwiches and a small fruit salad for us and brought coffee in a thermos. Instead of eating at our desks like we typically did, Everett set everything out on the previously unused coffee table in front of the couch. I sat on the floor facing the couch where the guys sat. They both had offered me their seat on the couch, but I wanted to look at them both. It felt like there was going to be some serious conversations about our relationship. Relationships? And I wanted to see them both when the discussion began.

I sat cross-legged on the tasseled throw rug and picked at my sandwich. The butterflies of both excitement and anxiety took up too much space in my stomach to eat anything. I kept looking from Everett to Nate and back as they ate their lunches happily and like nothing abnormal had happened. Nate talked to us about the video game he had been playing recently, and Everett took part, as usual, whenever Nate stopped talking long enough for someone else to get a word in.

Could I date both of them? Would one relationship eventually fracture under the strain of the other? What if I felt more for only one of them? It made me sick to my stomach to think about losing either one of the guys, and especially sick to think of it being my doing. It wasn't normal to care for two men at once. And I surely was no vixen. I could barely speak to another human, let alone flirt with one. I wasn't a blushing virgin, but I may as well have been with my level of understanding in this situation. While there were a few people who thought kindly about me in this world, nobody cared for me deeply. Maybe I was so confused when given care and friendship that I immediately labeled it as romance. Though, the way I felt when I kissed them both would suggest otherwise.

"Eva? Where'd you go off to?" Nate asked, snapping me back to the conversation.

"Hm?" I asked, sitting up straighter.

He smiled. "What were you thinking about?"

"Oh, uh, just- you know, like how this is going to work and all," I said and started picking at my sandwich again, not making eye contact. I felt the ever present blush burn hotter on my cheeks and chest.

"You mean the three of us?" Everett asked as he leaned back on the couch, his lunch finished. He draped his arm along the back of the couch behind Nate and crossed one boot clad ankle over his thigh.

I nodded once, nervously, and swallowed.

"We share you," Nate said with a shrug. "I think it's pretty simple."

"It's not," Everett amended.

Nate leaned back with a sigh on the couch. Everett's fingertips incidentally brushed the nape of Nate's neck below where his hair was tied back in a bun. Neither of them moved away from the contact.

"How is it not simple?" Nate asked. "We both kiss her, and we both sleep with her. We continue our normal lives in this project, but add in orgasms."

I bit my lip and looked down at my crossed legs.

"Is that what you want, baby girl?" Everett asked me in his quiet, calm voice.

I thought for a moment, looking at both of them and gauging my reaction to the idea. They were both looking at me with hooded eyes and smirks. My mouth salivated and my lower abdomen clenched. I nodded.

"Say it," Nate demanded in his low voice. He leaned forward in his seat towards me, keeping heated eye contact.

"I want you both," I whispered and licked my lips.

"Good," Everett said, and gave me a rare, full smile.

"But we're not telling Daisy," Nate said with a shiver. "She would have a fit."

I thought back to the pictures she'd been sending Nate and her bitchy texts to me. "Did you tell Daisy that Nate and I were hooking up?"

"No, I don't gossip. Besides, I haven't spoken to her more than a few words in weeks," Everett said, and something flashed over his eyes, but I couldn't make out what he was feeling.

"Then how did she know?" Nate asked, his eyes locked on mine where we were both sharing a confused and worried look.

"What do you mean?" Everett asked, looking wary.

I showed him the texts I had exchanged with Daisy a few nights ago. He was shaking his head in anger when he finished reading them. "She's truly chaotic," he said gruffly. "You should see the kinds of things she sends me, despite me asking her not to."

"Oh-ho-ho, I bet I do fuckin' know," Nate said loudly, his eyes wide. "She sends them to me, too."

I cringed, feeling bad for her despite our argument and falling out. "Well, if you didn't tell her, then how did she find out?"

"Did she see us in that parking lot?" Nate wondered.

Everett raised his eyebrows but said nothing.

"There were some people around, I guess. But there's no way she wouldn't have interrupted us," I said with a shake of my head.

"Yeah, she was desperate for a piece of you, too," Nate chuckled, and cleaned up our lunch. "She would have joined us or something."

Everett's eyebrows raised even further, and I rolled my eyes with a blush. "Okay, so we're definitely not telling her," I muttered.

We cleaned up our lunch and were about to go back into the lab when Nate's phone chimed. He checked it as Everett and I put on our protective gear. "Oh, my *god*!" Nate exclaimed. "What the *fuck*?"

Everett and I rushed to Nate, where he held out his phone for us to see. It was a picture of Daisy in front of a full-length mirror, wearing a pale pink and lacy thong and nothing else. Glossy lips puckered around a red lollipop and her makeup and hair perfectly styled and her perky boobs exposed. Below it was a text.

Daisy: Me and Everett broke up. I could use some company...

"I need to talk to her," I blurted out angrily. I was seeing red and ready for a fight. I'd never felt like this before, having opted to choose the "high road" when people had wronged me in the past. I cracked my knuckles reflexively.

"And say what?" Everett asked as he watched Nate pocket his phone.

I didn't answer him, just looked up at him and Nate with the rage fire burning within me.

"Oh shit, yeah, let's go. I gotta see this," Nate said, and turned to grab our coats to leave the lab.

We dressed in our coats and hats to leave. The picture of Daisy was seared into my mind's eye, and it filled me more and more with an indignant rage as the seconds passed. She knew me and Nate were together. And whether or not she liked it; he was not interested in her. She had to know doing this ruined all chances to repair our friendship. I stomped to the car and waited a few more seconds for the guys to come out. It felt like she was personally attacking me when I had done nothing to upset her. I tugged on the car door; I was on a mission to throw my very first punch.

13

We were technically in a restricted contact stage, so we could see Daisy. We weren't supposed to be anywhere public or on campus, though. Everett drove us to a part of campus that I had never been to in order to find Daisy's dorm.

"Do you know where she lives?" Nate asked from the passenger seat.

"I've dropped her off outside her building a couple times," Everett said as he navigated us into a parking spot. "But I never walked her in."

"Gasp! A Southern Gentleman didn't walk his lady friend to the door?" Nate exclaimed in false horror and accent. Ev shot him a Look before pulling into the parking lot. I was too angry to laugh.

As soon as the car stopped, I jumped out. I looked back once to see if the guys were following my angry walk towards the dorm building and saw them exchanging hesitant glances as they jogged to catch up.

I stopped outside the dorm building and tried to open the door. It was locked and required a school ID to swipe in. I dug mine out of my coat pocket and swiped it. It flashed red. I swiped again. Red flash.

"We're not residents of this building. It's probably not going to open," Everett explained before he took my hand to pull me back from the door.

I growled in frustration and looked around. A girl was coming towards the door from down the hall. She wore a heavy coat, a hat with the Truman Tiger logo on it, and carried her bookbag. She opened the door and her eyes swept over the three of us.

"Excuse me, I'm looking for Daisy. Do you happen to know if she's home?" Everett asked in a smooth voice. He wasn't wearing a cowboy hat, he was wearing a navy blue Carhart beanie, but when he spoke in that tone, he verbally was removing his Stetson with a polite bow.

"Who?" the girl asked with a tilt of her head.

"Daisy Rossi? Or Francesca Rossi? Red curly hair, blue eyes?" Everett asked as the girl shook her head.

"She must be in a different dorm. I'm an RA here and I know everyone in this building. Sorry," the girl said and carried on to her class.

"Are you sure it was this dorm?" Nate asked Everett.

"Absolutely sure. I always watched her go through these doors." Everett shook his head and looked around.

Another student was approaching the building. It was a chubby, red-faced guy. If anyone was going to know Daisy, it was a male. "Excuse me, do you know Daisy Rossi?" Nate asked him.

"Daisy? No, I don't know a Daisy," the guy said as he stopped in front of us.

"Curly red hair, blue eyes, big rack?" Nate asked. I punched him in the side.

"I wish I knew her," the guy shrugged. "Only one redhead here, and that's Sarah."

"Thanks anyway," Nate said as the guy swiped into the dorm. Nate turned to us. "Um, what the hell?"

"We must have the building wrong," I said. "It's the only thing that makes sense."

Everett nodded. "Let's ask Professor Hoffmann if he knows where she lives. I don't want to ask her in text where she lives. I have a feeling she'd lie or be weird about it."

We got back into the truck and Everett drove us to the building where we first met, assuming that was where Professor Hoffmann's office was. Upon entering the building, a different young receptionist than the last time we were here greeted us. Professor Hoffmann's office was not in this building and the receptionist did not know who he was to direct us.

Silently, we walked to the building that housed the science department of the college. Professor Hoffmann had to teach more than us and had to have a place for office hours with his students. Students were coming and going from the building, meaning classes were in session. I hoped we could catch him between classes or during office hours. We hadn't needed to swipe into the building since other students were around, but we had to look at the building directory to find where staff offices were located. We took the elevator to the top floor and exited into a quiet vestibule. A few teaching assistants were using the space to sort out papers. We walked up and down the hallways, reading the name plaques with no success.

Nate spoke to the teaching assistants in the vestibule when we couldn't find his office, and they said they didn't know him and had never heard of him. We rode the elevator back down in tense silence. Nobody wanted to even guess at what was happening or voice their concerns aloud. As soon as the doors opened, both guys stormed out and went to two different students and asked about both Daisy and Professor Hoffmann. Neither student knew who they were talking about. I caught sight of a professor coming down the hall, carrying a stack of papers and a coffee. He was checking his watch as I approached.

"Excuse me," I said, determined to contribute to the search. "I'm looking for Professor Hoffmann. Do you know where I might find him?"

The young professor's polite face faltered for a moment. "I am not sure who you're talking about," he said, and his eyes glanced up at Everett and Nate as they approached behind me.

"He's a science professor, and oversees the PhD program," I elaborated.

The professor straightened his stance and looked around. He was clearly nervous. "No, I don't know him. I'm sorry. You could always ask the registrar's office. Now if you'll excuse me…" he said before rushing off.

"Something's wrong," I said to the guys. They both nodded and looked around at the other students and professors moving through the lobby. "Are we going to the registrar's office? I kind of want to know where his office is now."

I forgot my anger with Daisy in my confusion over where she and Professor Hoffmann were.

"Yeah, I need to sort this out," Everett said, and led the way out to the registrar's office.

A squat, elderly woman manned the desk. "Good afternoon, dears. Registration for second semester classes has ended already. I hope that's not what you're here for," she said in a warm voice.

"No, we're looking for a professor's office," Everett said. "Professor Hoffmann, science department."

"Did you check the science building?" she asked as she peered through her bifocals at her computer screen, typing away.

"Yes, ma'am," Everett replied politely.

"Well, it looks like there's no Professor Hoffmann at this school, dear. There's Professor Holden, but he's in engineering," the woman said, looking at Everett, Nate, and me over her glasses.

My stomach dropped and my mouth went dry. Nate grabbed my hand and gripped it tightly.

"Can you look up a student for us?" Everett asked in his smooth accent.

"I shouldn't, but your faces- you three look like you've seen a ghost," she said, and her fingers rested back on the keyboard.

"Francesca Rossi, please," Everett directed her and looked back at us. He pressed his lips in a firm line and his blue eyes showed his unease.

"No, sorry dear. Nobody by that name," she said and looked over at us again. "Is something the matter?"

"Everett Monroe," Everett said, his voice barely a whisper.

She typed in his name, a crease in her brows. "Not a student."

My stomach roiled and I broke out in a sweat.

"Nathaniel Gibson," Everett whispered.

She typed and then shook her head.

"Evangeline Reid."

Another shake of her head. "Dears, do you need to sit down?"

A buzzing had begun in my ears, and I was sure I was about to faint. Black spots danced in my vision. I clutched Nate's hand harder with my sweat slick palm.

"Thank you, ma'am," Everett said hoarsely before stepping between me and Nate and grabbing us both by the arm and leading us outside. The cold air brought me back and cleared the black spots, but not the panic.

"What the fuck?" Nate asked as we raced to the truck across campus. I jogged to keep up with their long strides. Everett let go of our arms once we were a few feet from the building. "Why are we not students? And why do Daisy and Professor Hoffmann not exist?"

Everett shook his head. "I don't know, but something is going on"

"No shit, Sherlock," Nate snapped.

"Let's not talk out here," I said as a few people turned to look at us when Nate shouted.

We rushed back to the house and stood in the kitchen. I made a pot of coffee to have something to do with my hands. Nate was pacing the kitchen, running his hands through his freed hair, and Everett stood with his palms flat on the island and his head hanging between his shoulder blades. We didn't speak for many minutes as the coffee pot bubbled.

I couldn't think of any explanation other than someone had tricked us. There was no way the college let us use an entire lab for a project that wasn't part of the curriculum, right? The college wouldn't give us unlimited funds and a house right off campus and a golf cart for transportation if we weren't part of the college, right?

I poured everyone's coffee and prepared it in our preferred ways and passed it out. We each only took a sip or two, the anxiety running through our blood had fueled us enough. Everett then grabbed bottled water out for each of us. I chugged that down, anxiety always gave me cotton mouth.

Nate paced a few times before he chucked his half-drunk water bottle towards the sink. It bounced out of the sink, hit the bottom of the mug cabinet, and then fell onto the countertop before rolling to the floor. Something small clattered to the countertop, and I looked to see what it was as I bent to pick up the thrown bottle. I froze.

There was no way.

Icy fear poured through my body like a waterfall. Electric ice flushed through my veins as my breath hitched.

"What, Eva?" Everett asked.

I didn't respond. I couldn't. No sound came out when I opened my mouth.

"Spit it out, Eva," Nate said, irritated. If I didn't know him and I wasn't, in fact, gaping like a fish, I may have been offended.

"Camera," I whispered, trembling.

"A what?" Nate asked as both he and Everett raced around the island to me. They both put their hands on me as I pointed to the countertop.

They stared at the small, round and discreet camera. It was nearly the size of a pen, but had been fastened to our cabinet with what looked like a clear zip tie. It was wireless and didn't have any lights to suggest it was on or off. They had painted the camera to match our cabinets except for the lens.

"Field trip," Everett barked out before we raced to pull on shoes and coats. We took Everett's truck to our park. The parking lot was plowed, and the tree covered path had only a few inches of snow covering it, having been clearly travailed many times today. We made our way as quickly as we could to the field house. The little path leading up to it had a drift of snow and was too buried to get into the building. We stood outside of our secret sanctuary and looked at each other, panting from the exertion of getting there.

"What are we thinking?" Nate asked, his hands on his hips as he caught his breath.

"The simplest answer is typically the correct answer," Everett stated.

"The simplest answer to me is that we've hopped timelines and are in a different universe," Nate spat sarcastically. "What the hell do *you* think is the simplest answer?"

Everett stepped up to Nate, his shoulders back and chest forward, his face like angry stone. "You watch it-"

"Stop it!" I shouted at them. "This is not helping. We need to step back and- and form our questions. So, my first question is why aren't we students?"

"Why were we bugged?" Nate asked.

"Who are Daisy and Hoffmann?" Everett added.

"Is this a real program?" I asked.

"I think these questions can be summed up into one question: We've been tricked, but by whom?" Everett summarized, his hands on his hips.

"Then narrow it down to who would benefit from our research?" Nate said, pacing next to me.

"Even further; what part of our research is the intended project?" Everett pushed. "Our assigned project was so broad and far-fetched. Create the illness causing bacteria and then the cure? Not likely in the time span I assumed we were given."

"Then why didn't you say anything?" Nate asked, his face looking defeated as he paused his pacing.

"Oh, because you two didn't also have doubts about it?" Everett asked us and ran a hand over the back of his neck.

"I did," I said. "It seemed too good to be true."

"Same. And I also thought the secrecy aspect was a bit much," Nate added, resuming his pacing.

"The project seemed a bit over our capabilities, but I figured we'd get as far as we could and pass it on to the next PhD students," I said and sighed. "Out loud, I realize it makes little sense why we'd still get our diplomas if we didn't finish the project they tasked us with."

"It also still doesn't explain why we were bugged," Everett added.

Nate continued to pace the snow-covered ground around us, the crunch of the snow and ice almost echoing in our silence.

"What if-" I started and swallowed a few times. "What if *we* are the product?"

"Like our labor in the project?" Everett asked.

I nodded.

"Again, that leads to what part of the project? The illness or the cure?" Nate paced faster, kicking up snow. "Because they could get any grad student or even undergrad student to mess around with different bacteria and phages."

"Do you think someone wanted us to create an illness that wouldn't have a cure yet?" Everett asked, his voice stoic.

Nate nodded after a few seconds of thought. "I think so."

"Who would want that?" I asked, feeling small and used.

"Who would have the money for it?" Everett added.

"Who has the money and power to get us degrees, a house, a top-of-the-line lab, credit cards, and everything else?" Nate listed.

"The college," Everett suggested.

"For financial gain from the research or for prestige?" I asked.

"Neither," Nate said. "Especially not from unfinished research."

"We're not listed as students and Daisy and Hoffmann don't exist. Um," Everett said, and ran his hands through his hair while he thought.

"Pharmaceutical companies?" I suggested.

"Would they really pay students to do what they have their own teams of scientists doing?" Everett challenged.

"The uh, the- government?" I asked, my mouth void of all moisture again.

Silence. Nate stopped pacing.

"Don't they have their own people?" Nate asked.

"They do," Everett said confidently.

"Yeah, but this is a shady and unethical study if it's cut off at creating the illness. They wouldn't do that," Nate said, his voice trailing off as basic US history filtered back into his brain.

Silence.

"Well, whoever it is, I don't want to do this anymore. If they feel the need to spy on us and create this web of fake people and degrees, then I want nothing to do with it," I said after swallowing a few times.

"Agreed," Everett said, and Nate nodded.

"We'll sign more NDAs. We'll give up the alleged degrees," I added. "We'll even give back the paychecks."

"Let's go home to call Hoffmann and pack up. We can go to a hotel to plan out how we move forward," Everett suggested.

"Sounds good. It's fucking cold out here," Nate grumbled as he took my hand and we headed back to the truck.

"I guess that's how Daisy knew we had hooked up," I said quietly as Everett drove.

"Huh, I guess so," Nate said with a humorless laugh.

Once we were back home, Everett called and left a voicemail for Hoffmann about discussing the termination of our project. We went our separate ways to pack bags of our essentials, hoping we could send for our things once we had gotten back to our homes. Everett invited us back to his family farm to avoid being separated as we planned our next steps. Nate had music playing in his room, but I could hear when Everett's phone rang.

"Hello Professor Hoffmann," I heard Everett say as he came up the stairs to meet me and Nate.

Nate turned off his music and met me in the hallway as Everett reached the top of the stairs. Everett had an angry expression on his face as he pulled the phone away from his ear and pressed a button to put it on speakerphone.

"-will stay where you are. There will be no more digging into the college or the project. You will complete your assignment or forfeit your degrees and place at Truman College," Hoffmann said sternly.

"Sir, with all due respect, we've decided that because of the secrecy and deception, we would like to step down from the project and agree to forfeit the degrees," Everett said into the phone. He wrapped his arm around my shoulders as tears formed in my eyes. I had worked hard to get to where I was in my education, and giving it up was painful. "We understand the generosity of the college and will be out of the home by morning."

"You will remain in place or face severe consequences," Hoffmann spat.

"I don't understand, sir. We agree to give up the degrees, and stipend," Everett said, locking eyes with Nate as he spoke.

"I have men on their way-"

Everett hung up, cutting Hoffmann off.

"We need to run," Everett said abruptly. "Grab your overnight bag, leave everything you can't run carrying."

"Why? What do you think he means?" Nate asked.

"Whoever he is, he's not letting us go without a fight. Get your fucking bag and meet me at the truck," Everett shouted and ran down the stairs.

I shared one quick, fearful look with Nate before we both finished our bags and thundered down the stairs. We tugged on our boots and coats as Everett came out of his room carrying his bag. He ushered us out the door, pulling on his coat. Nate and I jumped into the truck, but Everett went into the shed. He came out with a can of gasoline we had for topping off Marie Curie, placed it in the truck bed, and got in the cab.

"What's that for?" Nate asked. Everett didn't respond.

14

Everett pulled up to the lab and hopped out of the truck. "Stay here," he barked at us.

Nate opened his door and got out to follow Ev. "What's the plan? What are you doing?"

Everett grabbed the gas can from the back of the truck and came around to the passenger side of the truck. I rolled down the window but followed the direction to stay.

"I need to make sure nothing survives," Everett explained, his eyes darting from me to Nate.

Nate opened his arms up in a *what the fuck* gesture. "And you're going to what? Set the place on fire?"

"I am," Everett said and walked towards the lab. "Stay in the truck."

"No!" Nate shouted and started to follow Everett. "I'm not letting you do it by yourself. It's not safe to go in there alone. What if there's someone in there looking for us?"

Everett spun on his heel and pushed Nate with a palm to his chest back against the truck. This was not the calm, smirking cowboy I knew and cared for. He was steel, vengeance, and undeterred rage. I gasped as Nate's back slammed against the truck at the front passenger door. Everett pressed his chest against Nate's and spoke clearly and in a demanding tone that allowed for no negotiation, his arms boxed in Nate at his shoulders. "Stay. In. The. Truck."

"You have five minutes before I come in and get you," Nate said in an argumentative tone.

Everett pushed away from Nate and picked up the gas can and jogged into the lab. Nate looked down at his watch to mark the beginning of five minutes. Neither of us spoke, but Nate kept looking from the doors to his watch as he paced next to the truck. As I stared at the building, I took a steadying breath. I had my seatbelt off and my hand on the door handle, ready to run into the building if needed. I saw Everett move from the lab to the office at a run, right as the fire alarm sounded and the sprinklers started. The lab room itself had a different type of fire deterrent where the doors would lock, and all the oxygen is sucked out of the room through the ventilation system, therefore cutting off the fuel for the fire. My stomach clenched at the realization Everett had been seconds from being stuck in that room without oxygen.

Nate had stopped pacing when the alarm sounded, and I knew he was waiting to see Everett not trapped in the lab. A blaze was visible from the open office door, and Everett came running out without the gas can. He had his shirt over the bottom half of his face to block the smoke as he ran out. "Get in the truck, Nate!" he bellowed as he sprinted to the driver's seat. Ev turned back to the lab and lifted both middle fingers to it. Nate and Ev both jumped into the truck at the same time and Nate and I both gave the building middle fingers as well, assuming cameras were watching us.

As Everett was slamming on the gas in reverse to get us away from the lab, the building exploded. I shrieked as the force rocked the truck. The sound was so loud it felt like my eardrums had burst. I knew vaguely that Nate was swearing as Everett sped us away from the decimated building. I fought back tears from the shock of it all and buckled into my seat with shaking hands.

"There was hardly any gas in that can! How'd you do that?" Nate shouted incredulously as he craned around to see the burning building.

"There were a lot of accelerants in that building. You just have to know how to use them," Everett muttered as he maneuvered us through Cleveland traffic.

"I guess so," Nate grumbled and buckled his seat belt.

"Wh-where are we going now?" I asked in a quiet voice after a few attempts to gather my speech.

"I need to find my brother," Everett said.

"Wait, he's in the-" Nate started to clarify, but Everett cut him off.

"Let's not talk about where we're going until we get rid of our phones," Ev said. "Call your families and say goodbye for a little while. Then toss your phone out the window."

"Eva, go ahead," Nate said and reached back a hand to pat my knee.

I pulled out my phone and with still shaking hands; I pressed my dad's contact. It rang and rang until it went to voicemail. I hiccupped a sob before swallowing it down when I heard the standard voicemail greeting. "Um, hey, dad. I uh- I think the school has tricked me. It seems like I was never actually a student there. I um- I had to leave quickly because I think it wasn't legal or ethical, but it's okay because nobody will be able to get the samples anymore. Um, I guess this is goodbye for a little while. So, bye."

Nate and Everett exchanged quick glances in the front seat, and I looked back down at my phone. What if he called back? I wasn't sure if I wanted to throw my last lifeline to my dad out the window. Should I call Caleb? But what would I say to him? I sighed and rolled down the window and threw my phone down onto the road as hard as I could. I heard it shatter as we sped away.

I listened to Nate call his mom and explain quickly what happened and then throw his phone out. The call was quick, as he didn't allow her to ask questions. He sat still and silent in the front seat, staring straight ahead. It was rare for Nate to be both quiet and unmoving, so I knew he was upset. I rubbed his shoulder over the seat, and he reached a hand back to place over mine, holding me to him.

Everett called his mom next. "Mama, there's been a mixup at school. I'm alright, but I had to leave. They had us doing something that wasn't right, and I needed to back out. It might be bigger than me, though. They might be after me, so I'm going to disappear- no, mama. No, I did nothing wrong. It's why I'm leaving... I'll see you soon. I love you," Everett said, and threw his phone out the window instead of hanging up. I could hear his mom's voice wailing on the other end of the phone as it sailed out the window and my heart clenched for her. She had lost contact with her oldest son before this, so this was difficult. But my heart also clenched at the absence of having someone in my own life that cared so deeply.

We drove in silence for a while as Everett sped down the highway in a direction I didn't pay attention to. When we all settled down enough to feel more comfortable in the car, Everett reached down to turn on the radio. "I say we should drive as far as we can tonight and then stop somewhere to sleep and use a payphone to call my brother in the mountains," Everett said as he found a station playing country music.

"Why your brother? I thought you said you hadn't had contact with him after he went crazy," Nate said.

"He might be able to help us figure out if this *was* the government ordering the project or if it was the college or someone else. I don't know who else to trust with this to help us. If anything, he'll help us hide out for a while," Everett explained.

I nodded when Everett looked at me in the rearview mirror. I certainly didn't have any other plans or ideas. If he trusted his brother, then I trusted him as well.

"Breaking news here in Cleveland tonight. An explosion on the campus of Truman College with three students on the run." A news report began on the radio. "Earlier this evening, three doctoral students fled the scene of their attack on Truman College. Video footage gathered from the scene shows them making obscene gestures after one student set the building ablaze. Sources say the students had created an alleged bioweapon instead of completing their assignments. Truman College and the surrounding area are in lockdown and quarantine to deter the spread of any illnesses. News Channel-"

"WHAT THE FUCK?!" Nate was roaring in the front seat. "YOU *HAD* TO BLOW IT UP!" Everett was screaming back at Nate, but I couldn't focus on their words anymore.

I couldn't hold back my tears now. Sobs wracked my body, and I curled in on myself as much as I could in the back seat. I felt sick. It felt like acid burning through my veins as I realized we were now wanted criminals. We would be hunted down and treated like terrorists. I couldn't catch my breath I was crying so hard. I was going to end up in prison or killed. The guys were arguing with each other, and red in the face. A vein pulsed in Everett's forehead as he bellowed back at Nate. Nate's fists clenched tightly in his lap before he punched the truck's dash.

"STOP IT!" I screamed and sobbed at them.

Everett quickly pulled over to the side of the highway, likely realizing it was not a smart idea to fight and drive at the same time. He turned off the radio that had played music again. "I'm sorry. I'm so sorry, baby girl," he said and reached over the center console to me.

I unbuckled with numb fingers and threw myself towards him and buried my face in his chest as he wrapped his arms around me. Nate unbuckled as well to hug me from behind, his forehead resting on my back between my shoulder blades. I clutched at both of them and sobbed while they both stroked over my arms and back. Thinking of them in prison or being killed and treated like terrorists made me almost sicker than thinking of myself in that situation. We had done nothing wrong. We realized the project was not what we thought it was. We tried to step out, and when that didn't work, we destroyed the experiment.

"We have to get to my brother as soon as we can," Everett murmured against my hair. "We can drive in shifts to get there faster. I don't think we're safe staying anywhere."

"Let's stop for gas now, before word spreads and there's a manhunt," Nate added. "I'll pump the gas and you find a pay phone."

"Use only cash, no paper trail," Everett said as he pulled back from me to drive again.

A crashing of glass behind me made me jump and squeal. I thought a car had hit us, but we were fully off the road and on the shoulder. I looked around as the window on my door exploded.

15

Everett's hold on me changed as he reached for Nate's head and pushed us both down on the center console. "Stay down!" Everett bellowed as he slammed the car into drive and took off. I could hear gravel flying as he tried to navigate back onto the road. The truck rocked and shook, and I dug my nails into the center console and Nate's coat sleeve.

"Are we being shot at?" Nate asked, his voice loud and in my ear.

"Yes!" Everett said as squealing tires sounded around us. All I could see was his hand flexing as he pushed the gear shift into reverse before he whipped the wheel around and put the car back into drive. Everett grunted as he desperately tried to get us away from the shooter. A few more gunshots sounded around us, making me think there was more than one shooter. I peeked upwards and saw the reflection of blue and white flashing lights, and my heart dropped to my stomach in panic. Nate's breath was hot and panting on my neck, and he was whispering to me to comfort me. But in my panic, I couldn't process what he was saying.

Everett was swearing as he tried to navigate us away from the police. Should we be running from the police? What if we explained everything we had experienced, and they let us go? I was about to say as much to Ev when he shouted, "Get out and run!"

I didn't question the authority in his voice as he threw the truck into park. I jumped out of the car, running for the tree line. Nate was right behind me, and Everett was only a few feet behind him. I could see people running after us, but I didn't focus on them. I jumped over a fallen log at the start of the woods that bordered the highway. It was dark and little light reached us as we got further and further into the woods that likely opened up into someone's backyard on the other side. My pulse pounded in my head as I pushed my body as fast as I could through the trees. I was aware of gunshots ringing out behind me. The sound barely echoed over the crash of branches and leaves under my feet and over my body as I ran. I chanced one look back to see if the guys were still with me. I was worried about them; I had been running almost every day since I regained the ability, so I knew I was a strong runner. Everett was fit from working on the farm, but he was not a natural runner and Nate had just started running with us this fall. They were also much bigger than me, running through this patch of forest in the dark, dodging branches and trees.

I heard a thump and a curse as one of them fell. My heart lurched as I turned around to find them. "Get up, get up!" I heard Everett say breathlessly.

Another thump and a grunt as someone tackled Everett to the ground. I ran back to where I saw them behind me. A man clad in a police uniform was wrestling Everett. A click of a gun next to me turned my blood ice-cold. I swallowed and looked over to see a man pointing a gun at my head.

"We got you, fuckers," a man's voice laughed. A flashlight blared into my face, and I flinched at the blinding light.

"Nate, Ev," I said hoarsely, needing to hear their voices to know they were alive. The flashlight was so bright I couldn't see them.

"You're going to be okay, baby girl," Everett replied, panting.

"We're here," Nate added.

"How nice. Now *move*," a man's voice barked.

The policemen spoke in hushed voices as they walked us back to the road, guns to our heads and blinding flashlights to our eyes the entire way. This didn't feel right. I knew a gun was at the back of my head because when I stumbled over a branch; the man jabbed me with it. I thought for sure I was going to vomit and pee my pants with fear. Tears streamed down my face as we approached the road where two cop cars were facing us. The tires of Everett's truck had been shot out, which had prompted our run into the woods. Lights flashed on top of the police cars and people were slowing to watch what happened. We were lit up like a stage under the police lights and big streetlamps. I looked around and saw that four policemen were arresting us.

The man walking with Everett kicked out the back of Ev's knees, causing him to fall on the gravel shoulder of the highway. The policeman kicked Ev in the back to get him to fall the rest of the way into the gravel and I briefly doubted that was standard police practice before the same thing happened to me and Nate.

Face down in the gravel, the police cuffed us roughly. I scraped my face on the gravel to look over at the guys. Before they took us to jail, I wanted to see them one more time. I met Everett's scared eyes, and he was shaking his head at me. Gravel was stuck in his beard and a cut on his eyebrow was bleeding into his eye. I only stared at him, wondering what he meant by his head shake. He looked pointedly down at the shoes of the policeman that was putting on his handcuffs. They were red basketball shoes. I wasn't sure what the standard issue of shoes was for the police, but I was pretty sure they weren't red Nikes. I looked over my shoulder at the shoes of the man straddling my back and saw tan work boots.

"I think we'll shoot you after we cuff you," the man over me laughed. "Maybe you are showing signs of sickness and we have to put you down."

Not exactly the speech police typically give as they arrest someone. In fact, none of them had read us our Miranda warning.

Nate's glasses were on the ground in front of him and I knew he probably couldn't see the shoes of our alleged police officers. I swallowed. "Nate," I rasped. "Nate, we're missing Miranda."

He was facing me on the ground, and he blinked up at me, likely not quite seeing my features. "What?"

"Miranda, our *friend*. She's missing," I rasped again.

Nate gave a sharp intake of breath as he realized what I was saying.

"Wait, I thought there were only three of them," one man said.

"Boss said only three. I don't know what they're talking about," another guy said.

"I'll call him," one guy grunted and walked away from us. "Gotta let him know we got them, anyway."

They roughly propped us against Everett's damaged truck tire. They wedged me between Nate and Everett while the fake police met up with the guy on the phone. The fake cops were on the other side of the second cop car, on the phone with their boss. The cold water and snow from the road seeped through my jeans and felt like needles in my skin.

"They're not police," Everett said quietly.

"I gathered," Nate replied.

"What are we going to do? If they aren't police, then who are they?" I asked, my throat still dry.

"How did they get the cop cars? And the uniforms?" Nate asked.

I shifted a bit where I was sitting to get off a stone that was hurting. The handcuffs were on terribly behind me. One was super tight, and one was loose enough that I was sure I could wiggle out of it. I spent a moment trying to do so, but the cuff kept getting stuck over my thumb. "I- I need lubricant," I huffed out.

"What?"

"Excuse me?"

"This hand," I said, shrugging my right shoulder. "I can get it out of the cuff. Just... like spit on me or something."

"This is not the way I imagined you saying that," Nate groaned.

Everett scoffed, but he was on my right, so he was the one that leaned over and spit on my hand. I felt the warm liquid slide over my palm, and I wiggled my hand around to get it where I needed it.

"Why was that so hot?" Nate moaned. "We're about to be murdered by fake police and I'm hard."

"Is it a library boner or a sexy time boner?" I asked quietly as I successfully slid my right hand out of the cuff.

Nate chuckled quietly. "Oh man, I fucking love you guys. I'm sorry we're about to die. We could have had an amazing threesome."

"Nathaniel," Everett warned halfheartedly.

"I'm sorry, too," I said, seeing my window of opportunity nearing a close. I needed to work fast.

"For what, baby girl?" Everett asked, sensing my change in tone.

I didn't respond before quietly getting up from my seat and running around to the first cop car where the door was still open. The guys didn't make a sound, and I didn't look back. But I could feel their angry and frantic eyes on my back as I slid into the driver's seat.

I hunched over in the driver's seat as I looked around for something to use as a weapon or maybe a handcuff key. A belt with a walkie talkie and a ring of keys was on the floor below the passenger seat. It was as if the fake police didn't put that part of the uniform on when they got dressed. A long club that rested between the car seats caught my attention. It would not be much against the guns these men carried, but maybe I could at least be a distraction for the guys to get away. The dash camera mounted above the two front seats was visible when I looked around in the car. I wasn't visible to it while being crouched down in the seat, but I hoped it had audio. I remembered a few viral videos featuring dashcam footage, and they had audio.

"My name is Eva Reid. I did not create a bioweapon with my partners, Nate and Everett. Someone tricked us, we're not sure who, to do this project. We were supposed to find a cure for the bacteria. We didn't get to finish. But burning the building destroyed the samples. Everyone is *safe*. Please, we've done nothing wrong, and we tried to leave when we got uncomfortable. Professor Hoffmann and Daisy Rossi- find them, they're the ones behind this," I whispered hoarsely before taking a deep breath and leaving the cop car with the key ring and nightstick. I passed in front of the car to return to my guys, and I stopped for a moment to give the dash camera a pleading look. It was a long shot that actual police would even see the footage if these guys didn't turn it off already or would destroy it later.

"What the fuck were you thinking?" Nate hissed at me as I returned to my spot between them. Crouching this time, like I was ready to pounce.

"I got the keys for the cuffs," I whispered. "And a nightstick."

"They have *guns*, Eva," Nate said like I was dense.

"I'll be a distraction for you guys to get out of here. You have families to get back to," I said, watching as one cop came around the other car.

"Eva, no," Everett warned.

"Your dad-" Nate started.

"Died the day my mom died. Now when I say go, you need to go," I muttered quietly to them as the fake cop approached.

The fake cop approached us with a bored expression and raised his gun to Nate. I lunged at him with the club ready to strike. I got a solid blow to the guy's head before he could do more than take a shocked breath. The man dropped to his knees, and the handgun clattered to the gravel. He fell to the ground after I hit him again with the nightstick. I looked to see both Nate and Everett tense with anticipation watching me, and our eyes all dropped to the fallen gun. I'd never shot a gun before.

"Go," I told the guys.

"No," they both said.

"I'm not leaving here without you," Everett added gruffly, straining against his handcuffs. "Get me out of these cuffs."

I scrambled to the key ring and looked for a key that probably didn't look like any other key. I tried a few odd-looking keys before I found one that had a small rectangle at the bottom. Everett's handcuffs successfully opened, and he lunged for the gun, holding it out as I unlocked Nate's cuffs. Footsteps were approaching as we scrambled to stand.

"Go go go go," Everett commanded quietly as we took off quietly towards the trees again.

I heard the fake police shout as they found their bloodied partner. They started running, following our footsteps in the snow towards the tree line. This time, I held Everett's hand, and he grabbed Nate's as we quickly made our way through the woods together. Once we were in the trees, there was no snow to track our footsteps. We stopped hearing the sounds of our would-be attackers as we went further and further into the woods. We didn't let go of each other until we stumbled out of the woods and into what seemed like the back of a strip mall.

Panting, we all turned to each other and assessed the damage. We brushed our hands over each other, knocking off twigs and leaves and checking for blood. We were bruised and scraped, but no major injuries. I still had the tight handcuff on my left hand, having dropped the key ring in our dash through the woods. Everett used the sleeve of his coat to wipe at the blood on his eyebrow with a hiss. Nate rolled his shoulders stiffly and tried to adjust his broken glasses on his nose. I was still numb and was unsure of any injuries I had suffered. Nate reached out and thumbed blood away from my lip and I winced.

"Are we all okay?" Everett asked.

I nodded.

"Yeah, we're good," Nate replied with a relieved sigh.

Everett reached out and pulled us both into a tight hug, and kissed the top of my head. "We're okay," he said, as if he was convincing himself. He stepped back and patted down his waistband and pockets. "I'm sorry, I dropped the gun. I thought it was in my waistband."

"I dropped the handcuff key," I added.

"Yikes," Nate said, looking down at the handcuffs hanging from my left hand. Everett reached for me and tucked the metal into the sleeve of my coat so it wasn't dangling any more.

"We need to get out of here, though," Nate reminded us.

We carefully walked around the front of the building and saw it was an empty strip mall. Graffiti covered the walls, and the windows were boarded up. It was facing a large road that had residential streets intersecting it. We found a quiet street with cars parked along the curb. Nate looked around, assessing our surroundings, and tugged on a few cars' door handles. Only one car was left unlocked on the street, and it was a small, black sedan. "Perfect," he muttered contentedly to himself as he slid into the driver's seat. I looked around nervously, waiting for someone to come running out of their house. But it was late and a cold, dark weeknight in December. Nobody was paying attention. I had only been looking around for a minute before the engine of the car started.

"Nice," Everett said to Nate. "Where'd you learn to do that?"

I got in the back seat, and Everett quickly followed me in. The car was clean but had a slightly moldy smell, like a window had been left open in the rain once and the fabric got musty. The beige cloth interior was cold against my hands as I clutched the seat beneath me.

"I played a lot of the Grand Theft Auto games during some formative years," Nate said nonchalantly.

"Uh, I didn't think the game taught you *how* to hotwire a car," Everett scoffed as Nate quickly navigated us out of street parking and to the main road.

"It doesn't. But I took an interest. Like I said, formative," Nate said with a shrug. "So, Tennessee?"

"Yeah, head that way. When we stop for gas, I'll call him," Everett said.

I was still tense, sitting on the edge of the seat. Everett reached for my hand below where the handcuff was tight against my skin. "Hey, we're okay. We're all safe. We got away," he said soothingly. I realized I was shaking.

Nate glanced at me in the rearview mirror, his brow furrowed in concern.

"I know," I said after a moment.

"You're in shock, I think," Nate suggested. He turned on the heating to full blast.

"Here, let's get you warmed up," Everett said and helped me out of my coat after shrugging his own off. Our coats were wet from snow and covered in gravel. He pulled me to him, letting my head rest on his chest and draping my coat over us. His body heat radiated into me and I slowly felt my body again. He stroked over my hair as he leaned back against the car door.

"You are so brave," Everett murmured softly into my ear. "I'm so proud of you."

"I spoke to the dash cam. I hope the real police hear it," I said. My voice sounded sleepy, and I noticed my adrenaline crashing.

As soon as I could feel my hands and fingers again, I was drowsy with the heat of the car and the steady thump of Everett's heartbeat under my cheek. We were safe for now; I had saved my guys.

16

I woke up with a start when I heard a car door shut. The buzzing lights of a gas station made me blink as I sat up. Everett gripped my hips tightly as he sat up with a start, too. I whirled around, taking in our surroundings and looking frantically for Nate. We were in a gas station, a major chain that had a little store inside. We were the only car in sight, and it was still dark. The blaring tv that played at the pump screamed to life with an advertisement for hot dogs and ICEEs and I heard Nate swear at it as if it had also startled him. Everett smirked and exhaled his relief when he heard Nate's voice. He knocked twice with his knuckles against the window over his shoulder. He smoothed my knotted hair back from my face with his other hand.

"Oh hey, you're up," Nate said, peering down through the window.

"Where are we?" Everett asked in his raspy sleep voice. I looked him over as he sat up in the car. He had been leaning against the car door and holding me as we slept. His t-shirt was rumpled and pushed up, exposing a strip of tan lower abs. My core clenched at the sight of him and his raspy voice.

"We're outside of another college in Ohio. I wanted to get us somewhere we might be overlooked," Nate said with a yawn.

"What time is it?" Everett asked, catching Nate's yawn.

"It's about three. It's only been like two hours," Nate answered as he pulled out his wallet from his back pocket. "I gotta go inside to pay in cash."

"I'll go," I said, my bladder complaining. "I'll put money on the pump, and you fill up while I grab us some food and coffee."

Nate handed me some cash, since I didn't have my wallet or a purse. "Be careful. Wait, here, wear this hat I found in the car." He handed me a red beanie hat that smelled strongly of cologne. I wrinkled my nose at it and tucked the handcuffs back into my coat sleeve.

"Take Nate's glasses, too," Everett said. "You'll be less recognizable if our pictures are out there."

"Then I can't see shit, bro. They're broken anyway," Nate grumbled, but handed them over.

I put them on and blinked to adjust. They were thick black Ray-Ban frames, and he truly had terrible eyesight. I adjusted their placement on my nose and ears, as they were now crooked where they had broken.

"Jinkies Scoob, Velma would surely love to see this sexy librarian," Everett joked, and smacked me on the butt as I climbed out of the car. Nate groaned like he was in pain.

I rolled my eyes and went into the gas station, the bell above the door tinkling cheerfully. The half-asleep attendant only briefly looked up and saw I was a small female, not a large man wielding a gun and robbing the place. "Thirty on pump 6, please," I said with surprising ease as I handed over some of the cash. The attendant wordlessly nodded, and I stepped away. I kept my face turned away from the clerk and looked for the bathrooms. The bathrooms were eerily quiet and echoed when I ripped off the toilet paper. Nothing was abnormal, but I was waiting on bated breath for the next attack.

The gas station had a pretty good selection of bottled coffees and waters, and I grabbed the containers most closely resembling our normal coffees and cradled them in my arms. A small TV was playing over the beer cooler, and I stopped when I saw my own face smiling back next to Nate and Everett's. It was our grad school graduation pictures, showing us proudly smiling for the cameras. It flicked over to grainy and dark dashcam footage from two hours earlier. I stepped closer to the cooler and pretended to browse in order to hear the news better. I heard the tail end of what I said to the dash cam and the reporter said dispatchers watched it live after alleged car jackers stole the cop cruisers. Those were not average car jackers, though. Someone had sent them specifically to kill the three of us. My heart hammered painfully in my chest, and I clutched the bottles of coffee and water.

"This statement made by Reid is believed to be false, as Truman College officials state there is no Professor Hoffmann at their school. A student has come forward and claims to have been in classes with the trio and that they often joked about using their knowledge to hurt others," the news report continued.

The video flashed to me hitting the fake cop with the nightstick twice until he fell and Everett holding the gun. "Experts in behavior assert they believe that Reid, Monroe, and Gibson thought these carjackers to be actual police officers and attacked to avoid arrest. The tip lines are open and will remain open until these individuals are apprehended. Cleveland police believe them to be armed and dangerous as most of Truman College and its surrounding neighborhoods remain on lock down."

With a steadying breath, I turned away from the tv as the news continued to another story. I grabbed a small glasses repair kit, a few bags of chips and granola bars, a pair of sunglasses, and a baseball hat with a bird mascot on it. I placed them on the counter with shaking hands. The attendant had not been watching the news, and therefore likely had not seen my face plastered all over it. He didn't even pay any attention to me other than to tell me the total and take the money I slid across the counter. He gave me my change and slid everything into a plastic bag and handed it to me. Neither of us said anything else as I made my way quickly out of the store. I saw Nate finishing up at the pump and Everett was snapping his fingers to get my attention from where he was at an old and crusty looking pay phone near the ice box.

I went to his side as he spoke into the black receiver. "Cookie Monster?"

An angry yell came from the other side, and Everett hung up. "I can't quite remember his phone number. And now I'm panicking because what if the number he had is no longer his?"

"You'll get it," I whispered with a hard swallow. "You have to."

He peered at me with narrowed eyes as he dialed again. "Cookie Monster?"

Another confused and angry shout. I didn't blame them. It was the middle of the night, after all.

Everett growled in frustration and tried again, shoving the coin into the slot, as Nate approached us. He took his glasses off my nose and held out a hand for the bag. "You okay?" Nate asked, concern etched his features.

I shook my head. "Our pictures are on the news. The police saw what happened with the fake cops. Said they were carjackers, and we thought they were real police and attacked them to avoid being arrested. They have some kid saying we were in classes with him and we talked about hurting people. They- they said I was lying when I talked to the dash cam when I said someone tricked us."

"Fucking hell," Nate swore and snapped open a bottle of coffee. "I knew that was going to happen. I fucking knew it."

"Cookie Monster?" Everett grunted into the phone. He was about to hang up when his eyes popped open and he clenched the phone in his fist. "Yeah, it's me. I need your help."

Everett was quiet for a moment, and I could tell someone was talking on the other end, but I couldn't make out their words. Everett's eyes glistened with unshed tears, and I tightened my hold on his hand. I went on my tiptoes to hear, and Everett leaned down to accommodate me.

"First, what are you using to call me?" came a voice like Everett's.

"A pay phone outside a gas station," Everett answered. "We ditched our phones and we're driving a stolen car."

"Good thinking. Listen, I've been following your story on the radio. I know it's not true. I know you, little brother. You were right to call me." Easton's voice was strong and full of emotion. Everett's shoulders relaxed, and the tension in my stomach lessened. Nate couldn't hear the conversation, so I turned to him and gave him a thumbs up. He let out a breath and put an arm around me and Everett.

Everett sniffed and took his hand back to wipe his eyes. "I don't know what to do."

"So far, you're doing fine. There are no leads. Are all three of you together?" Easton asked.

"Yeah, they're both here," Everett said, and glanced over at me and Nate.

"Okay, don't be seen all together. Couples and singles will get overlooked; threes get attention. Especially since everyone's looking out," Easton said. "And you're going to come to me. I'm in the Smoky Mountains. This is a secure line, and hiding is kind of my specialty. Ask Mom and Dad. You're going to meet me here in Tennessee, but I'm going to need you to do this in segments. You're not coming straight here, and I can't give you where to meet me yet."

"Okay," Everett said with a shaky exhale.

"Hey, stay strong and stay smart and you'll be here with me in less than twenty-four hours," Easton said, and Everett's shoulders visibly relaxed even more. I squeezed him around his middle and felt his still rapid breathing expanding against my arms.

Easton gave us instructions to head towards Indianapolis and to stop for gas outside the city, and then to call him once we got there. He said it would take about four hours if we stayed off toll roads and major highways. He gave Everett directions that he wrote with a pen that had been shoved into the pay phone dock on the soft side of Nate's arm.

We got back into the car and pulled around to the side parking lot where the lights didn't quite reach. One empty car sat against the side of the building, and we assumed it belonged to the gas station attendant. No other cars were on the road and all the surrounding businesses were closed for the night. We drank our coffees and ate some of the granola bars while Nate repaired his glasses in the dim interior car lights with the little kit I had picked up.

"We could be safe in less than twenty-four hours," Everett said quietly, leaning back against the seat. All three of us were in the back seat, needing to be close to each other.

"Safe... ish," Nate said hesitantly.

"Nobody has figured out where Easton lives for years," Everett clarified. "He's very good at hiding."

"Hiding. Is that what we'll be doing forever?" Nate asked contemptuously.

"Better than dead, don't you think?" Everett shot back.

"Please," I said tiredly from between them. "Don't fight." They both reached out for a hand, and I squeezed them both. My handcuffs jingled. "Let's get to Easton first and then figure out what to do next."

We were quiet again for a moment, all three of us staring out the windows and thinking. Everett sniffed, and I looked at him to see his eyes fill with tears again. I reached out and pulled him down to rest his head on my shoulder in a hug. He sniffed and sighed into my neck and tangled hair but cried no more. He caught his breath and nuzzled against my neck. I pulled back to kiss Everett softly. His lips moved against mine and my heart soared. We were going to be safe together. We were going to get out of this mess. We had to. I could not lose these men. And right now, I needed to touch them. I needed to feel them in case this was the last time. I needed something positive.

Nate tugged at my hair until I pulled away from Ev and turned toward him. He smirked down at me before kissing me. His kiss became more heated as he gripped my hair at the base of my neck and held me to him. My breath hitched and I grabbed at the front of his shirt. Nate pulled back and smiled at me mischievously before lifting my shirt over my head. As soon as my shirt was off, I was being tugged back to Everett. His mouth was hot on my lips and he licked into my mouth. I turned fully to him, and he pulled me up onto his lap.

"Hey," Nate complained.

"You've had more time with her like this," Everett said, not even shooting Nate a glance as he looked up at me and stroked my hair away from my face.

Nate made a noise of disagreement as I leaned down and kissed Everett again. Everett stroked his hands over my torso, stopping to cup my breasts in my cotton bra. He groaned against my lips as he gently squeezed me. I ground down against him with a roll of my hips and his breath caught in his throat. I felt him harden beneath me and I suddenly felt very hot. Everett pulled away from the kiss, his hands coming to rest on the waistband and buttons of my jeans. His knuckles brushed warmly against the skin below my navel. He lifted one eyebrow in question, his expression smoldering and wanting. I nodded once before he flicked open my jeans and Nate reached over and yanked my jeans down over my ass, exposing my black panties that he also roughly pushed down. Everett lifted me by my hips and Nate pulled my panties and dirty jeans off my legs. I blushed at the awkward position in the car as Nate yanked my clothes off, but neither of them seemed to care. They placed me back down on Everett's lap, and I kissed him again.

Everett slid his hands over my ass and thighs with a groan. Nate chuckled next to me and kissed my shoulder. "Her ass is perfect, isn't it?"

Everett grunted his agreement, not moving his lips from my skin. Arousal covered my inner thighs just thinking about being with both of them. Everett's fingertips inched closer to where I needed him most, and my breathing quickened in anticipation.

"You should see what it looks like fucking her from behind," Nate said in his deep, sexy voice.

"I intend to find out. Not in the backseat of a stolen car," Everett said gruffly. "I want to lay you down in a bed and devour you." His fingers brushed over my wetness, and I let out a sound that was like a squeal but ended in a breathy moan. "But that's not to say I won't make you come right here."

"Hell yeah," Nate said and returned to kissing his way up my shoulder to my neck.

Everett's long fingers slid through my slick folds and he moaned.

"She gets so fucking wet," Nate said breathlessly.

Everett pushed two fingers into me and I gasped and arched my back. I reached the headrest of the driver's seat behind me and held on with both hands, while I wantonly rode Everett's fingers. The handcuffs still dangled from my left wrist and clanked as I moved. One or both of the guys swore. I couldn't tell who. But another hand snaked its way down to my clit and began rubbing in circles. I cried out and rode Everett's hand faster. He leaned forward and latched his mouth around a nipple that was poking through my cotton bra. He tapped out a quick rhythm against the soft spot within me for a few seconds before pulling in and out and doing it again. Sweat broke out against my skin and Nate leaned down to kiss my open and gasping mouth.

There were so many hands and mouths on me. I knew it was only four hands and two mouths, but the sensations felt like more. I tried not to come so fast, but when I looked down and saw them both touching and kissing me, it sent me over the edge. I screamed against Nate's mouth as the world around me completely disappeared and shock waves of pleasure spread through my body. They gently placed my body against Everett's chest as I panted. I was vaguely aware of the low vibration of Everett speaking below me and Nate chuckling behind me.

"I told you so, man," Nate was saying when my brain regained the ability to process information.

"It's unbelievable," Everett rumbled, stoking up my arms.

There was still work to be done, so I sat back on Everett's lap. I reached out to both guys' jeans and popped the buttons. I bit my lower lip as I thought about the logistics, but said nothing. Both guys' eyes snapped between where I was unbuttoning their pants and the other's pants. Everett audibly swallowed.

"Sit next to him," I whispered to Nate who obeyed. I got off Everett's lap and kneeled on the mostly clean carpet between them. I admired their eager expressions and straining erections in their jeans. "Pull down your pants."

They both lifted their hips, pulling down their boxers and jeans, neither one looking away from me on my knees before them. I smiled as they both settled back into their seats, cocks bobbing before me. I was in trouble. I stared at their lengths for a moment, admiring them. My mouth watered. Nate pumped his cock with his hand- not shy at all. Everett looked over at Nate and smirked smugly at me. Everett was longer than Nate, but even without touching them I knew Nate was thicker. I rolled my eyes playfully at Everett.

Nate realized what was happening and looked over at Everett's length. "What?!" he exclaimed. "How are you real?"

Everett gruffed out a laugh as I leaned forward. I gripped both of their lengths at the same time, one in each hand. It was an odd experience, holding two cocks like that, but arousal flooded to my thighs again. Everett tipped his head back against the seat, but kept his eyes on me. Nate's eyes darted between me and my hands on both cocks. I smirked and pumped them both simultaneously a few times. My handcuffs jingled as I moved, and they knocked against Nate's thigh. Nate and Ev's breathing was heavy, and they both moaned as I squeezed at the bases of their cocks. I clenched my thighs together, admiring my men and feeling powerful.

Even though they each had a leg pressed against me and I had my hands around them, I felt too far away. I licked my lips and looked up at Everett. He noted my tongue and gave a sharp intake of breath and nodded. I smiled and leaned over to take him into my mouth. He moaned hoarsely and rested a hand softly at the back of my head like he wanted to push me down on him, but was holding back. The dry corners of my mouth caught against his skin, and I pulled back to spit on him before returning. Nate's cock twitched in my hand as he cursed. I stroked him in time with my head bobbing on Everett.

Everett's skin was soft under my tongue as I swirled around his tip. He hissed and gripped my hair almost painfully.

"Do that thing with your tongue," Nate commanded.

I raised an eyebrow in question, my mouth still around Ev.

"You know, like-" Nate said and stuck his tongue out and undulated it like a wave. "It's so good. He's going to love it."

I turned my eyes back to Everett, who had watched Nate wiggle his tongue about, and then looked back down at me. "Show me what you got, baby girl."

I smiled with my eyes, then sank back down as far as I could on Everett, gave a swallow, and then made my tongue a wave against the underside of Everett's cock. He jerked in his seat below me and I heard him smack Nate in the chest while he grabbed the back of my neck with the other. He let out a shuddering moan as his hips rolled.

I pulled off him without warning and turned to Nate. I had been pumping my hand on Nate and was ready to get my mouth on him, too. Nate sat up and pulled me in for a kiss, likely tasting Everett on my tongue. I pressed my thighs together even tighter at the thought. Everett's hand had still been clenched in Nate's shirt, and he quickly pulled it away to grab my right hand and place it on his cock. I had accidentally forgotten to keep touching him. Handling two cocks at once was apparently an art form that required practice.

Nate broke the kiss off and shoved my head down towards his lap. "Suck my fucking cock like you sucked his," he demanded. I opened my mouth to take him in, but Nate stopped me by shoving this thumb into my mouth and hooking it against my cheek and wrenching me to the side. "Say it," he growled.

"I'm going to suck your cock as well as I sucked his," I said in almost a whisper around his thumb, and looked up at him from under my lashes.

Nate grinned darkly and removed his thumb, stroked his hand over my hair, and sat back. I spit over his dick, getting it wet before I lowered my mouth over him, taking him in as far as I could before pulling back up. While Everett was longer and hit the back of my throat quicker, Nate was thicker, and my jaw clicked as I worked him up and down. I did the same tongue movement on Nate and he cried out and pushed my head down on him and thrusted up into my mouth. I gagged and my eyes streamed with tears, but I did the tongue movement as much as I could without gagging repeatedly.

Everett gripped my hand on his cock and helped me move at a quicker pace.

"Good girl, my fucking good girl," Nate moaned out as he stroked my hair with one hand and gripped the back of my head with the other. I rubbed my clenched thighs together to get even the tiniest bit of friction.

At the telltale signs of Nate about to come, Ev forcefully batted away Nate's hands from my head and grabbed me with both hands around my jaw and neck like my head was a basketball. He was up in a kneeling position, one knee on the car seat and one foot on the floor, and he brought me up to his waiting cock. I swallowed him down as he pumped into my mouth a few times before coming with a shout. He almost fell over with the force of his orgasm, and Nate shot out a hand to hold him up at his chest. Streams of come shot down my throat and I swallowed repeatedly. When Everett pulled out of my mouth, I moved my mouth back down to Nate. I slowly let some of Everett's come drip out of my mouth out onto Nate's dick. Slow and deliberate enough that Nate and Everett both saw exactly what I was doing. Their eyes both flared and Everett sat back down, panting, to watch.

I took Nate into my mouth as far as I could go, relaxing my muscles as much as I could. Nate took over and thrust up into my mouth, making my eyes stream again, but he grunted repeatedly as he thrust, and his balls drew up before he came with a long, deep groan. I swallowed down his come and sat back with a smile at both of them.

Nate only rested for a moment before hauling me up onto the seat and laying me out on my back over his lap. He wrenched my legs apart, so my pussy was facing Everett. "Taste her," Nate demanded, still breathless. Everett launched himself off of the seat and to the cramped floor in a crouch, just enough to get to my pussy. He buried his face between my thighs with no teasing and licked a hot, wet circle from my opening to my clit and back down. I cried out and bucked against his face. Nate held me down against him. "That's right, fucking lap her up," Nate said to Everett in that deep sexy voice he gets. "Fucking drink her."

Everett followed directions like a straight-A student and had me gasping and arching against Nate's hold in seconds. Everett returned his fingers to my pussy and quickly found a rhythm that had me sweating and swearing unintelligibly. I had never come this hard or long. These men had me so unbelievably turned on I couldn't think past this car and their bodies. I could hear the start of my release dripping onto the car's floor. Nate bent to kiss my panting and moaning mouth, his tongue probing and aggressive. I grabbed his neck and used it as my anchor as the tidal wave of an orgasm started. "Yeah, beautiful. Come on his face. Look down and watch as he eats your pussy."

I did as Nate commanded and saw Everett between my thighs, eyes looking up at me and Nate. He winked at me before taking my clit into his mouth and sucking while undulating his tongue not unlike my signature blow job move. It was the ultimate breaking point that sent me completely over the edge. My mind went totally blank, and my eyes closed as sensation took over.

When I came back to my senses, Everett was lazily kissing the inside of my thighs and Nate was stroking my hair. "Wow," I said hoarsely.

"Yeah, wow is right," Everett chuckled and slid into the seat, pulling his jeans and boxer briefs back up. I sat up and kissed him. He was likely tasting himself and Nate on my tongue while I tasted myself. "You're so beautiful, baby girl. Are you alright?"

"Um, yeah. Very alright. Why?" I asked, looking down at my mostly naked body to check.

"After care," Nate said casually. "You just sucked off two guys for the first time. He's checking in to make sure you're not freaking."

"Oh, uh, honestly, freaking like a little bit. But not in a bad way," I added in a hurry when I noticed the worried expressions creep onto their faces. "I was thinking taking two cocks was an art form I needed to practice."

"Holy shit," Nate groaned and leaned his head back against the car seat. "That's so fucking hot."

Everett chucked, gave me a quick peck, and helped me get back into my panties and jeans. Nate pulled his pants back up and said, "I need a nap now. Ev, drive us to Indianapolis."

"Yes, sir," Everett said with a tinge of sarcasm as he opened the car door to get back into the front seat.

"Stop, I'm getting hard again," Nate joked with a whine.

I wasn't tired, so I moved up to the front seat to sit with Everett while he drove and Nate napped in the back. We listened to music quietly and sipped our coffee, giving each other smiles and grins whenever we thought back to what we did in the back seat, but mostly not talking other than quiet driving directions. The sun rose behind us as we drove, and Everett reached for my hand and pressed a kiss to the back of it while the surrounding light was golden and promising.

17

We stopped in an Indianapolis suburb at another gas station. I stayed in the car, having peed on the side of the highway an hour ago, and to avoid having all three of us seen. Our car had Ohio plates, making us a target as it was. There was no need to draw further attention with three people. I stayed reclined in the passenger seat and waited.

I felt bad that I didn't drive. I wished I could have contributed to the journey more than watching for cops and nosey drivers. The guys never complained about my lack of driving, but I felt their thoughts about it every time they yawned.

A few minutes after we stopped, Nate came back with gas station coffee and water for us, having paid for gas with cash and used the restroom. Everett finished pumping the gas and then used the pay phone to call Easton. He got back in the car and was visibly grossed out. "That phone-" he stopped to stifle a gag. "I need hand sanitizer or something."

Nate laughed as he and I rummaged through the stolen car. I found a takeout wet nap still in its little foil square. Everett quickly ripped it open and rubbed it over his ear and hands.

"Okay, so we need to take I-65 to get to Lexington. We're going to skip around Louisville and go to Lexington proper. Easton says it'll be about another 4 hours," Everett said after he was sufficiently clean.

Nate passed back a coffee to Everett, who thanked him. It was seven thirty in the morning, and people started to fill the roads. A car pulled up next to us at another pump. We didn't stick around and left as soon as we were done. The sunlight streaming through the clouds renewed our hope of getting to Easton and to safety.

It was near eight when a news report came on the radio and halted our conversation about the fantasy Xbox game Nate had been playing for weeks. "Breaking News coming out of Cleveland, Ohio, this morning. After last night's attacks on Truman College, the families of the perpetrators are cooperating with police and investigators to find college students Evangeline Reid, Nathaniel Gibson, and Everett Monroe. It is believed they would have headed North to Canada to flee local authorities. More as it comes on News Channel 5."

"That doesn't make any sense. Why would we flee to Canada? They would send us right back. Don't people run to Mexico to hide?" Nate asked.

"The weather is nicer in Mexico. They extradite American criminals the same as Canada, though. There are also more places to hide in Mexico. And we could pass as tourists easier in their cities," Everett mumbled. "So, people go there more often to hide."

"Huh," Nate considered. "I do love me some tacos."

"Let's get to Easton before we plan our next move, please," Everett said, clearly not in a mood to joke around.

"They're talking to our parents," I said quietly, thinking of my dad in an interrogation room.

"Of course, they are. They're going to get nothing. Other than my dad telling them we went to Canada," Nate shrugged.

"Why do you think it was your dad that gave them that idea?" I asked.

"My family went to Canada a lot for vacations. We often tried to guess how many American criminals were in line at the border to get over and what their crimes were," Nate explained. "It was how we passed the time if the lines were long as a kid. He would think that would be my first thought."

"What *was* your first thought?" I asked him. We had let Everett take charge, so I wondered what Nate had been thinking.

"Mostly screaming internally," Nate replied with a shy grin.

"Thank god one of us has a brain," Everett smirked.

We made it to Lexington around noon, and there was enough hustle and bustle that nobody spared us a glance. Nate stayed reclined in the car while Everett and I went inside the gas station. I used the restroom and paid the attendant for gas while Everett used the restroom and grabbed some food for lunch. Someone was in the men's room, so he was a few minutes behind me to get to the car.

"So, Everett will call Easton, and I think he'll give us the last leg of instructions," Nate said through the open window while I pumped the gas. He was lying across the back seat, so someone did not easily see him.

I nodded and looked around quickly to make sure no eyes lingered on me. "Yeah, I can't wait for a full night's rest. I'll be able to think so much better about all of this once I sleep," I said, and yawned.

A car pulled into the gas station, and I looked up. It was a cop car. My heart sank to my stomach, and I looked at Nate. He was watching me with fear in his eyes. "What?"

"A cop just pulled in," I breathed as I watched the car pull around to the other side of the station to where the parking spots were. "He might be just getting a coffee; he's going to park."

"Is Ev at the phone?" Nate asked, trying to look around without being visible.

I shook my head. I looked into the store through the glass windows and didn't see his head over the top of the shelves, and he wasn't at the counter.

"Fuck," Nate said. "We wait another minute while the pump finishes and then you drive us out of here."

"I can't drive, remember? And I'm not leaving him," I said, my voice shaking.

"If he saw the cop, he's probably hiding in the bathroom or down an aisle. We will have to get out of here, Eva. I can't let you get arrested," Nate said and sat up, getting out of the car.

He got into the driver's seat, looking around as discreetly as he could. Nobody was paying us any attention, and the cop was still sitting in his car. The pump clicked off, and Nate mumbled, "Get in the passenger seat. Quick, but don't run."

I followed his direction on shaky knees, sinking into the beige material. "We can't," I said to Nate desperately.

Nate swallowed and started the engine, both of us looking at the gas station to hopefully find Everett. The cop got out of his car and looked around, his eyes settling on us for a second before moving on. I hoped my fear wasn't showing in my eyes, but it seemed he didn't notice as he went into the station. Where Everett was.

"Fucking fuck. Fucking hell. God damn it," Nate swore incoherently as he slowly maneuvered us away from the gas pump and out of the gas station. Tears streamed down my face as I looked back at the gas station and still didn't see Ev.

Nate drove us down the street to a busy Starbucks parking lot and we waited ten silent, tense minutes before heading back to the gas station. I felt sick to my stomach with nerves. Tears welled in my eyes as Nate drove us back down the street. I had heard no sirens or seen any more police come through, so I hoped that was a good sign. We neared the gas station, and it looked like the cop was gone. I didn't see Everett outside the gas station as I sat up straight in the car and peered out the windows.

"There he is!" Nate shouted so suddenly it made me jump. Nate pulled into the grocery store parking lot next to the gas station and whipped around to where there was a covered bus stop. Everett was standing against the bus stop pavilion, a plastic bag at his feet, and smoking a cigarette. He was alone at the bus stop and his shoulders relaxed as we stopped outside the bus stop. He threw the cigarette and got into the back seat. I spun around in my seat and leaned over the center console to reach Everett in the backseat. He reached for me, and we held each other while Nate drove away from the busy roads and stores.

18

I held Everett tightly and cried into his neck while he stroked my hair and kissed the side of my face over and over. The car stopped suddenly and Nate got out of the car. I looked up to see that we were in a park we passed when we drove into town. Nate had pulled us over into the grass near where the bike path had started. Nobody was around. It was still a cold December weekday. Everett and I pulled away from each other when Nate got out of the car and we watched him come around to the passenger side. Everett got out of the car, and the serious expressions on both of their faces made me think they were about to fight.

My heart was in my throat as I watched them approach each other, stormy expressions in both of their eyes. I got out of the car quickly, thinking I was going to have to break up a fight. But instead of fighting, Nate launched towards Everett and hugged him tightly around his shoulders. Everett wrapped his arms around Nate's torso, and they turned their noses towards each other's neck. Nate mumbled in Everett's neck. Everett said something back and clutched Nate tightly. This wasn't a back thumping, turn your pelvis to the side, bro hug. This was an embrace.

Nate pulled back, his hands still on Ev's shoulders. "I'm so sorry for leaving you. You have no idea, man. I had to get Eva out of there, though. Fuck, that was the hardest decision I've ever made," Nate said with a sniff.

"I'm not mad at you," Ev insisted. "I'm proud of you for getting her out of there. Nate, I'm not mad at you."

Nate shook his head and sniffed again. He let out a loud exhale and hugged Everett again, then gestured for me to join them. We stood there clutching each other tightly as we caught our breaths and relaxed our anxiety. They were both at least a foot taller than me, so I had to reach up to tell them to bend down to kiss me. They both kissed me gently before I caught them both sharing a long look. I thought maybe they were about to kiss for a moment before they pulled away and we walked back to the car.

Everett got into the driver's seat since it was his turn to drive, and he knew the next set of directions. "Easton has us meeting him in a parking lot of a grocery store in Pigeon Forge, Tennessee," Everett said as he adjusted the mirror and drove us out of the park.

"Finally," I said with a relieved sigh.

"Almost there, baby girl," he said, and patted my thigh in the passenger seat. He glanced at Nate in the rearview mirror, but I didn't turn around to see Nate's expression, allowing them to have that moment to themselves. I wondered if they were growing to have feelings for each other. The idea of them together made me clench my thighs together in my seat, but their relationship wasn't about me. Running from the law seemed to have a bonding effect on us, and I wouldn't put it past my guys to have expanded their feelings for each other. I, for one, was having to take a moment to evaluate the way I was feeling about these men.

"Easton is meeting us at 6:30, so we'll need to be careful. He wants us to get off every few exits to lose our lane neighbors and to look like normal traffic," Everett explained in his calm voice. "We're going to make it; we have to be watchful and move with caution like we did earlier. We're not being seen together and we're paying in cash everywhere. Though, I am running low. I don't have enough for gas *and* dinner."

"I'm not hungry, anyway. I only want to sleep somewhere safe," I said.

"Me neither," Nate agreed from the back. Everett raised an eyebrow in the mirror and Nate *tsked* back at him.

The radio was playing quietly as we drove for the next few hours, Nate and I occasionally dozing in our seats, and Everett occasionally humming to the music. It was nearing five and traffic was becoming more congested, so Nate laid down across the back seat. I reclined in the passenger seat and sunk down, and Everett put on a pair of reflective sunglasses he picked up at a gas station. Everett's hand shot out and turned up the volume on a news report. My stomach dropped hearing the familiar cadence of a news reporter's voice.

"Breaking news update: Cleveland Police have encouraged a 'nationwide manhunt' for three suspected terrorists on the run from Truman College. Evangeline Reid, Everett Monroe, and Nathaniel Gibson are suspected of creating a bioweapon in their school lab before setting it ablaze. Another student has come forth and shed some light on their potential motives," the report switched to an audio clip of a young man speaking. "Yeah, I was in their group in class, and they were *always* talking about how they hated this country and wanted to wipe everyone out. Like Evangeline was one time talking about how she wanted to kill every other woman in the country, so she would be the only one left and all men would love her. It was weird because she never talks." The news report switched back to the news anchor. "Sources have revealed Evangeline was present when her mother died as a young teen. Sources have also said Everett Monroe has a brother who was dishonorably discharged from the army some years ago. Could a disdain for our country be the motive for their attacks? To prepare, all national monuments have closed early for the weekend and any potential attacks. Follow our Twitter account for live updates at-"

"'A disdain for our country?!' Most of my family has served our country in the armed forces!" Everett shouted. I shushed him and placed a hand on his leg to calm him. "Where are they even getting these students to give statements? I never once interacted with any students outside of you two."

"Neither did we, Ev. Anyone who knows you, knows about your family's service and your plans to make America's food safer," Nate soothed him.

"Are they trying to say that I killed my mom and hate all women?" My lip trembled, but I bit it to hold myself together. A sob escaped before I could swallow it down.

"I think it's a way for whoever is after us to tell us they know we're both sleeping with you, Eva," Nate suggested, squeezing my shoulder. "It's their way of saying they saw us at the lab when you and I were in the locker room and when you and Ev kissed out front."

"How was that only yesterday?" I sighed, realizing he was right. Whoever had planted that camera in our house, of course, must have had them throughout the lab. It only made sense to have them in both places.

"A surreal twenty-four hours, that's for sure," Everett agreed, and tightened his grip on my hand.

"Someone is paying people to come out and say very specific things, I think," Nate continued the conversation. "Whether they're taking part in the investigation or just giving statements to the media to piss us off- they're not real."

I nodded again as Everett got back on the highway for our last stretch of driving. We got off the highway at Pigeon Forge and looked around for the specific grocery store Easton had directed us to. It was in a strip mall with stores of varying hours of operation and a large parking lot. Neither of us spoke other than directions for the last part of the ride, with Nate and I peeking out the windows.

Everett spotted his brother and quickly maneuvered the car to park next to him in a parking spot closest to the street. Easton rolled down his window, and Everett did the same. “Hey there, little brother!” Easton called. I peered up to see him. He looked a lot like Easton. Dark blonde hair, red beard, and bright blue eyes. His smile crinkled his eyes in a way that Everett’s didn’t yet and spoke of heartache. He got out of the car and Everett met him behind the cars in a back slapping hug.

“Evangeline and Nathaniel, can you two hop in the truck? Go quickly,” Easton directed us.

“It’s Eva and Nate,” Everett corrected his brother as he climbed into the truck’s passenger seat.

Nate and I both left our stolen car and got into the small back-seat of Easton’s truck. It was almost identical to Everett’s, though appeared to be a model or two older and much dirtier. Easton quickly used a screwdriver he had in his pocket to take the license plate off of the stolen car. He placed a “For Sale” sign in the window and shut the door. The number to call on the sign was almost illegible. He got into the truck and pulled away from the curb. I settled back into the seat and Nate took my hand, rubbing it in circles.

“Nobody is going to notice how long that car’s been there until well after Christmas. And when they call about it, they get the front desk of one of the area’s tourist attractions. It certainly buys us extra time,” Easton said to the three of us. “Man, little brother. How long has it been? Four years since I saw you?”

“Something like that,” Everett said quietly.

“You sure have grown,” Easton said affectionately.

“Yes, he’s not so little anymore,” Nate said dismissively. “Can you tell us where we’re going?”

"To my home," Easton said, looking back at Nate and me in the rearview mirror. He was studying us and trying to get a read. "In the mountains."

"Why do you think it's safe there?" Nate asked further. "What's your security?"

"I live where there are no roads, there are no stores, there are no other people. I am what you would call Off the Grid," Easton explained easily. "I'm as good'n'gone as you can get good'n'gone in America. There are a few other vets living in the woods, and we watch out for each other and trade. We are self-contained in our area."

"How'd you follow our case, then?" Everett asked.

"I have a battery powered radio and a few police scanners," Easton explained. "I can show it all to you when we get there."

I leaned against Nate in the seat and let his arms close around me. This felt closer to safety than I had felt in a long time. I closed my eyes as Everett told his brother the story of how we got to this point. Hearing our story reacted to by Easton was validating and helped put a few things to light.

"And you thought blowing the place up was a good idea?" Easton asked Everett like he was an idiot.

Nate snorted next to me, where he was leaning back against the door and window with his eyes closed. We smiled, listening to Easton rip into Everett for being 'a dramatic dumbass.' Everett looked back at us hesitantly, seemingly worried that we'd also be disappointed in him. He found us laughing at him being scolded and crossed his arms over his chest with his jaw clenched.

"Hey, don't be so smug back there," Easton called to me and Nate. "You two are dumbasses, too, for believing the horse shit Hoffmann threw at you. I mean, *come on*! Nothing is free! You all thought you were *so special* to get all this free shit if you did one little experiment? Dumb."

I felt thoroughly scolded and looked down at my hands.

"We each had our reasons to believe it," Nate countered irritably. "It's not like we had anyone to run the contracts by before we signed them."

"True," Easton agreed. "But when anyone offers you that much free shit, you *have* to question it."

"If the product is free, then it's the bait and you are the actual product," I said, after taking a few steadying breaths.

"Correct," Easton murmured.

Everett and Easton chatted quietly, and I fell asleep leaning against Nate, listening to his steady whoosh of breath and the thump of his heart. It wasn't a deep sleep, and I was still partially aware of the sound of the truck rumbling along the road and the guys' voices up front. When the truck bounced off the road, I awoke with a start. We were driving into a small cutout of the forest, and Everett was outside the car, moving brush and branches back over the path behind us. He came and hopped back into the truck after Easton stopped for him.

"Unbuckle your seatbelts and roll down your windows," Easton instructed. "We're about to go over a river in a minute."

Easton drove us through some trees I assumed to be marked in a way that Easton could decipher where to go. It was dark and the clock on the dash said it was near nine thirty, so we'd driven for at least an hour and a half from our meeting space. I wasn't sure if we'd driven in circles or gone straight there, so I had even less of an idea where in the mountains we were. It was a few minutes before we reached the wide, shallow river. Ice had clogged up a few of the shallow areas of the river and rocks jutted out of other areas.

"Hold on," Easton mumbled before driving the truck over the river, navigating left and right to avoid ice and large rocks. I held my breath as he drove, thinking for sure we were going to tip over. At one point, freezing water splashed over the hood of the truck, but Easton maneuvered us over the river with skill.

I let out a breath once we were solidly on the other side of the river and driving through a path that Easton knew, but I could not see. No visible tracks were before us in the dark. Our windows were still down, and the only sounds were the truck's engine, tires cracking over branches, and water dripping from the truck. The night was almost silent other than the sounds of the truck. We drove for a few more minutes through a path I still could not see before the trees opened to about an acre of space. Everett pulled up closer and shut off the engine. A small, rustic cabin sat in the center of it all, an RV off to the side, a sizeable chicken coop near the cabin, and a few patches of dirt, large enough to be gardens. A few rows seemed to have things overwintering in freshly tilled soil. The air was crisp and cold and smelled of pine trees and soil. I inhaled deeply before we rolled up the windows. We were finally well and truly hidden away and my stomach relaxed the hard clench it had taken up since Cleveland.

19

Home sweet home," Easton said as he climbed out of the truck. The three of us followed, stretching out our arms and legs. We looked around, taking in our surroundings. "You three are welcome to stay in the RV. Don't ask how I got it up here. I'll put on some supper for you to have before you go to bed. And Eva, I'll get those cuffs off of you. Come on in."

Easton's cabin was mostly one room with a small bathroom off to the side. He had a few mismatched chairs he told the guys to get around the table while he lit a gas lamp, then stoked a wood stove to a roaring fire. Easton had a small twin bed against the far wall of the cabin, but in direct view of the wood stove, a small dining table with four mismatched chairs, a kitchenette that comprised a steel basin working as a sink, and a few cabinets. Easton pulled out a small toolbox and rummaged through it on the table for a moment before he pulled out a handcuff key. He held out his hand for my wrist and I placed my hand over his.

Up close, I saw how similar he and Everett were in appearance. Everett's callused hands had softened some during the months we worked in the lab, but Easton's were still rough against my skin. He was gentle as he unlocked the cuff and an instant relief swept through me.

"You'll want to bandage that after dinner. It looks raw," Easton advised. He was right, the handcuff on this wrist had been so tight that my skin had rubbed raw underneath. Bright red skin circled my wrist and the air of the cabin bit at it.

"Thank you," I whispered before joining my guys.

Easton opened a jar of beef stew and added it and some carrots he had in a basket on the table to a cast-iron pot he placed on a grate in the wood stove. I watched Everett eying Easton's cooking and smiled, remembering his books on primitive cooking. I had borrowed one and read some of it, so I knew this was right up Everett's alley.

Once Easton finished preparing the stew, he ladled it out for us and grabbed a loaf of crusty bread out of the cabinet. I heard both my guys' stomachs rumbling as Easton tore chunks off for each of us. He popped the cork off a home brew bottle and poured each of us a glass of a dark beer. We tucked in eagerly and barely spoke as we ate. We had eaten little more than granola and coffee in twenty-four stressful and exhausting hours. Easton watched us devour the salty and savory meal before speaking.

"I know you're tired, but I need to know some more information about who you think set up the assignment before you go to sleep," Easton said as we finished eating.

I sipped at the smooth, bitter beer and waited for one of the guys to talk.

"Well, we have a few ideas. It's either the college, the government, or a pharmaceutical company," Nate recalled.

"I'm almost a hundred percent sure it is not the government. They are not this sloppy with their work. And I have heard nothing about it," Easton said.

"I thought you weren't in the Army anymore," Everett said.

Easton only smiled at his brother. "Let's just say that I still have contacts. And none of my contacts have made anything known.

And they would have if this was the government and involving my baby brother."

"So, who do you think it is?" Nate asked.

"We're looking at a private group with their own interests. I have more people I need to talk to, but I'll keep digging. I've already got a few people following some trails," Easton said, and sipped his beer.

"How do you know you can trust them?" Everett asked his brother, his concern etched into his brow.

"We all have worked together for a very long time, little brother. We look out for each other. Many of them live here in these mountains with me. I trade with them almost every week," Easton explained.

"Are they Army, too?" Everett asked.

Easton only smiled that same secretive smile. "We're connected."

Everett sat back in his seat with a sigh and looked at his brother for a long time. "You know you had Mom and Dad thinking you'd run off and were living in the woods like a squirrel or something."

Easton shook his head. "No, I'm living *with* the squirrels, not *like* a squirrel."

"Why?" Everett asked. His one word question held years of family heartache and my chest constricted.

"To protect you."

"From what?"

"What I know. What I've seen."

"That's bullshit."

"I'm sorry," Easton said, and leaned toward Everett in his sincerity.

"You broke Mom's heart," Everett added. I leaned over and placed my hand on Everett's forearm to break his stare down with his brother.

"I know," Easton said quietly.

Everett shook his head and looked at me and Nate like he was coming out of a trance. "Where do we sleep again?"

"The RV. There's only electricity if you start the engine, and very little water in the tank. Sorry, I didn't exactly prepare for guests. But there's probably enough for one shower tonight if you're quick. Start the engine and warm the place and get washed up, but turn the engine back off. Don't keep it on long," Easton said and stood and gathered some clothes for us and a battery-powered lantern.

He walked us to the RV and opened it up for us. Everett hugged his brother and mumbled his thanks before heading into the RV and starting it up. Easton looked at me as I approached him. "Thank you for your kindness and your help," I said and reached up to hug Easton, who stiffly hugged me back. I assumed it had been a while since anyone had hugged him. Nate shook his hand and thanked him before following me into the RV.

We looked around while the engine rumbled. I could hear the heating whirring around us, and I shrugged off my coat and left it on the seat of the small dinette. The guys followed suit. A small dinette was nestled next to a kitchenette that had a mini-fridge and a microwave and sink. A small bathroom with a toilet, sink, and shower stall was across from a closet, and a bedroom was along the back. There was only a bed and a small closet in the room and Everett set down the clean clothes and lantern there.

"Marie Curie 2.0," Nate said with a grin.

"Marie Curie's bigger, older sister," Everett half heartedly chuckled.

"Last one to the shower is a rotten egg," Nate said and started stripping his clothes off.

I giggled and started stripping as well. I heard Everett rustling behind me as Nate and I sprinted around the corner into the little bathroom, where Nate turned on the water. The water smelled metallic, but it was clear as Nate and I wedged ourselves into the tiny shower stall. It was barely big enough for one person to shower, so there was no way the three of us would fit. The water was ice cold for a few seconds, and I squealed at the temperature. Nate laughed and shuddered before the water warmed, and Everett squeezed in behind me. They pressed me between their wet naked bodies, and I shivered again, though I was no longer cold. The laughing stopped abruptly when we realized we were naked and smashed together. Nate reached down awkwardly to grab the generic shampoo bottle that was on the edge of the shower. He couldn't bend down fully because of how tightly we were packed in the stall. He opened the bottle and squirted it directly onto my wet head. I tipped my head back and closed my eyes when he started massaging it into my hair. The shampoo smelled heavily perfumed and like the standard "ocean" scent, but it would be effective to clean the dirt from our hair.

"Nate, hand me that bar of soap," Everett murmured, and Nate stopped washing my hair for a second to grab the soap.

Everett lathered up his hands with the old bar of soap and ran his hands over my body gently and with purpose. It also was an overly perfumed soap, but smelled clean. I moaned at their ministrations and Nate leaned down to kiss me. I was as tall as their nipples, so the water didn't rain down on me as much. His wet hair slid down and curtained around us in curled sections. Everett ran his soapy hands down over the front of my stomach and over my hips, reaching for my core. I inched my legs apart, my ankles touching the sides of the shower stall as he caressed me between my legs. I sighed and held on to Nate's hips for support. Everett caressed me slowly, his fingers slipping past my entrance and back out, teasing me.

Nate leaned to the side in a slight crouch to allow my hair to be rinsed with the shower. I opened my eyes when he finished and picked up the shampoo to wash his long hair. He tilted his head down while I massaged his scalp with a slight scratch of my nails. He sighed in pleasure and tilted his head back to rinse out the suds.

Behind me, Everett was hard against the small of my back and was still caressing my pussy, teasing me. I trembled at the intensity of the sensations.

"Want to wash your hair, Ev?" Nate asked.

"My hands are a bit busy right now," Ev said, his voice husky.

"Wait, are you fingering her right now?" Nate asked, shocked.

I moaned out my answer.

"Oh, I thought you just really liked showers," Nate chuckled. He opened the shampoo and poured some in his hand. "I guess I'll have to help then."

Nate massaged shampoo into Everett's shorter hair and my pussy spasmed around Everett's fingers. Everett leaned his head into the shower and rinsed out the shampoo, and handed Nate the bar of soap with his free hand.

"I'm not washing your ass for you," Nate insisted.

"You would if I asked. But no, it's for you. I'm done with it," Everett countered.

Nate ran the soap over his skin, and I watched him intently. My mouth watered at the sight of bubbles sliding down him and tangling in his chest hair before sliding down his stomach to his hard cock. I melted back against Everett's chest as my pleasure crested and I came around his fingers. My knees turned to jelly as I sagged in his hold. I remembered Everett's promise to lay me down on the bed and devour me and I knew I wasn't finished for the night despite the exhaustion deep in my bones.

"Ev," I gasped. "The bed, please."

"Of course, baby girl," Everett said, and lifted me out of the shower as Nate turned off the spray.

"Get her dry and in the bed," Nate commanded.

Everett found towels in the little hall closet and wrapped one around me, handed one to Nate, and then dried himself off quickly. Nate ran to turn the engine off while Ev rubbed the towel over my skin and picked me up and carried me the few steps to the bedroom. He dropped me on the bed as Nate turned on the lantern. The light was dim, but I could clearly see both Everett and Nate's erections beneath their towels and their hungry expressions. Nate took my discarded towel and dried his hair with it. I watched his chest and arms flex as he did it, and caught Everett looking as well.

"Further back on the bed," Everett told me, and I backed into the center of the bed, which I figured to be a full-size mattress. I watched Everett crawl towards me with his signature smirk before his lips crashed down on mine. I gripped him at his jaw with both hands as I deepened the kiss. After our time in the shower, I was well and truly ready for him.

I looked over to where Nate was settling against the wall, his cock in his hand. There were windows on three of the walls in this room, allowing in streams of moonlight that slipped through the trees. The moonlight shone across his eyes and over to the expanse of smooth skin on Everett's back. I watched his muscles shift and bunch as he kissed down my body to my pussy.

"I'm ready, Ev, please," I begged.

Everett and Nate both chuckled. But the aching emptiness I felt was not funny and I pouted. Ev licked a circle around my clit slowly, teasingly. He looked over at Nate. "You want a taste?"

"I'm watching you have her this time. It's your turn," Nate said and spit into his hand before slowly stroking his cock.

"Okay, so have me," I said and rolled my hips.

"So impatient," Everett taunted, and then sucked my clit into his mouth.

I let out a small shriek and my head fell back, my wet hair slapping against the plain white blanket on the bed beneath me. Everett worked me up to another leg shaking orgasm with his mouth and fingers, and my eyes caught Nate's as I came with a long moan. He was pumping his cock in his fist at a steady rhythm, looking at me, down to where Everett's mouth was on me, and then lower to where Everett was also stroking his length. Nate's attention to Everett kept my arousal high as my orgasm subsided.

"Please- pl- please, Ev," I shuddered and whined as he kissed the inside of my thigh.

"Please what?" Ev asked teasingly, his eyes dark and mischievous as he looked up at me.

"I-I need you inside me," I said, still trembling and breathless.

"The sweetest fucking sound I've ever heard," Nate groaned.

Everett chuckled his agreement and got up to a kneeling position in front of me. He held his length at the base, and I understood the silent demand. I sat forward and took him deep into my mouth. I hummed in pleasure as he pumped in and out of my mouth, gliding against my tongue. Remembering the way he had reacted to my tongue move in the car, I did it again to much the same effect. Everett cried out, and his thighs trembled at the effort of remaining upright.

I pulled back; I would not allow him to come in my mouth when I still needed him elsewhere. "Now?" I pleaded, looking up at him with my best puppy eyes.

"On your back, baby girl. Nate, hand me that pillow," Everett said, his voice calm and quiet but commanding.

Nate quickly handed him the pillow that was then shoved roughly under my ass and hips. Everett lifted my legs and hooked them over his shoulder before quickly burying himself inside me. I cried out at the sudden, but welcome, intrusion. Everett didn't move once he was fully seated inside me. His eyes rolled back, and he gripped my thighs tighter. I clenched him with the muscles inside me a few times, and he groaned and looked down at me. "You play dirty, baby girl."

I smiled up at him and did it again.

He raised one eyebrow in challenge and moved his hips in a slow roll. I was staring at his abs as they clenched and relaxed with his movement. It was mesmerizing, and one of the hottest things I'd ever seen. He continued the up and down roll of his hips, but started doing it with a bit more force. He was repeatedly sliding against the soft spot within me that caused me to break out in a sweat and my moans turn high pitched.

Nate was jerking himself much quicker in my peripheral. I wanted to turn to watch, but I couldn't control my body at the moment. "Fuck man, she's going to come so hard." I heard Nate say breathlessly.

"That's the point," Everett huffed from above me.

Nate grunted out his release, and I watched Everett watch him. My pussy clenched and flooded again, and Everett looked back down at me with a slightly sheepish expression. Everett kept up the hard roll and then wrapped his arms around my trembling thighs and placed one hand flat against my lower stomach and applied pressure while the other hand gently pinched my folds together below my clit and moved it in a motion as if he were jerking me off in time with his thrusts. My third orgasm of the night rolled through me so ferociously that Nate covered my mouth and laughed as he shushed me. I wasn't even aware I had been screaming. My body felt like tv static after the roar of pleasure ripped through me. My release puddled below us as Ev's pumping pulled it out of me. Ev was gripping my thighs tightly and thrusting into me hard enough I slipped off the pillow more and more with each pound into me. Sweat was beaded on his forehead, and I watched a drop of sweat move between his pecs. He bent to kiss me, folding me almost in half as he gave a few quick, deep thrusts and came with a shout of his own. Nate covered his mouth, too.

"You're going to have to teach me that move," Nate said as Everett rolled off me and kissed my forehead.

"Which one?" Ev asked between panting breaths.

"The one where you held her pussy like a taco," Nate clarified.

Everett laughed, and I groaned in embarrassment. "You literally grab it like a little hamburger and jack it off." Everett lifted a hand in the air and mimicked the way he had held me.

"Aw, a little slider," Nate crooned.

I groaned again and covered my face with my hands. The guys chuckled, and Nate handed us towels to get cleaned up.

We crawled into the bed as the temperature dipped, since they shut the engine off. The bed was small and probably would fit two people semi comfortably. I was wedged between two large men again, all of us wearing clean boxers Easton had given us and nothing else, hoping our body heat would keep us warm enough through the night. Everett had found us another fleece blanket to throw over the bed before we settled into our cocoon of blankets and body heat. We shuffled around, murmuring to each other, trying to get comfortable in the small bed before we found a suitable arrangement. The feeling of their skin against mine was intoxicating. The linens of the bed had a slight dusty scent from not being used recently and the soaps from the shower still scented our skin and hair. I fell asleep quickly with my head on Everett's chest and Nate spooning me, their breathing creating a calming rhythm.

20

I woke the next morning feeling too warm next to the human furnace named Nate. The sun was bright and shone in the windows that almost surrounded the bed at the back of the RV. A few birds chirped outside, and I inhaled deeply, enjoying the peaceful surroundings and the masculine smell of slightly sweaty men. Nate kissed my bare shoulder from behind me. "Good morning, beautiful."

"Good morning, handsome," I replied. He reached over and found his glasses on the window ledge and put them on.

"Ohh, handsome?" Nate asked, running his nose lightly along my skin from my shoulder to my neck. "I thought Ev was the handsome one."

"You are both handsome," I said and turned over to face Nate.

"Hmm," Nate said, and kissed me lightly on the lips once I settled. "I know it's wrong, but this feels like a vacation."

I smiled. "I haven't been on vacation since before the accident, so yeah, I get it."

"It's been a while since my family went on one. Maybe six or seven years," Nate said with a yawn. He was quiet for a moment. "Last night was so hot, seeing you with Ev."

I blushed. "Hey, um, it's okay if you have feelings for him, too. I've noticed the way you two are with each other and wanted to throw that out there. It's- um, it's okay," I said awkwardly.

"I think I might," Nate said after another moment. "It would be a first for me to have feelings for another dude, but I don't know. Maybe that's why I was cool with sharing you with him."

Nate sat up in bed next to me, a nervous expression on his face. I felt Everett sit up before he smiled down at me and kissed me lightly. "Hey," I said to Everett.

"How'd you sleep, baby girl?" he asked me and pushed my hair out of my face.

"Snug as a bug," I said and smiled up at him, trying to get a read on how much he had heard me and Nate talking.

"Good," Everett said and looked to Nate, who had his arms up to finger comb his air-dried and tangled hair. Everett took in Nate's muscular torso and arms, and his eyes darkened.

My breath caught in my throat. He had heard everything.

Everett sat up all the way in bed and reached over and grabbed Nate roughly around the back of his neck and pulled Nate's mouth to his. Nate froze for a second and Everett slowed like they were both taking a moment to consider their feelings towards the kiss. I didn't dare move or make a sound. Nate's lips relaxed against Everett's, and he kissed him back. Their kiss quickly deepened and was a clashing of tongues and lips and their hands grabbing for a better hold on each other. It was searing, and I could feel their emotions and desperation for each other rolling off them. Everett pulled back, breaking the kiss with a pop. They shared a look, and I averted my eyes to be respectful. Even though they were leaning over my legs, and about a foot away from me, I felt like I needed to give them some privacy.

The sound of their breathing changed, and I looked back to see them both looking at me with concerned expressions. As if I was going to scream and run out of here. I swallowed. "That... was the hottest thing I've ever seen in my entire life."

Both smiled simultaneously with relieved exhales. I blushed at the attention from both of them.

Nate opened his mouth to speak, but there was a sharp knock on the RV's door. "Hey, I have news!" came Easton's voice, so like Everett's.

We scrambled to get our borrowed clothes on before meeting Easton at a campfire outside his cabin. Chickens were roaming the area, at least twenty of them, and pecking at the ground. Over the fire was an iron grate on a stand, a navy and white speckled metal kettle on the grates, and a slightly smoking cast iron pan. Easton prepared fresh eggs, more crusty bread, and thick slabs of bacon in the pan and coffee in the kettle.

"I've had some friends stop by in the night to let us know their news," Easton said as he plated us breakfast. "So, it's not government, official or otherwise. Nobody had heard of it until the fire. *Now* they're interested, of course, mind you. It's not the college either. But here's the kicker. My buddy accessed their financials and the science department staff's financials and found that the department and staff were getting huge checks in their accounts every month. It's all from different shell companies and none of them even visibly connect with each other, except for the fact they've been sending thousands and thousands of dollars to the staff and the school since December of last year."

"That's when they contacted me for the program," Everett said.

Nate and I nodded that we were also contacted around then.

"I figured as much," Easton said and continued. "And I've also talked it over with my partners and we don't believe it to be any sort of pharmaceutical company. They're much more covert and have this kind of stuff already."

"What makes you think that?" Nate asked.

"No offense, but you weren't exactly doing anything groundbreaking," Easton said as he poured another cup of coffee. "You don't think these companies aren't paying millions of dollars to create new illnesses to cure people of? Come on. It's supply and demand. If you want to sell your supply, you must create a demand. And they wouldn't be having college kids to do it out of a college lab. Again, no offense."

"I don't think either of us takes offense. We knew we weren't creating anything revolutionary, but the appeal of a free education was too much to pass up," Everett grumbled regretfully. "So, who do you and your partners think it is?"

"We think it's a militia group with their own mission. Someone with a lot of money and considerable pull and know-how by the looks of it. Figuring out their motive could be the key to figuring out who they are. But figuring out who they are might be the key to figuring out their motive, too. I have a buddy coming over to help draw sketches of this Hoffmann and Daisy. He has worked in surveillance for as long as I've known him. He lives a few miles away from here, so he'll be here early this afternoon. In the meantime, I need your help to gather and chop wood. I've promised him a truckload."

After breakfast, I gathered branches and kindling to dry and save while the guys worked together to chop wood on a large stump that served as a chopping block. I tried not to stare too much at shirtless Nate and Everett as they chopped wood. Easton was also incredibly fit and was wearing a white tank top tucked into thick work pants. Their breath puffed in front of them as they swung their axes and chatted about Easton's way of life in the mountains and taking occasional sips of their blue and white speckled metal coffee mugs.

I found myself to be irrationally angry when Easton's friend arrived to work on the sketches of Daisy and Hoffmann. It was a shame for the shirts to go back on. Easton made more coffee for us inside the cabin as we sat with a man who introduced himself as "Tommy." I knew this wasn't his real name based on the bark of a laugh Easton made when he told us. Tommy was an incredible artist and had portraits drawn in all angles of both Daisy and Hoffmann by sunset. His red and black checkered flannel, dirty work overalls, mud encrusted boots, and unruly black beard had him looking like a stereotypical "mountain man." I supposed he blended in by standing out if he were to go into town. The people who saw him would look at his stereotypical appearance and would look less at his identifying features. They would likely see his overalls and beard and not that he had warm brown eyes and a scar slanting across his lips. We had loaded his truck with split wood during a break and he left after dinner with a full truck bed. He told us his plan was to fix up these sketches and run them through some software and look out for Hoffmann and Daisy or find their real names if they're using fake ones. Easton scoffed and said, "Oh, is that all you do, Tommy?" when Tommy said this, so I knew there was more to the story. I didn't mind the teasing if they were truly helping us.

21

We tidied up after dinner for Easton as he sat in front of the woodstove, looking pensive. Once we finished, we each pulled up a seat to enjoy the warmth of the fire and the smell of the yellow birch that was burning. "Tommy is going to work up some finished sketches and start looking for Hoffmann and Daisy. But I'm thinking more about your own backgrounds," Easton said when we settled. "You were all specifically chosen for this project for a reason. Knowing those reasons might help us find who this organization is."

I shifted uncomfortably. Digging into my life and psyche was not on my list of fun things to do.

"Ev, we can assume they thought you were not going to walk away or ask questions for fear of looking like your big brother," Easton stated, and Everett's eyes narrowed on his brother. "They thought you'd fear the backlash of backing away from something that was labeled as 'doing good.'" Everett glowered at his brother, his jaw clenching and his fists balling on his lap. "They were obviously wrong, little brother. Now, Nate, tell me about your life."

Nate took a hesitant breath and launched into his story about his parents, his family life, his friends, his love of science, and his dad's staunch expectations of his work and success. Easton asked about all the schools he's gone to, the competitions he's won, his participation in rugby, and his past relationship.

"They looked at you and thought you were too damaged by your old man to see the value in your own time and efforts. You would never back out and look like you fucked up and go back home," Easton said, watching Nate carefully.

Nate huffed.

"Again, they were wrong," Easton reminded. "What about you, little one?"

"Eva doesn't really talk much," Nate said in defense of my silence as I was slow to gather my words to respond.

"I can do it," I said hoarsely to Nate. I was trembling with nerves, but I told Easton about the accident, my mom's death, the way my dad had been since her death, Caleb, my schools, competitions, and social life.

"Well, it's obvious they thought you would never speak up for yourself and would never go against the contract to get out. They thought you'd live in the uncomfortable feelings until you completed the project to avoid the confrontation. And they were wrong, yet again," Easton said with a smirk that was like his brother's, only lacking the heat Ev's had.

"They picked us because we're fucked up," Nate summarized dejectedly.

"Yeah, I mean you're capable, intelligent, and hardworking scientists. But you seemed flawed enough in ways they needed to complete the assignment, and gullible enough to agree to sign in the first place," Easton said. His tone had been casual and kind, but his words still stung.

"Well, we walked away," Everett said with a bite of aggression to his words.

"You blew up a building after seemingly creating a bioweapon. You're a little too late to just 'walk away,'" Easton shot back angrily.

"Oh, because you know all about walkin' away," Everett shouted and stood, his shoulders bunched.

"Is that what you still think I did?" Easton shouted in return and stood to face Everett. He was taller than his little brother by maybe an inch, and he used it to his advantage.

"Ev," Nate warned, standing up from his seat, ready to intervene.

"There are things that I know, that I have seen, that I'm still involved with," Easton said vaguely. "It's nothing that could be around you and our parents."

"What the fuck does that even mean?" Everett demanded.

"I can't tell you!" Easton shouted into Everett's unflinching face. He sighed and stepped back, running his hands through his hair. "Have you not noticed the connections? Have you not noticed the hiding and secrecy?"

"Of course I have," Everett spat.

"Well," Easton said quietly. "That all comes at a cost to my safety and the safety of the people around me. My separation from society and my family had to be dramatic enough to not warrant any of my… enemies a reason to go after you," Easton said in a hushed tone.

Everett shook his head and turned away.

"Now," Easton said, and sat back down in his chair by the fire. He cleared his throat. "What made you all walk away?"

"It was when we realized nothing was real. We weren't real students, our degrees would not be real, the people we spoke to were not real, and our work likely would not get finished," Nate said, breaking the tense silence.

"I think you're right, Nate," Easton added. "I think they were going to kill you after you finished with the illness causing bacteria. You were probably never going to find the cure, and you probably would never get your degree."

My nervous trembling became more pronounced, and my jaw chattered. Ev got up and found me a knitted throw blanket and put it around my shoulders like a little old lady. Though my shivering was not from the temperature, it was from hearing we may have narrowly escaped being murdered.

"For me, it was not knowing who and what my work was for. I wanted to be able to be honest with myself when I said that what I was doing was to help others," I replied after prompting.

"I didn't want to be attached to something terrible or be remembered as someone who helped something terrible happen. I didn't want to be like a scientist who helped create the atom bomb," Everett ground out when he was asked. "I did it to protect them." He gestured to me and Nate.

Easton looked confused about what Everett meant when he said he wanted to protect both Nate and I. Nate looked strong enough to easily beat Everett in a fight, so it was an odd statement. "I think it's only a matter of time before they use your history and your flaws against you. They need to keep you in the news and well hated if they're ever going to find you."

My teeth chattered loudly with my nerves. I clenched my mouth shut to stifle it.

"Beautiful, you're shaking like a chihuahua," Nate laughed.

"I'll find you another blanket," Ev said and jumped up from his seat.

"She's not cold, she's freaking out," Easton said, eyeing me like he was seeing through me.

Nate and Everett both moved their chairs to my side, but Easton's searching gaze held mine. When both guys rushed to my side, Easton's eyes narrowed in thought, like he was trying to figure out my relationship with them. I didn't want to get kicked out for having a weird relationship status, so I broke eye contact with

Easton and looked at Everett. "Yeah, I'm kind of freaking out. Can you take me to bed?"

"Yeah, let's go, baby girl," Everett said and stood, offering me his hand. "We can all talk more in the morning."

"In the morning, I'm going to need more information about your involvements with Daisy," Easton said, his eyes on me again. His tone suggested he was giving me a warning to avoid freaking out again.

We said our goodnights, and I walked out the cabin door and made it two steps before I crumpled. I sobbed into my hands, my newly washed jean clad knees sinking into the cold mud. Everett was close and tried to catch me as I sank to the ground. This was all our fault. My fault. I had had questions in the beginning about the motives and sources for this project. If I wasn't so damaged and unable to speak up, then I could have prevented this whole thing. We could be safe in our homes and looking into other education options rather than hiding in the woods as suspected terrorists.

Everett picked me up and carried me towards the RV as sobs wracked my body so hard my chest hurt.

"At the risk of upsetting Eva more, I need to say I think something big is about to happen and our faces are going to be plastered to the front of it," Nate said quietly as we approached the RV.

"I know," Everett whispered

22

The next morning, Everett woke me and Nate up with soft kisses to our lips before he left to help Easton with the morning work. I knew we should get up and help as well, but I couldn't get my body to move.

"Come on," Nate said, groggily. "We have to go milk the chickens or whatever these cowboys do at the ass crack of dawn."

I smiled and curled against Nate. "I think they're gathering the eggs and, like... mucking the stalls."

"There are no horses here," Nate said. "And I don't think chickens have stalls."

"I don't know. I guess we should go find out," I sighed.

We dressed and joined the brothers out by the campfire. The air was crisply cold and smelled of pine and snow. The sun was creeping into the sky and the brothers were standing and drinking coffee, planning out their morning. Nate and I were handed a basket and a mug of coffee each and sent into the chicken coop to gather eggs.

Everett and Easton went off to the river to get water and then came back to get it boiling. They were talking as they worked about their parents and the family farm they grew up on. It was nice to see them catching up and laughing, even though they were both hesitant around each other.

When we were finally sitting down to eat breakfast and drink more coffee, I was starving. Everett set up the radio near us and we listened to a local country station and waited for the news and weather reports. When the news finally came on, we stopped talking and eating entirely. Easton set his plate on the ground next to him and leaned forward and put his elbows on his knees as the local news played.

"News out of Cleveland, Ohio today sheds new light on the Truman College attack. Students from Truman College and the alleged attackers' previous schools have come forth to speak out against the three people involved. Reports quote that Everett Monroe had often made extremist comments and had a strong hatred for the United States. Experts suspect Nathaniel Gibson and Evangeline Reid had underlying mental health concerns that allowed them to be swayed by Monroe's extreme thinking. Other students have come forth and reported Gibson was often angry and spoke of hurting others, while Reid was antisocial and disconnected from others. The search for them continues and now includes the two people Reid mentioned in her escape from carjackers dressed as police. Sources say two of the suspect's families had also mentioned the names of these individuals. They have supplied no pictures of a Professor Hoffmann or a Daisy Rossi at this time."

Everett put his head in his hands, and Nate scoffed. I was numb to it. It wasn't true, and the reports people were giving were false. There was nothing I could do to fight false information. I was tired of it all.

"How about you three head over to the river and do some fishing? Stay on this side of the river and don't go where you can see the road," Easton said and stood to gather breakfast dishes. "I'll check in with my contacts and we'll see if I can find anything else out. You seem burnt out, and I don't want you making any more stupid decisions." His tone was that of a big brother, but I knew it held judgment for our situation. It wasn't an unwarranted judgment, but it still chafed.

Supplied with fishing poles, a cooler packed with snow, and a thermos of coffee, we set off to the river. Nate and Everett chatted about fishing, when they'd last gone, the fish they've caught in the past, and their personal records. I trailed behind them, crunching in the dead leaves and snow.

We spent a few hours fishing in the river together. It was calm, and a bit too cold. We had quickly drunk all the coffee and walked down the stream looking for some sunlight to warm us. Trout and bass populated the river, and we had caught a few that could be dinner tonight. I was sitting atop a boulder where the sun was shining while the boys laughed at me. Nate was down the riverbank further, but within shouting distance, and Everett was wearing Easton's tall rubber boots and standing in the river.

"Looking like a princess on her throne," Nate called down to me.

Everett laughed as I struck a pose.

"Queens have thrones," I called back, posing regally.

"Nah, she's like a mermaid," Everett laughed.

"Yeah, that part of Little Mermaid when she doesn't have a voice, but she's got killer legs," Nate added.

I giggled and kicked my borrowed sweat pant clad legs in front of me and arched my back. I could see Nate smiling from far away, and Everett winked at me.

A sound of cracking branches and a revving engine sounded somewhere in the distance. My heart leapt in my chest, and I looked around. Everett had also heard it and was looking warily through the trees. The sound of an engine and the cracking of branches got closer to the river, and I slid down off the rock to the side facing away from where the car was approaching. I landed with a small splash in the icy, knee-deep water. Everett was scrambling to the edge of the river in his tall boots and rushed up through the mud.

Nate had heard the car approach now and was running backwards down the stream, waving his hands to get our attention. I knew I couldn't make it up the riverbank and into the brush before the car was in view. I shook my head and waved them on frantically as I crouched behind the boulder.

"Go!" I urged them when they were looking between me and the woods as if they were debating their chances of being seen or leaving me.

With a regretful look, Everett dashed into the woods and I at once lost sight of him as he crashed through the trees. I couldn't see Nate's expression from my position, but he turned and ran after Ev did and jumped over a log to get to the woods. I hoped they both ran further than hiding in the brush.

The car stopped before the muddy riverbed, likely where Easton had driven us across almost two days ago. I heard a door open after the engine shut off and a person walking over the wet rocks and mud towards the river. I made myself as small as possible, completely soaked from the waist down, as I hid behind the rock. The cold-water bit into my skin, but my fear kept me from feeling it as adrenaline shot through my veins. I heard them make it to the side of the river behind me and my rock and start up the small hill towards Easton's cabin. I hoped it was Tommy coming back or someone else Easton knew, but my gut told me to stay hidden.

Once I heard the footsteps retreat out of earshot, I peeked around to see the car parked at the river's edge. The feelings of adrenaline and terror mixed in my stomach and made me want to vomit. Bile rose in my throat as I looked at the car of a park ranger.

I took my chance to get to the edge of the river, still in a crouch. The riverbed proved to be an obstacle when I slipped going up the riverbed and my fingers caught in the frigid, slimy clay. I scrambled my way up and ran downstream to where Nate had been fishing. I jumped over the same log he had and crouched behind it and listened. There was nothing moving around me or voices in the distance. Where were Nate and Everett? I waited a moment to catch my breath before I made my way through the woods to find them.

I heard shouting in the distance and dread filled me. I stifled a sob with my gray clay covered hands before I crouched down and hid next to a tree. Who had been caught? Was it both of them? Was the ranger now calling for backup? Images of the guys being shoved into the back of a cop car or cornered and shot flashed through my mind. I felt helpless and alone, shivering on the floor of the forest. More shouting sounded in the distance, this time two voices. I couldn't tell who it was, only that both voices were male.

This was it; the gig was up. We were about to be carted away and treated like terrorists. I was going to die in prison away from Nate and Ev. I laid down on the cold, damp forest floor and cried. It had been only three or four days since we went looking for Daisy on campus, but I was tired. Those days felt endless and exhausting as I reflected on them. It was too much for me, and I felt weak. I should have been able to protect the guys better. We should have only spent the night here with Easton and then left for another hiding spot. I felt unsettled and sick with anticipation as I waited for everything to blow up in my face even further.

It had to be near an hour on the ground of the forest before I heard the distinct sound of someone starting up an engine and driving away through the woods. It was only the one car, and I wondered if the ranger was leaving on his own or with one or both of my guys in the back. Wouldn't he have called in back up to look for the rest of us?

On unsteady feet, I stood and walked stiffly through the forest. My joints and surgery sites were achy and cold, limiting my range of mobility. I was lost in the forest, but I could smell the birch smoke of Easton's campfire, so I knew I was close. The desperation to get to the cabin and see Nate and Everett was so strong I didn't feel the ache of my bones and the cold anymore. I trampled through the brush until I emerged on the side of Easton's parcel, not where I thought I'd come out, but safe.

Easton's eyes widened as he saw me approaching, covered in mud and leaves, soaked with river water, and wild desperation on my face. "There you are," he said, relief in his voice as he rushed to me. I was sure I was a sight to see limping out of the forest like I'd been attacked by a bear.

"Where?" was all I could hoarsely say, looking around me.

Easton shook his head and grabbed my arm to help me to the fire. "They're not back yet. I take it you got separated?"

I nodded and craned my neck around to look for Everett and Nate.

"Sit by the fire, I'll find them. They're probably still hiding. Relax," Easton said and pushed me into a chair by the fire.

He was calm as he spoke to me, but I was feeling anything but relaxed as I almost tipped over in the chair looking into the woods. My back and knees were screaming in pain, so I aggressively scooted the chair closer to the fire to warm up. It would be days before my knees recovered from this. I knew my limits, and I had surpassed them by kneeling on the cold forest floor.

A crash of branches sounded on the other side of the parcel and Nate stumbled out, brushing debris off of his coat sleeves. I was up and limping to him despite Easton's warning to stay in my chair.

Nate jogged to me, seeing my struggle, and opened his arms to hug me. My dried clay caked hands gripped him tightly, and he kissed me roughly. "Did you see?" he asked against my lips. "It was a ranger."

I nodded. "I saw. Where's Ev? Did you hear yelling?"

"He's not here yet?" Nate asked, his brows drawing together. "I thought I was last because I got lost."

Behind him, I caught sight of movement and I looked around him to see Everett walking up the path, tall boots in his hands. I gasped when I saw him, and Nate turned around with me still in his arms. Ev dropped his boots and ran barefoot in the snow to us and wrapped his arms around both Nate and me. I clung to them both, tears of relief falling now. Everett kissed us both as we all clung to each other and caught our breaths and relished in the feel of being reunited.

"I get it now," Easton said from behind us. I startled, forgetting he was there. "I understand what you said about protecting them both."

Everett swallowed as he studied his brother's expression. "They're... mine," he admitted. The words were simple but said so much about how he was feeling about our relationship, and I knew I felt the same. A look at Nate to see him standing tall while holding me and Ev told me he felt the same as us.

Easton nodded and gave his brother a soft smile before looking at me and Nate. "Well, you are all probably wondering what the hell that was all about, so come warm up by the fire."

He put a pot on for coffee as we sat with our chairs pushed together and wrapped in knitted blankets. I wondered if Easton knitted them himself since he had so many.

"Rick is a friend of mine," Easton began.

"His name is Ranger Rick?" Nate asked.

"It is. He felt it worked better than Ranger Dick," Easton shrugged. "Anyway, I live here on national park property. Not really supposed to be here, but Rick knows about me and the others who live in the woods. We don't cause any problems and we've helped him out a few times, so he lets us be. He's also a vet, so he understands that some of us have this drive for seclusion and privacy. I go with him to the VFW every so often to keep a good relationship going. He's good people. That's not to say I trust him. He doesn't know what we do, and he doesn't know you're here. As far as he knows, I'm a veteran with PTSD living in peace in the forest. He came here today to check in, as he does occasionally, and inform me of what major media believes you guys have done. He was, indeed, looking for you."

The guys held my hands on either side of me. Another close call. Though this time it was with real law enforcement. I swallowed tightly.

"What was the yelling about?" Ev asked. "I couldn't hear what was being said."

"Oh, sorry about that. I figured it might freak you out," Easton chuckled. "He knows I'm off the grid up here and asked if I had listened to the radio lately. I said I had not, and he gently informed me that my baby brother was a terrorist on the loose. I got dramatic."

Everett rolled his eyes. "You get the dramatics from Mom."

"You obviously didn't see Dad on the sidelines of your football games," Easton chuckled.

"You played football?" Nate asked Ev, his eyes wide.

"He did," Easton answered.

"Let me guess, quarterback?" Nate asked in a teasing voice.

"The best our school had seen in decades," Easton praised. Everett sat back in his seat, looking like the attention had embarrassed him.

"Of course you were. Fucking hell," Nate laughed. "I'm in love with the star quarterback cowboy. How is this real life?"

Everett blushed a deep red and I shifted in my seat. I had suspected it would be Nate who said the L word first. He wore his heart on his sleeve and didn't seem to do anything halfway. A twinge of jealousy zipped around my stomach since he said it to Ev and not me, but I tamped it down. There was no point in getting worked up over something that was said in a joking way with Ev's brother. I could be happy about the progression for Ev without sulking.

"How is it real life that we're suspected terrorists when we were just trying to get our degrees?" Everett rasped, changing the subject. "We need to think of a new plan. We can't stay here much longer if the rangers are already looking."

I sighed. "Back to the drawing board."

"You have time here, yet. I think you should wait until we get more information on who was controlling the project," Easton said.

"I think we need to talk this over," Everett said, gesturing to me and Nate.

"Absolutely. Go get washed up. Did you catch any fish? I'll grab the cooler and the rods from by the river and I'll call you when dinner is ready. Go rest your legs, Eva," Easton said and stood.

Everett had to carry me to the RV while Nate grabbed our clothes that had been drying by the woodstove in the cabin from yesterday.

"Nate said he loved you," I whispered to Ev as he walked me to the RV.

A blush creeped up Ev's cheeks again. "I heard him."

I squealed and wiggled excitedly in Ev's arms, and he shushed me with a laugh.

23

We dressed and sat at the dinette table in the RV after Nate came back with our clean and wood fire warmed clothes. The vinyl bench seat was a half-circle around a small table and reminded me of a roadside diner. I sat between them on the bench, and Everett rubbed my knees to massage the muscles and scar tissue.

"Okay, so what are your ideas?" Nate said with an exhale as he settled into the bench.

"One option is to wait until Daisy and Hoffmann make a move or more information comes out, then we come out of hiding. Easton backs this one. He thinks we should catch Hoffmann or Daisy or whoever is running the show and then come out and tell everyone what happened to us," Everett explained. It was difficult to determine his thoughts on that plan because he said it without feeling.

"Another option is to keep working with Easton and his… friends to try to stop anything major from happening," I added. "We could work more intentionally with them to find where our research is going to be used and stop it."

"Hmm, or we could get moving and find somewhere else to hide indefinitely," Nate offered. His voice was dark as he spoke. "And not risk getting executed or locked up."

We were quiet for a few minutes as we each considered our options. A thought occurred to me, and my heart sank. It wasn't the healthiest thought to have, and I knew it. I swallowed thickly. "The way I see it, we're already dead. If either Hoffman and Daisy's people or the police don't kill us on sight, we're never going to have lives without this over our heads. So, if we're going to go out, we might as well go out helping other people."

The guys were quiet, and they exchanged a long, serious glance. I felt like they agreed with me. It felt like I had said what we were all thinking. This felt deeply and heart-wrenchingly hopeless.

"Whatever we do, whatever we decide, we're doing it together," Everett said quietly.

"Fucking duh," Nate scoffed.

"I don't like being separated from you guys." I looked at the tabletop, avoiding their eyes. "I've never-" I swallowed a gulp of air and huffed a sigh. "I've never felt like I needed another person before. They were right on the news to say that I lived disconnected from people. It's like... it's like if I wasn't talking, nobody was listening, and I wasn't on anyone's mind. A girl who doesn't talk probably sounded like a lot of work to have a relationship with, so... hardly anybody ever tried. Friendship or otherwise. So, there was never anyone I felt was worth it to need. Maybe that doesn't make sense. I don't know."

"It makes perfect sense, baby girl," Everett said and held my hand. "Little did they know that getting to know you was the key to your voice."

"I need you, too," Nate said and took my other hand. "I need both of you."

"Like I said to Easton earlier, you're both mine," Everett said, his eyes flashing as he looked between me and Nate.

Nate cleared his throat and sat up straight, clenching his jaw. "Both of you need to get to the bed now."

Everett cocked a brow. "No."

Nate stood, slowly and menacingly. I fought a grin, biting my lower lip.

"Fine, then you can listen," Nate taunted and held a hand out for me to take. He roughly pulled me to him and swept me up into his arms, considering my nearly unusable legs.

"Hell no," Everett growled and got up from his seat.

I peeked at him over Nate's shoulder as I was carried to the tiny bedroom. I raised my eyebrows suggestively at Ev and he smirked back.

"Can you stand?" Nate asked me.

I nodded.

"Then strip," Nate commanded and sat on the bed against the back wall of the RV. Everett crawled onto the bed to sit next to him in the same position, legs stretched in front of them in wide Vs. Both of them palmed themselves through their jeans and looked at me expectantly.

I swallowed and looked down. I was wearing the same clothes and underwear they've seen me take off a few times already, so I felt self-conscious. My clothes were clean and I had bathed, but they had to be getting bored. Their intense gazes told me otherwise, so I had to believe them.

I bent down and kicked off my shoes and slowly peeled off my socks. The slowness was partially to be teasing and partially because the movement was stiff and painful. When I stood back up, I hooked my hands under the hem of my shirt and lifted it over my head and off my arms. When the fabric of my shirt was no longer blocking my view, I saw their hooded eyes and straining jeans. This strip tease was hardly a tease. I didn't exactly know how to do it sensually. But I hoped it was working well enough for them. Getting inspiration from their faces, I turned away from them and unbuttoned my jeans and unzipped them slowly. The sound was a soft shush of metal. Smirking to myself, I bent and pushed my jeans down my legs. I was bent over in front of them in only my plain black panties with a blush creeping over my face and chest. I heard Nate moan softly while I was still bent in half and getting my jeans over my feet.

Turning around to face them, my blush crept lower and my core warmed. They were both still fully dressed, but their eyes were alight with arousal and their cocks straining against the zippers of their jeans. My mouth watered, and I smiled at them.

"Take the rest of it off," Nate demanded, his voice deep like a growl.

"Uh-uh, not until you guys are naked, too," I teased and fluttered my eyelashes.

Both of them scrambled up to get their clothes off until they were both sitting back where they started, fully naked and with cocks standing tall. I licked my lips while they both returned to watching me.

"Continue," Nate instructed with a low growl.

Everett chucked. "Has anyone ever told you that your hardware doesn't match your software?"

"Me?" Nate asked, taken out of his dominant persona for a moment.

"Yeah, you," Everett laughed. "What the hell is that?"

"Like it or get out," Nate barked.

"Oh, I like it," Ev assured him. "It's just not what I was expecting."

Nate shrugged, then looked back at me and gestured for me to keep going.

I unhooked my bra and slipped the straps down my arms and stood before them in only my panties. The elastic hair band that Nate had been using on and off the last few days caught my attention on the small dresser. I picked it up and put my hair into a ponytail while bouncing my eye contact between both of them.

Nate swore and stroked himself. The movement caught Everett's eyes, and he watched Nate for a moment. I hooked my fingers into my panties to slide them down.

"Wait," Nate ordered. "Turn around and do it."

"Fuck yeah," Everett agreed.

I obeyed. I slid my panties down my legs at the same dramatic speed as I had on my jeans. Both guys groaned behind me, and I heard the sound of skin moving against skin. Were they touching each other? My pussy flooded, and I spun around, standing up. They were not touching each other, only themselves, but it gave me the idea.

"Touch each other," I whispered.

Both of their fists on their cocks halted.

"Right now?" Ev asked.

"Yes, I want to see it," I said, my blush getting even deeper.

They looked at each other almost shyly and I wondered for a moment if they weren't ready. But then Nate reached out to Ev and Ev didn't tell him no, so my worry dropped. Nate looked Ev in the eyes as he wrapped his hand around Ev's cock. Ev gasped and his head tipped back against the wall. Nate scooted closer to him for better access, and Ev reached out and grasped Nate's cock. Nate groaned low in his throat, and they kept eye contact as they pumped their hands in tandem. Evening sunlight streamed through the windows above their heads and made their hair and eyes glow with warm, golden light. Both of their mouths were open as they breathed heavily and adjusted to the sensation of touching another man's cock. They were truly beautiful at that moment, glowing in the sun and enjoying themselves. My heart swelled and my pussy clenched. I realized I was in love.

"Wait, fuck, spit on it," Ev hissed and looked down at his cock.

Nate hesitated for a moment, looking down as well. I swooped in under their arms and took Ev into my mouth. I knew that was what he was hesitating to do. I'd give him the opportunity in a moment to try it if he wanted to. The sensation of having a cock in my mouth caused my pussy to flood in anticipation again. My arousal dripped down the inside of my thighs and I hummed against Ev's cock. He stroked my hair and used my ponytail to guide me up and down.

I pulled back and stroked Ev a few times and looked over at Nate. He licked his lips and looked at Ev, then down at me. I smiled and sat back. Nate took a breath and leaned down. Ev's abs tensed when he realized what was happening. They only relaxed marginally as Nate bobbed his head a few times.

"Fuck!" Ev shouted and his torso jerked, and he grabbed Nate's head. "He did your tongue thing!"

"Hey, that's my move!" I laughed and swatted Nate on the head playfully.

Nate pulled up and wiped his mouth. "That wasn't as weird as I thought it was going to be. Who's going to suck my dick now? Both of you?"

Ev and I both converged on Nate as he sat back against the wall again. I licked a stripe up Nate's cock. Ev watched and copied the move. Everett and I both laid on our stomachs in front of Nate and between his outstretched legs. After a few experimental licks and sucks, Ev seemed more confident. Our tongues and mouths worked together on Nate, who was twitching and moaning and gripping our hair. He was mumbling semi-incoherent dirty things as he watched. My tongue battled with Ev's like we were making out as we slid up and down Nate's cock, alternating who would take his head into our mouth and suck.

Nate tugged on our hair to get us to back up. "I'm about to come," he panted. He looked at me, "Suck his cock while I fuck you."

Everett got up onto the bed and kneeled. I got on all fours before him, and his cock slid into my mouth and he moaned deep in his throat. Nate got behind me and smacked me on the ass so hard I yelped.

"You're fucking dripping," Nate mused, and used his fingers to catch the drips on my thighs. He stretched his hand out to Ev, who took Nate's fingers into his mouth. I wasn't just clenching in anticipation now; I was throbbing and desperate. To take away some of the pressure, I reached down to my clit.

"Baby girl is impatient," Ev said after letting Nate's fingers go with a pop.

Nate growled in the back of his throat and smacked me on the ass again. Ev hissed as this impact caused me to lightly scrape my teeth over him. I made up for it by doing The Tongue Thing. He buckled at the waist and almost collapsed over my back. I giggled around him as he grabbed my ass cheeks to stand back up.

"No, spread them," Nate commanded Ev.

Ev spread my ass cheeks, and I felt embarrassed for a split second. But Ev's cock twitching in my mouth and the salty, sweet taste of pre-cum told me I had no reason to be self-conscious. Nate moved behind me and I kept up the pace on my clit as I waited. Nate gathered more juices on two fingers and then pressed them into me. The stretch felt good, but wasn't enough. I moaned and tried to push back, but Ev's hands braced me. The angle of his cock in my mouth with him bent over my back caused more weight to rest on my tongue, so it was difficult not to gag on him, especially since I couldn't move to control the depth. He pumped into my mouth slowly and gripped my ass cheeks apart. It was hotter than I could have ever imagined being at the complete mercy of two men. I had trusted them with my life, but letting them aggressively spit roast me felt like a whole different level of trust.

Nate curled his fingers inside of me and I instantly broke out in a sweat. He amped up the pace and intensity of those finger curls and I was moaning, high pitched and uncontrollable around Ev's cock.

He pumped into my mouth with his hips snapping as my release made rivers down my thighs. Nate pulled his fingers out of me mid orgasm and slammed his cock into me. I screamed around Ev's cock as my eyes watered. Nate slammed into me repeatedly from behind and Ev continued to pump my mouth. I heard sounds of kissing above me and Ev's hands on my ass clenched painfully.

"Fuck, beautiful, you're doing so good. Taking both our dicks at the same time," Nate panted above me. He grunted low and long in his throat. "So wet for us. Such a pretty pussy."

My first orgasm hadn't had time to wind down, so my second one started at the level of pleasure at which the first one ended. My vision went black for a second as fire and tv static coursed through my body. I was trembling, sweating, and soaked when I came back to my body.

Nate's thrusts became uneven, and he elongated the word "Fuck," into a whole breath as he came inside me. I felt the throbbing of his cock near my entrance as he filled me. Everett pulled out of my mouth, and I thought he was going to come on my face, so I tipped my face up to him, but he quickly moved behind me to take Nate's place. Nate, realizing what was happening, pulled out of me as he finished coming and moved over so Ev could press into me. He drove into me at a punishing pace, and I put my head down on the mattress and gripped the sheets in my fists to anchor myself. Within a few seconds, he was shouting his own release. When he pulled out of me, he collapsed over onto Nate, and I flopped onto the mattress. But Nate heaved Ev off him and said "No, I wanna see the cream pie."

Nate wrenched my thighs apart and peered at my swollen pussy. Ev chuckled, and I rolled my eyes. "It'll all come out later. I'll be walking and it, like... pours out."

Everett's chuckle turned into a full laugh at Nate's wide-eyed look. "Really?"

"Yeah," I laughed. "I mean, sometimes it comes out as soon as I stand up, but sometimes it's later."

"Why is that so hot?" Nate asked, his eyes still wide.

"Because it means whenever a bit comes out, she remembers what we did," Ev explained as he got up to get towels.

Nate hummed in understanding and pulled me to him in a cuddle. He kissed my sweaty shoulder. "I love you," he murmured against my skin.

I spun around in his arms to face him. "What?"

"I said I love you," he repeated, his green eyes locked on mine.

"I love you, too," I said, and tears welled in my eyes. I wasn't sure I'd said that to anyone before.

Nate smiled and kissed my forehead as Everett returned with warm, damp washcloths. Nate looked up at Everett. "I love you, Ev."

I turned and looked at Everett. He was frozen, holding the washcloths. "Ev, I also love you."

Everett exhaled low in his throat. "I love both of you, too."

I grinned widely.

"Now we have to come out of this alive," Nate said, and took a cloth from Everett. "We need to give Eva here a white picket fence in the suburbs."

"No way," Everett said with a smirk. "She's getting a farmhouse and a chicken coop."

I crinkled my nose, remembering the chicken coop smell.

"Alright, goats?" Ev chuckled.

"Yes, please," I smiled.

"Why not the suburbs? I think it could be hot. Eva's out planting a little flower garden at our new house and some nosy bitch in a tennis skirt carrying a casserole comes over and asks where her husband is and we *both* come out," Nate mused.

"No, you've got it all wrong," Everett said as we finished cleaning ourselves up. "We've got acres of land with no neighbors, the animals are all tended to, the work is done, and Eva is sunbathing naked by the pond, waiting for us."

"Why aren't I doing work on the farm?" I asked, laughing at their stories.

"Because you're pregnant and can't lift heavy things and you needed a nap," Ev said with a smoldering look.

I laughed as I put my shirt back on. "You guys have some grand ideas."

"Well, what do you picture?" Nate asked me.

I considered his question as I put my jeans back on. I felt a wave of sadness and grief for what I had lost when my mom died and for what I could have had. "I... don't care where we go. Suburb or farm or city. I just want to be together and in love. I don't want to be without this feeling ever again."

"Never," Everett said quietly.

And I knew he meant it.

24

It was midafternoon the next day when we were startled out of our tasks by the sound of a vehicle coming over the river. My knees and back had felt better that afternoon, so I was helping Easton turn and harvest potatoes while he talked me through the process of growing them. When I heard the crashing of branches and crunching of stone, I looked up to see both Everett and Nate running toward me. I was crouched down in the soil with Easton and was getting up stiffly as Nate and Ev reached me at the same time, heaving me under the arms and carrying me awkwardly between them to the woods behind the RV. I was still facing Easton as they ran with me, so I saw him brush his hand over my footprints in the soft soil. We hid in the woods, crouched behind a fallen tree, and peeked over to see who approached.

A dark gray pickup truck pulled up next to Easton's and Tommy hopped out of the passenger seat. The fear that had gripped my heart relaxed when I saw the mountain man approach Easton. Easton turned to where we had run and gestured for us to come out, which we were already doing.

"Hey is this Hoffmann and Daisy?" Tommy called to us, holding out some paper.

Nate and Everett jogged to him and looked at the paper. They looked at each other and then over at me as I approached. Ev handed me the paper, and I looked down to see a few pages of pictures of Daisy and Hoffmann in varying qualities. I gasped.

"It's them," Everett told Tommy. "One hundred percent. Where are they?"

Tommy looked serious when he replied. "New York City. This building is where they're storing the merchandise and decorations for New Year's Eve celebrations. You know, the dumb ass glasses with the year on them and the beads and shit."

"How'd they get in?" Nate asked.

"A swipe card," Tommy sighed. "Can't tell if they've stolen it or if they work there."

"What can we do?" I asked quietly.

"I have to make some calls. Wait here, but be ready to move if you want to stop them," Tommy said, and pulled his phone out of his pocket. "I have a feeling they're planting something."

"I burned everything. Nothing survived," Everett insisted. "It's not ours."

"Did they have access to the slides or test tubes or whatever before the fire?" Tommy asked with an eyebrow raised.

Everett's shoulders slumped in defeat.

"That's okay because you'll be able to identify what they have," Tommy said, and stepped away to make a call.

Easton turned to us. "Have you made your mind up on what you're going to do? Here's your opportunity to stop them and whatever they are planning. Or you can stay here. I can't tell you what to do."

Nate, Everett, and I looked at each other. We hadn't exactly planned out what we wanted to do. Or come to a full agreement on it.

"We're going to help," Everett said, and looked back at Easton. "Whatever we need to do."

Tommy hung up the phone and made another call while we waited. He yelled back to us to pack to leave, but we had nothing to pack. Easton went into his cabin and came back out with a heavy black backpack. He handed it to Everett and explained that it was food for the road, water, a change of clothes for each of us, a few knives, and a first aid kit. He'd had it packed since the night we arrived, in case we needed to leave quickly.

"Alright," Tommy said as he approached us and put his phone back in his pocket. "You three have official clearance to move to New York. Though, local cops and highway patrol along the way will still pose a problem if you get caught by them. I recommend that you not do as such. The general public will also be an issue, so avoid being recognized. You can prove that you are not terrorists by catching and turning in Hoffmann and Daisy."

My heart was beating in my throat. We had official clearance. Did that mean they did not consider us to be terrorists anymore? Or did it mean that we had the chance to prove we were not? I didn't care. I needed to try.

"I want you three to take my truck, too," Easton said. "It's got Tennessee plates and I won't report it stolen."

Ev nodded in understanding. "Thank you. We owe you so much."

Easton waved off the offer and shook his head. "It's the least I can do after abandoning you and our parents and apparently sort of fucking you up."

Everett snorted a laugh and rubbed the back of his neck.

"I've already got people on water and sanitation in the city," Tommy continued, businesslike. "We need to make some calls, and you'll be out of here within the hour."

The guys and I washed up after being outside all day and met Easton and Tommy by the trucks. "Alright, it'll take you a little over 12 hours to get there so you'll get into the city at about four in the morning," Easton briefed us in a tone that sounded practiced.

"We've got points of contact in sanitation, water, Times Square, airports, and other tourist locations. We've got a secure lab in New York City for you to check samples and determine if it's your bacteria or not."

"While you have clearance to get there, you are not out of trouble yet. We have been informed that if you help in the investigation, your consequences will be lessened," Tommy added in a similar tone to Easton. I realized that this was their job. They were experts in this, and I was eternally grateful that they were on our side.

"Take direct routes, alternate drivers, and go straight there," Easton said. He handed Everett a phone. "Answer every call. It'll be one of us."

"Got it?" Tommy asked.

"Yes," Everett said. Nate agreed, and I nodded once.

Tommy and Easton stepped aside for us. Nate, Everett, and I got in the truck. I was up in the passenger seat to allow Nate to nap in the backseat before his turn to drive. We were about to leave when Easton came up to Everett's window. He spoke lowly to his brother, but I could hear him. "Ev, if you're only going to go try to stop them because you want to bring back glory to the family, then don't do it. I know how you want to show the world that only *one* of the Monroe boys is a fuck up who can't help his country- who can't keep the family in good name. But it's not about the glory. It can't be about the glory. Glory is about how others think of you, but *honor* is how you feel doing what you think or feel to be right. Glory serves *yourself,* and honor serves *others.* I want you to consider which one you want before you make any more decisions."

"I want to do what's right. I can't continue thinking I may have been responsible for people getting sick," Everett replied.

"We don't know that anybody is sick yet. We don't know that they've made a move," Easton assured Everett. "Get there and do what you can."

We said our goodbyes, and Everett drove us over the river and out of the woods. Once on the road, we remained in a tense silence until we hit the open highway.

25

We had been on the road and silent for about an hour when the phone rang. Nate was trying to sleep in the back seat, so I answered.

"Hello?" My voice was small and hesitant.

"Take the next exit for gas. There are no police in the area," a man's voice directed me. It wasn't Easton or Tommy.

"Um, thank you," I said and relayed the message to Ev. "Who is this?"

"A friend of Easton's," the man said, and hung up.

Ev shrugged and moved lanes as directed. We filled the tank that had been less than half full when we got in the truck.

I wore a baseball hat and sunglasses to pay in cash that Easton had provided for gas and returned to the truck without incident. I had been alone in the store and didn't draw attention to myself, so nobody paid me any mind. It was hard to remember that people were out here living their own day-to-day lives and weren't actively looking for three suspected terrorists. They may have seen us on tv, but they weren't expecting to see us in their town.

We drove until close to nine at night, before Everett needed a break from driving. We stopped at a rest stop to use the restroom and stretch our legs. I was doing some of my physical therapy exercises with the guys when the phone rang again. This time, Everett answered it, leaning against the truck and watching Nate and I finish stretching.

"We're taking a stretch break," Everett said to whomever was on the phone. "Yeah, we'll be back on the road in five... Nate will drive... How are you watching us?" He looked up at the streetlight poles in the parking lot. The person must have hung up because he rolled his eyes and put the phone in his pocket.

Once we were back in the car, we were a little more awake than when we had stopped. Nate was driving and had the music on a rock station. As we drove North, more and more snow was visible on the ground. While there had been snow on Easton's property, there had been none in Gatlinburg when we left. It felt like as the amount of snow grew, our anticipation and feeling of dread also grew.

"So, why are we doing this? What are our motivations?" Nate asked us as we sped down the highway.

"You two probably heard what my brother said when we were leaving. He said I needed to figure out if I was doing this for glory or for honor, and I said it was honor. But I'd be lying if it wasn't a little for regaining glory, too. I want to help Easton's friends and the authorities find the real terrorists, and I also want to not be labeled as a bad person and have my family dragged down with me," Everett contemplated. He huffed out a harsh sigh and shook his head and looked at me in the passenger seat. "And I'm doing it for you two. Neither of you would do well in prison."

Nate and I smiled at his joke, but my heart wrenched at his explanation. "I want another chance," I answered next. "I feel like I've spent the last decade of my life recovering and not doing anything with the life I'm honestly lucky to still have. It's like I've spent the last decade waiting for my mom to come back, my body to heal, or my dad to give a shit. I guess it's not until I might not have my life or my freedom anymore that I suddenly want it."

"I feel similar to both of you," Nate said, only glancing at me and back to the road. "I've spent my whole life waiting for my dad to realize that I'm a hard worker and a good person, but he's probably never going to tell me what I want to hear. I need to do something without thinking about how he will react. But I also want him to see my name cleared and feel proud of my choices. We're so damaged."

"We're not that bad," Everett conceded. "We're just easily manipulated."

"Oh, because that's much better," Nate laughed wryly.

"We'll find therapists when this is all over," I added with a smirk.

It was near two in the morning when I was jerked awake by the phone ringing. Nate answered it while driving. "Hello?... Okay... Yeah... They'll let us do that?... Holy shit, no way!... Okay, got it."

"What's going on?" Ev's sleepy voice grumbled.

"We're getting out in Trenton, up ahead, and we're getting on a helicopter the rest of the way," Nate explained excitedly.

"A helicopter?" My eyes were wide.

"Yeah, this is a little badass," Nate said, his eyes alight.

Everett and I sat up as Nate navigated us to a hospital. I could hear the propellers of a helicopter as we got out of the truck. A hospital employee had a side door open near where we parked the truck. He was gesturing for us to follow him. The three of us hurried through the door and followed him to the elevator. This end of the hospital was dark and quiet, and I heard only the squeaks of our shoes.

"Thank you for helping us," Everett told the employee as we approached the elevator.

"Honestly, I don't know who you are. They offered me money to get you to the helicopter," the guy said with a chuckle. He swiped his badge on the elevator control panel and pressed the button with the helicopter pad signal.

"Well, thank you anyway," Everett said as the elevator door closed.

The elevator opened right out to the roof, and a helicopter was indeed waiting for us. A pilot was already in his seat and a door was open for us. We got into the helicopter and donned helmets that had been on our seats. They had little speakers and microphones for us to communicate.

"Hey guys, I'm Jimmy. I'll be your pilot this morning." His voice was calm and friendly. We mumbled our hellos, but left out our names, just in case. We buckled into our seats and my hands shook with nerves.

Taking off was like nothing I've ever experienced before, and I felt mildly ill. I swallowed down the feeling and clutched the seat beneath me.

"Where are we going?" Everett asked.

"Hospital in New York," Jimmy replied. "Easton said it would be faster to get you guys there this way, since a few samples are there waiting for you."

"So, you know who we are?" Nate asked cautiously. "And why are we are going to New York?"

Jimmy laughed like we were missing something. "Yes, I am aware. In fact, I know a little more than you guys."

"Like what?" Ev asked.

"I know that Hoffmann and Daisy are part of a group that wants to wipe out most of our country. We've been looking for them for quite a while and this is the closest we've gotten. They want to get rid of almost all women and much of the male population. They would use the women as breeding stock and the men would rule the country," Jimmy explained.

"Um, so like The Handmaid's Tale?" I asked, thinking of the novel by Margaret Atwood and the tv show.

"Sort of. You'd be surprised by how many people and groups want something similar," Jimmy said with a shake of his head.

"Why would they want that?" I asked as Nate took my hand in his.

"They think women make men aggressive and therefore we should get rid of most of the women and use the ones left as breeders and maids," Jimmy explained, not sounding happy to inform us of what we were inadvertently involved in.

"Daisy was for that?" Nate asked Ev.

Ev shifted in his seat and glanced at me. "She would say stuff sometimes. I thought it was only something that got her going."

"You thought killing off most of the population was her *kink*?" Nate asked incredulously.

"No, man! She would talk sometimes about me getting her pregnant and her being the only woman that a bunch of guys had kids with." Everett rubbed his hands over his jeans like his palms were sweaty and shifted in his seat again. "It sounded like orgy stuff. But I never really thought about it."

"I knew there was something wrong with that chick," Nate said.

"Yeah, right," I laughed to diffuse the tension.

"Anyway, we think her job was to keep you three focused on her. If you focused on her and all her antics, you had less time to focus on each other and people outside of your house," Jimmy continued.

"She was always trying to make me and Nate jealous of each other," Everett said and took Nate's hand that wasn't holding mine.

"She tried to make me think you guys would never like me and I shouldn't try to be your friend and especially not more than friends," I said, looking to Nate, who had seen the texts.

"We've seen her texts and pictures to you three and her flirting nature to each of you have us thinking that she was trying to keep you occupied, as separate as possible, and loyal to her," Jimmy said, and his tone suggested finality to the topic.

"Good thing none of it worked," Nate said with a relieved sigh.

"For long, you mean," Everett corrected.

"Eh, I think having to blow up a building before going on the run constitutes as too long," I mumbled. I heard Jimmy huff a laugh in response while both Ev and Nate looked gloomily out the windows.

26

Jimmy dropped us off on the helicopter pad of a hospital in New York City with the instruction to go with the person waiting for us. We landed smoothly, though it was still a nerve-wracking experience. Once we settled on the ground, we looked out the windows and saw three New York City police officers waiting. My stomach churned, and I reached for my guys.

"What the hell?" Everett demanded of Jimmy. His voice was harsh and angry. "I thought we had clearance!"

"You do, for now, until you can prove otherwise," Jimmy said easily. "The cops in the city have been briefed on the situation. Going forward, you will work with them to not only catch the group that Daisy and Hoffmann are a part of, but to prove yourselves innocent. Good luck."

And with that, we hopped out of the helicopter and the police escorted us into the lab in the hospital's basement. Nobody spoke on the way, and it wasn't a comfortable silence. In the basement, they had sectioned a part of the lab off with clear plastic for us to use. A few lab techs were there, but only glanced at us as we entered. They must have known we were coming.

"You are to identify the samples in there and let us know if they are your bacteria," one cop informed us.

"How were these samples found?" Everett asked as we suited up. "I mean to ask- how were the samples gathered? Saliva? Blood?"

"Petri dishes," another cop replied.

"Wait, they were already plated?" Nate asked, getting his gloves on.

"We found them in a location that one suspect had been hiding," the first cop elaborated.

My stomach jumped at the thought of them being close to catching Daisy or Hoffmann. My hands shook slightly as I put my gloves on and I closed my eyes to take steadying breaths. It was looking at some slides and running a few samples through the PCR machine. I could do this.

We worked quietly and diligently as we ran tests on the three samples they had supplied us. We ran the tests a few times to be sure and only found three common bacteria. They could make someone sick but were not life threatening. Basically, what they found in Hoffman or Daisy's hiding spot were three strains of bacteria that would give someone a cold or an upset stomach.

"Why would they have those?" a cop asked us after focusing his body camera on us.

"Well, it's hard to say exactly." Everett ran a hand over his hair and sighed. "Maybe they thought they had something more dangerous. They could be looking for co-infections, so bacteria that will infect a person at the same time as our bacteria and potentially make a person sicker. Or they could be trying to release something that presents with similar symptoms as our bacteria to incite more panic. Honestly, it's difficult to figure out without knowing what their plans were in the first place."

The cops were satisfied with his answer and asked nothing else before escorting us out of the hospital. We walked with our three police escorts to a hotel a few blocks from the hospital and up to the fifth floor. One cop opened the door and gestured for us to enter.

"How long are we here for?" Ev asked, holding the door open.

"I don't know. My orders were to keep you three here until further notice," one of the police said.

"Are we being arrested?" Nate asked.

"Not currently. You're still people of interest and also assets to the investigation, so we'll always have police outside this door. If you think of anything integral to the investigation, let one of us know. Otherwise, we'll let you know when something comes up," the cop said before closing the door with a "Oh, and uh, Merry Christmas."

Nate exhaled sharply. "So, we're just going to wait around until something happens? We should have stayed at East-"

"Shh!" Ev covered Nate's mouth. "I don't know if we're bugged. Let's... I don't know- relax or whatever. It's fucking Christmas Eve. Let's watch some movies and get some rest. We'll be ready when they need us again."

I sat on the edge of the bed and my body felt heavy and drained at the same time. I fought the tears that welled in my eyes. The exhaustion and anxiety had been getting to me and making my ability to manage my emotions difficult. I felt weak and stupid and worthless. All I could think about were my mistakes and the consequences of my mistakes. I wanted to stand up and take responsibility for what I had a hand in, but without finding Daisy and Hoffmann, it would put me and the guys even more in trouble. "If we don't find them, it's our asses on the line. They need closure to this story."

"I know, baby girl," Ev said and sat with me on the bed.

Nate turned on the tv and flipped through the stations before he found a classic Christmas movie. He tossed the remote to us and then headed to the bathroom with the backpack, saying he wanted a shower. Everett ordered some room service since we couldn't leave, and we took turns showering. I napped between them on the bed while they watched movies.

When I woke up, the guys were asleep, and someone had turned the tv off. It was late afternoon, and the sun was shining through the window. I used the single serve coffee machine in our room to make a cup and sat on the couch. While the guys slept, I turned on the TV to watch the news. I wanted to see if any more updates were being aired since we got to New York. A few local stories and a few world news stories played. When my face bracketed by Nate's and Everett's showed on the screen, my stomach lurched. It was a surreal experience to see my face on the news. I had heard the news on the radio and seen a quick news report on the gas station TV, but I hadn't seen our faces on the tv quite like this. "Breaking News update on the situation out of Truman College in Cleveland. New York authorities report the three suspects Evangeline Reid, Nathaniel Gibson, and Everett Monroe have surrendered and are actively working with police to locate remaining suspects Francesca Rossi and Gerald Hoffmann. Authorities believe the remaining suspects to be in New York City and encourage citizens to be aware of their surroundings. More at eleven and on Twitter."

I let out a shaky breath and switched the station to more Christmas movies. I couldn't focus or relax. The whiplash of feeling like my life was about to end, then feeling safe, then feeling like I was being hunted again, was draining. The only time I felt relaxed was when I was in bed with the guys. So, I crawled into bed between them and woke them both up with my hands around their cocks. Nate startled awake slightly but smiled and said, "Hell yeah." Everett woke up smirking at me with a raised eyebrow.

"Good morning, baby girl," Everett rasped.

"It's almost five pm," I informed him. "On Christmas Eve."

"Oh, well Merry Christmas," Everett chuckled.

"Jingle my bells, baby," Nate laughed and settled back onto the pillows.

I took my hand off Nate and gave him a dissatisfied look. He stopped laughing and sat up. His hand shot out and wrapped around my throat, pulling me to look at him closer, almost nose to nose. I wasn't sure if the closeness was part of his dominant persona or because he wasn't wearing his glasses. I got the message either way. "Do not take your hand off my dick until I say so," he growled.

"Yes, sir," I choked out, and his eyes flashed with appreciation.

He let go of me and I returned my hand to his cock, stroking in time with Everett's.

"She needs to be naked," Everett grunted.

Nate gave permission for me to undress, and I did it quickly as the guys also stripped off their clothes. They overwhelmed me in the best way, looking between the two of them. I felt like a child let loose in a candy shop. I wanted to do so many things to and with them and now was my opportunity. Nate grinned darkly when I looked to him for the next demand.

"Good girl, looking to me for directions," he said. "Now, bend over the foot of the bed."

I obeyed and arched my back. Both guys hummed their appreciation. "Ev, eat her out. I want to watch her face as she unravels."

Everett kneeled behind me and tapped the insides of my knees to get me to open my legs further. He licked me slowly in a zigzag from my clit to my pussy, dipped his tongue in, and then slowly zigzagged back. He did this until my legs trembled while Nate sat before me, his hand on his cock. I was panting and my hands fisted in the hotel blanket. Watching Nate while Ev touched me was great, but I needed more. I opened my mouth and looked at Nate and he smiled before sitting up and sliding quickly into my mouth. I gagged when he hit the back of my throat and he pulled back and used my hair to anchor my head as he fucked my mouth.

I was about to come when Nate ordered Ev to stop. I glared up at Nate, who was still fucking into my mouth. "Come up here and let me taste her."

Ev did as he was told and kneeled next to Nate and kissed him. It was hot and wet, and Nate's hips stuttered in their thrusts as he kissed Ev. I reached a hand down to my clit to finish the job, but Nate, who saw what I was doing, stopped me. "No way, beautiful. I want you to ride Ev."

Ev laid down quickly on the bed and looked at me expectantly. I smiled and climbed up the bed, kissing Everett's body as I went. He was hard and ready, his pre-cum leaking down his shaft, and I licked it up before continuing along his body. I kissed him deeply as I straddled him. I tasted myself on his tongue and felt his length press against my entrance. Nate came up behind me and smacked my ass. I jolted at the impact and moaned as Nate pushed me down on Ev's dick. He moved back to allow me to ride Ev. I moved my hips in an oval shape so that I briefly ground my clit against his lower abs before rising, tipping a little for the g-spot stimulation, then lowering back down to do it again. Ev's hands were on my hips, gripping tightly as I moved. I was sweating and dripping with arousal as I rode him with increasing speed and desperation.

Again, as I was about to come, Nate told us to stop. I could have hit him if I wasn't desperate for him to fuck me. Instead, I bit my lip and glowered at him.

Nate came around behind me and also straddled Everett's thighs. He ran his hands lightly over my arms and shoulders, making goosebumps rise. Then he said in my ear so low and quiet that I had to concentrate on his words and not just the vibrations, "I want you to take both of us, beautiful. Think your pretty pussy can handle it?"

I looked down at Everett, my eyes wide. We were both intimately aware of the thickness of Nate's dick. I thought for sure it wouldn't fit with Ev's dick already in me, but I was willing to try.

Nate lowered a hand to my pussy and pressed a finger in alongside Ev's cock. Ev twitched beneath me as Nate's finger also pressed against his cock. Nate pumped in and out a few times before adding a second. I felt the stretch with two fingers. It felt like a slight burn near my opening, and I was worried. Though not enough to stop my arousal from covering his hand and coursing down my thighs. I panted and held on to Everett's shoulders as I felt Nate pull his fingers out of me and replace them with the head of his dick. He was slick as he pressed against my pussy. Nate pushed the head of his dick into me, and I cried out. The burn of the stretch hurt, but faded quickly. I was so focused on the sensation, I didn't realize that both guys were whispering words of encouragement and praise.

"That's a good job, baby girl. You can take it," Everett strained and whispered.

"Your pussy is so amazing, beautiful," Nate panted.

Sweat dripped down my spine and I felt like my lungs were going to burst with how heavy I was breathing. Another part of me felt like it was going to burst, as well. I knew I was going to be sore after this. The guys held still as I gathered myself and got used to the overwhelming stretch and filled feeling.

I opened my eyes and saw Everett below me, his eyes on Nate. They were having a silent, angry conversation, mouthing words to each other. "I don't know! You hurt her!" Everett was mouthing to Nate over my shoulder. I felt Nate respond, his loose hair tickling my back as he shook his head.

"I'm okay," I breathed with a smile.

Ev's eyes snapped back to me and I felt them both relax.

"Okay, so how do we do this?" Nate asked, halfway between his normal voice and his dominant voice. "Do we alternate our pumps?"

I was about to share my thoughts when they moved in opposite directions. For once, they were too impatient to wait for me to speak. Everett pulled out of me, and Nate pushed up into me. I shook my head. "No, it has to be me moving."

Everett lined himself back up and carefully pushed back into me. Since I was more prepared this time, it didn't burn more than a second as he pressed past my opening alongside Nate.

"Woah that's a weird feeling," Nate said with a shudder.

"Yeah, but let's not say anything while we're inside our girlfriend," Everett shot back.

I giggled past my held breath as I again adjusted to the full feeling. I moved up and down on them. For a moment it felt like my insides were about to become outsides, but after lowering back down and lifting again, it began to feel good. Like amazingly good. Sweat beaded on Everett's chest and his face flushed red as his breaths heaved. I heard Nate behind me in a similar state as he rested his head against mine.

As I moved up and down on their dicks, the movement became easier and more pleasurable. I assumed it was because my muscles were loosening, and I hoped they would go back to normal after we were done. Each pump of my hips came with a grunted exhale from Everett and a groan from Nate. I was so focused on the sounds they were making; I didn't realize I was almost squealing. Nate had an arm banded around my middle and a hand above Everett's shoulder on the mattress to brace himself. Everett's hands gripped my thighs tightly as Nate kissed my neck.

It was a few more trembling thrusts before the rushing tidal wave of orgasm ripped through my body. I had stopped moving, and Nate used the arm around my body to move me up and down more for him and Everett. Everett was chanting "Yes, yes," over and over as he watched where our bodies joined. Moisture was pooling between us, a combination of our arousals, sweat, and my release.

Not long after I came, Nate cried out and his hips snapped into me over and over while Ev and I held still to avoid one of them coming out of me again. "Oh my god," Ev groaned, almost pained. "I can feel you coming, man."

"Come with me," Nate demanded, deep and breathless.

Ev chanced a few pumps of his hips and his grunting joined Nate's as he came alongside him, their dicks rubbing against each other within me. Seeing and hearing and feeling them come apart surrounding me kick-started another orgasm that had me clenching down on them, my whole body contracting as I fought down a scream.

When my body relaxed and I was more aware of my surroundings, they leaned me back against Nate's sweaty chest and they both were stroking their hands over me. "Wow," was all I could whisper breathlessly.

They both chuckled. Nate pulled slowly out of me, and Ev hissed in a breath and shivered below me. "My dick is so sensitive right now," he laughed in explanation before he also pulled out. They settled me between them on the bed, and we rested our heads on the pillows. I felt empty now that they were no longer filling me.

"That was amazing," Nate said as I cuddled against him.

"Incredible," Everett said and kissed the back of my neck.

"I didn't know it was possible for us all to do that at the same time," I admitted. "I thought we'd be taking turns forever."

"Well, I don't think we can do that every time," Everett explained. "I think that could hurt you- you're so small. It'll be a sometimes thing."

"It looked like you guys were in pain," I giggled, stroking lines with one finger down Nate's side and watching as goosebumps rose.

The guys shared amused and knowing glances. "Uh, no. We were trying not to blow our loads as soon as we got into you," Nate chuckled.

"Hmm," was all I could hum as an overwhelming feeling of tiredness encompassed me. I yawned and cuddled further into the guys.

I was vaguely aware of them getting up to shower, order food, and turn on the tv. One of them cleaned me up and brushed back my hair while I dozed.

"Baby girl," Ev said softly and trailed a fingertip over my cheek. "Come and eat and get washed up."

I got up and sat with them on the pullout couch while they turned the tv to the news. "Oh, um, apparently we've surrendered to police," I informed them as Ev handed us our plated burgers delivered by room service. "I saw it on the news while you guys were sleeping."

Ev looked thoughtful for a moment. "Well, I guess we technically did."

"Makes us sound guilty still," Nate muttered.

I picked at my burger and fries, barely eating, while the guys wolfed theirs down. They both grabbed food off my plate after I pushed it out. I smiled and looked at them both next to me as they ate and watched the local news. They both had clean, wet hair and had freshly groomed beards. My chest felt like it was going to crack with the weight of affection and love I had for them both.

Nothing had changed on the news, but video of us walking down a hallway with police had been added to the story and the news anchor reported we had been hiding separately from Daisy and Hoffmann and were now working to find them. While the narrative wasn't that we were innocent, it was more forgiving than the earlier reports. There were no fake eyewitness reports, no speculation on our personalities, and no mention of us as "suspected terrorists."

When the news report ended with no updates on Daisy or Hoffmann, I got up for a shower. It was a steaming hot shower, in silence, with real shampoo and conditioner. The shower was certainly an upgrade from the one in the RV and I relished in it. A good shower did wonders for my outlook and as I got out and dried my hair, I felt more positive about finding Daisy and Hoffmann and clearing our names. We needed to think about how our bacteria could spread the most and find Daisy and Hoffmann before they planted it. While I styled my hair, I thought back to the data we had turned in. I opened the bathroom door and called out to the guys. They appeared in the doorway with red, swollen lips. I smiled. "Sorry, I didn't mean to interrupt. I was just thinking about ways to catch Daisy and Hoffmann."

"What did you come up with?" Everett asked, his tone serious. "I've been thinking about it, too."

"Well, I was thinking about the data we turned in to Daisy. We had often added speculations on the ways the bacteria could transmit quickest. I can't remember what all we said since it didn't really matter yet in our research," I said as I braided my hair.

"The work I had turned in last mentioned vehicular as the initial infection," Nate said, his brow furrowed. "I figured that's why they were around the New Year's merchandise."

"The three bacteria we looked at this morning had different modes of transportation," Everett added. "All were low in virulence."

"Yeah, but our bacteria would cause a buildup of pus in the lungs, one of those bacteria was dermatologic and one was gastrointestinal. The other would likely only cause a small fever," I added, my stomach clenching in anxiety. "Together it would cause enough of a confusion and panic that there would be little to no effective treatment soon enough before our bacteria killed the host."

The guys thought about it for a few moments, and we went back to the bed. We sat cross legged and looking at each other, Nate cleaned his glasses on his shirt.

Everett got up after a few silent moments and opened the hotel room door. I heard him quietly tell the police outside that all major tourist areas and events needed to be sanitized with a high alcohol content cleaner regularly and the hospitals should contact us if anyone with suspected lung infections came in. I heard the beeping of their radios as they relayed that information to dispatch.

When Everett returned to us, he had a pen and paper in hand.

"If you were Daisy and Hoffmann and you thought transmission was only going to be vehicular, where would you start?" Nate asked with a sigh.

We worked diligently together and relayed random bits of speculation and information to the police outside. At one point we consulted via a cop's phone with a doctor in a nearby hospital about a lung infection. It ended up being a different pneumonia and not our bacteria after the lab looked at it and verified.

A loud knock woke us near eight in the morning and we were quickly and quietly escorted back to the hospital lab where we had worked the day before.

"Did someone get sick?" Everett asked one cop that had arrived to relieve the overnight shift. "Or are there more plates?"

"They found these on petri dishes," the cop said with finality, meaning we would not get any more information.

I wondered if they were still going through the first location that we had examined bacteria from yesterday or if these were from somewhere else.

Once inside the lab, the door locked behind us, and we suited up silently. The cordoned off area remained for our use. We started preparing the different tests for bacteria identification with little speaking beyond directions. We worked for a few hours before anything got interesting. Nate stepped back from the microscope he was working on and took a shaking breath. "One identify," he whispered. We had come up with our own way of speaking in the lab when we found something interesting, partially out of the need for efficiency and partially out of the need for very little speaking because of my anxiety at the beginning of our project. His call back of that was comforting, but also raised my heart rate at the realization of what he was saying.

Everett rushed over to him and looked through the microscope for a few minutes as he adjusted and looked at more than one place in the sample. “Two confirm,” he said, his jaw tight as he looked at me.

I stepped up to the microscope on my tiptoes and adjusted it to my eye preference and looked at multiple cells within the sample. The stain for the third sample showed similar, if not the same, structures to the bacteria we had been staring at for weeks. “Three absolute,” I whispered.

Nate moved to the radio they left us to communicate to the waiting police, who were sitting in office chairs and on their phones outside of our walled in area. “Hey, um, we might have something. We don’t have our research to compare it to, but we think this is our bacteria. We’ll do more tests to get a more confident answer, but sample number three might be it.”

“Thank you,” one cop replied.

“Where did you find this, anyway?” Nate asked as an afterthought.

“On the suspect we apprehended last night,” was the called back answer.

27

My heart hammered in my throat as we confirmed the similar or the same morphology of the bacteria we had worked on. It was difficult to say with not being able to compare it to our research, but we'd stared at the bacteria in our project for days and weeks. If anyone could identify it based on simple observations, it would be us. It likely would not hold up in court, that much I could gather. But it was going to be a step in the right direction to potentially get a confession out of Daisy or Hoffmann.

We ran a few more tests, so we had more data to present to the police before they asked us to come with them to the station. "Are we going to help identify your suspect?" Everett asked warily as he handed the folder of our data to the police.

The three cops approached us and put handcuffs on us simultaneously. I felt like I was about to vomit. At least, this time someone appropriately read us our Miranda rights and the metal handcuffs were on correctly. My eyes filled with tears as I looked up to see Nate and Everett also being cuffed. They were looking at me and each other with sorrowful but determined expressions. I saw the shimmer of tears in Nate's eyes and Everett's jaw was clenched so tight it shocked me he wasn't cracking teeth.

"It's okay guys," I said to them despite being in front of the police. "We helped the police; we did the right thing."

Nate nodded with a sniff, and Everett's shoulders straightened as they escorted us out of the hospital and into a waiting police van. It was Christmas Day, but teams of media outlets stood beyond a barricade and started shouting questions as the police led us to the van. The media trained cameras on our every move. The cold New York air whipped around me and made my eyes water more. I didn't want to cry in front of the cameras, so I blinked the tears away and stood tall. They pushed Nate into the back of the van in front of me, and I followed him up with Everett behind me. The shouts of the media were loud, and I couldn't pick out any words or phrases. It was one loud roaring in my head. They fastened us to our seats, and the van moved.

"We're going to be alright," Everett whispered. "We helped them today. This is probably a formality."

Somehow that made little sense and didn't seem correct, so I remained quiet and looked down at my jean clad knees. The feeling of being about to vomit didn't go away as they transported us to the police station. I was going to jail. I was going to prison. I was about to be named as a fucking terrorist. I was about to be separated from Nate and Everett. Possibly forever. I couldn't look at them for fear of falling apart. A tightness of my chest and stomach was the only thing that held me upright as it was. The guys were murmuring back and forth, but I couldn't listen to their words. I needed to get ahold of myself. I could not get out of this mess if I couldn't speak. It was going to be necessary to speak to the police and other investigators. I closed my eyes and swallowed a few gulps of air. This is something I could do. We were innocent, and I needed to be able to tell everyone.

We were pulling up to the police station and stopping by the time I had control over my body and mind again. The back doors of the van opened, and bright light and cold air swirled around us.

While we waited to be escorted into the station, I sat up straight. I could do this. I *needed* to do this.

Almost as soon as we stepped onto the slushy sidewalk amidst the shouting media, we were separated. I didn't even see where the guys were taken. They brought me into the station and into an investigation room. The cop that brought me in and undid my handcuffs offered me a coffee. This was a great opportunity to speak with little consequence. "Yes, please. Just milk, if you have it," I said with a confidence only slightly betrayed by the crack in my voice. The cop gave a curt nod and left the room, shutting the door behind him.

They did not handcuff me in the room, and I rubbed at my wrists as I stood in front of the table and chairs. I stretched out my knees, warming my muscles as I warily expected to be sitting in the chair for hours. The clock read three in the afternoon, and I yawned. The door opened and a man who wore a pair of khakis, a crisp white button down, and suspenders delivered my coffee.

"Miss Reid, I'm Agent Allen. I'll be talking with you today," he said. His voice was friendly but assertive as he sat at the table. "Please, come sit."

"Thank you for the coffee," I said and cleared my throat after hearing how hoarse it sounded. I sat at the table and sipped the coffee. It was surprisingly fresh but had clumps of powdered creamer still in it. I sipped slowly, warming my throat. It was quiet as the agent watched me. "Um Agent, as in FBI?"

"Correct," he said. He steepled his dark hands in front of him on the table after showing me his badge.

"Oh," I whispered. "Wow."

"Did you have any plans for the Christmas holiday?" he asked me, his eyes roving over my face and hands. His voice was smooth as he eased into our interrogation with small talk.

I shook my head. "Not really. The project was supposed to still be happening, so I could not go home. I- I'm sorry to keep you from your family."

The corner of his mouth lifted. "Dinner will wait for me. Speaking of family, tell me what Christmas was like with your family."

I sighed and then swallowed some air. "Well, it's only me and my dad since my mom died. We haven't done much to celebrate anything after she passed. We might pick up one of those pre-made dinners at the grocery and eat together. No gifts or anything like that. Not since I graduated high school," I explained with a shrug.

"That sounds sad," he said, clearly baiting me. "It might change someone's outlook on life."

"It did. I'm not going to lie and say I was the happiest person. But my schooling was going to get me somewhere," I said with all honesty.

"I heard you were mute," Agent Allen said after a moment.

"Not mute. I've had speech anxiety since my recovery from the car accident that killed my mom," I replied.

"You seem able to speak right now," he pointed out.

"This is not easy for me. At all." I took another sip of coffee. "I'm... sucking it up."

His mouth lifted into a smirk again. "So, tell me how science was going to get you out of a sad home life?"

"I always liked science growing up. The experiments, finding the unknown, and learning about the world around me. I found the medical world very interesting and inspiring after being in the hospital for a long time and wanted to contribute in a way that I felt comfortable doing. And that was working in labs and creating medicine," I explained, my voice becoming hoarse as I went on.

"How'd you get involved in all this, then?" He asked and gestured around us with a long-fingered hand.

"One of my grad school teachers, Mr. Harris, recommended me for the program. He had sent them some of my work," I replied.

"Who did he send it to?"

"I'm assuming Hoffmann. He told us he was the Professor who oversaw the science PhD students. And he referenced specific parts of my research, so he had read it," I said and then swallowed before continuing. "He's the only person I spoke to from Truman College."

"He's not from the college," Agent Allen said and watched my reaction.

"Oh, I know that now," I said with a slow nod. "I know he wasn't a professor, Daisy wasn't a student, and neither were we. It was all fake." Tears rose to my eyes, and I blinked fiercely. This was the single most important conversation I would ever have in my entire life. I needed to get it together.

"Let's start at the beginning. Tell me how you got involved with the project," Agent Allen said and sat back in his chair.

I told him the story of getting an email from Hoffmann, the interview, and the information that was sent to me. My heart raced when I realized I still had a packet of school and program information at my dad's house. It wasn't the stuff we signed NDAs for, but it was *something* to show that we were unaware and innocent. I told Agent Allen where I had left that packet and he didn't look impressed or interested and I wondered if my dad had already given them that information. I also told the agent about meeting at the school, the NDA paperwork, the promises to pay for our education and degrees, cost of living, stipend, the credit card, Marie Curie, and the lab. My voice was rasping, and I finished my coffee.

"None of that sounded suspicious to you?" Agent Allen asked me, his eyebrows raised.

I smiled at him. "Yes. It sounded too good to be true. A phrase my dad used to say kept popping into my head. He said something like 'If something is free, then you are the real product.' I guess I should have listened to that advice, but I was so excited to have a chance."

He nodded in understanding. "Tell me about your relationship with Daisy."

"She was my friend. Or… I *thought* she was my friend. I've not had many friends in my life on account of not talking much. She was outgoing and outspoken, and I admired that about her. She was good to me for a while until she thought I was romantically involved with Nate, and then she got mad and said some terrible things. And the fact that there were cameras in our house, and I think she was watching us," I said and looked down at my hands.

"Was she involved with Nate?" he asked. "Was she jealous?"

"No, she wasn't involved with Nate. And I don't *know* if she was jealous, but I think she was."

The door opened, and a cop delivered another Styrofoam cup of coffee. I hadn't asked for anything, and Agent Allen hadn't asked for anything, so I knew I was being watched through the mirrors. "Thank you," I told the cop as he left.

"Was she involved with Everett?" Agent Allen asked.

"In the beginning, they hooked up. But it wasn't anything serious," I said with a shake of my head. I sipped the fresh coffee, relishing in the hot liquid on my sore throat.

"How do you know?" he asked.

"The three of us are close. We lived together and could only speak to and see each other for most of that time," I explained.

"Define close."

No sense in lying to a fucking Federal Agent.

"We love each other."

"The three of you?"

"Yes."

"Okay."

"Being isolated then going through a trauma and being named as terrorists together has a bonding effect," I said with a small smile and shifted in my seat, feeling sweaty and uncomfortable.

He chuckled. "You could say that."

He asked a few more questions about the experiment, getting some specifics on our findings and the bacteria we were working with. He asked about the intentions we had with the bacteria, and our plan for finding a cure for it. I was more comfortable talking to him than I had expected. But it's what I needed to do to get to Ev and Nate again. Then we continued discussing the timeline of our project and what it was like finding out it wasn't real. We spoke for another hour about what the bacteria we had been working with would do to a person and how we knew that. We talked about the samples we had studied the past few days and how we arrived at our conclusions. He didn't ask about where we ran to or the stolen car, and I wondered if he already knew about it and maybe worked with Easton. I definitely didn't bring it up.

"Now, let me ask you this: why blow up the lab?" He sat back in his seat again, studying me.

"To destroy the bacteria and our research. If it wasn't being used the way we had intended it to be used, and if Hoffmann had threatened us after we tried to back out, we knew it couldn't continue to exist," I replied. "I know it's not good to blow up a building. I know I'm going to get in trouble for being involved in that. But I need you to know it was either that or potentially have a risk of the bacteria getting out."

"Nothing got out in Cleveland, then?" he asked.

"Nothing as a result of the fire," I said with confidence. "But if they've had samples this whole time, then I can't be sure. I'm sorry."

Agent Allen was quiet as he considered me for some time. "Why'd you go along for so long and then change your mind? I know the steps you went through, but tell me *why* you wanted out when you got out."

I considered this for a moment. It's what I'd been mulling over for days. "I've never had a purpose other than getting out of my home life. And I've never been a person of value to anyone. This project was supposed to give me value and purpose by creating something novel and helping others. I would get my PhD, get my schooling done, and then I'd continue that purpose. If it weren't for Everett and Nate, I'd have likely stayed to be completely honest. But not because I agreed with the mission, but because I feared the confrontation and losing something I had worked towards. Nate and Ev showed me that I, my time, and my work have purpose and value simply by being mine and not only because of my contributions. They gave me what I needed to say 'no, thanks' and try to leave."

Agent Allen was quiet again as he looked me over. "Thank you, Miss Reid." He stood and shook my hand before leaving me alone in the room.

I waited in the room, anxiously stretching out my knees and my back. The door opened about fifteen minutes later and a cop handcuffed me again before he escorted me to a jail cell. It was a holding cell, so it wasn't far from the interrogation room. I was alone in the cell, and I sat on the cot near the back. Talking with Agent Allen had exhausted me, but I didn't want to sleep. A few minutes later, I was leaning against the cool painted cement brick wall, and I heard footsteps coming down the hall outside my cell. Nate was being escorted past me, and I assumed he was going to the interrogation rooms. I said nothing, but he looked up and our eyes made contact. I tried to smile soothingly, knowing he had been waiting in his cell for hours, probably anxiety ridden over what was going to happen. His lips quirked up in a little smile, and I saw his posture relax slightly as he left my field of vision.

I nodded off a few times as I waited for Nate to come back. When the doors beeped open and he came back through, I stood at my door. I raised my eyebrows at him as if to ask if he was okay. He gave a small nod and smile as he went past me. He looked more relaxed than when he went by the first time. I supposed it was a relief to get his story out and to tell it from start to finish, with no confusion.

Everett was next to go by, and the first exchange was like Nate's. I had fallen fast asleep by the time he came back through after his own interrogation. I didn't see any sign of the suspect they had taken in before us. Agent Allen's questions about Daisy made me think it was her they had caught, but I had no confirmation.

Despite the cot being uncomfortable, I slept deeply and soundly, feeling like someone had lifted a weight from my shoulders. If they had gotten enough incriminating evidence against us, we'd be in prison and not a holding cell. Maybe Everett had been right in saying it was only a formality to keep us there. The hope of being acquitted held my dreams until morning.

28

They held us for the full seventy-two hours they could legally hold us for without enough evidence. I had not seen Ev or Nate since we were separated for interrogations. But I knew they were down the hall from me- waiting for our time to leave, like I was. Knowing they were with me was the only thing that comforted me.

Agent Allen had us brought to a meeting room on that third day. I finger combed my hair and wiped my face on my shirt sleeve before I saw the guys, knowing I *looked* like I'd been in a jail cell for three days. My heart lifted when I saw them, grungy and stinky, but standing with me free of handcuffs. I refrained from running to them when I saw them and settled for holding both of their hands and smiling. I would properly greet them… later.

"Francesca Rossi, aka Daisy, was arrested," Agent Allen told us.

The three of us let out relieved sighs and nods.

"Your stories were on track and cleared you three of charges other than arson. Mr. Monroe, your public defender reached out to the school and let them know you were not guilty of the other charges, and the school has dropped their case against you," Agent Allen said, and Everett's hand tightened in mine. "Not to mention, they're facing their own charges."

"Thank you, sir," Everett said to one man in the room with us. I had been so excited to get back to my guys that I hadn't even noticed who was in the room with us. I looked around now and saw a few police officers, a few people dressed similarly to Agent Allen, and a few people who dressed more casually. Three of the cops in the room had been with us the past few days.

"We had apprehended Miss Rossi before we brought you three in. Our own investigators substantiated your contributions in analyzing the samples and the data you provided. Your identification of the bacteria led to her arrest, and she is awaiting trial for her crimes. Gerald Hoffmann remains at large, though Miss Rossi alleges he does not have possession of the bacteria," Agent Allen continued.

My heart was soaring. We were free. We helped. Daisy was behind bars.

We were *free.*

"What's the next step?" Nate asked, his palm was sweaty in mine. He was still nervous. I squeezed him.

"You three are free to go. Your research was recovered and is in evidence. We will handle creating a cure for it if they release it. We may contact you about the investigation, but you are free to go home. Again, Hoffmann is still at large, and I suggest you be aware of your surroundings until we apprehend him," Agent Allen said with a smile on his face, despite his warning.

"Thank you," I said, my voice catching.

"I hope to see good things from you three," he said, and people around us murmured their agreements.

We left the meeting room escorted by one cop who brought us to the lobby and returned our belongings to us. It was only the guys' wallets and the backpack with spare clothes and a first aid kit that Easton had given us. The news was playing, and the cop pointed it out to us while he turned the volume up with a remote that was behind the front desk. "Take a look at that," he said good-naturedly.

It was a national news station playing the latest update to our story. The same pictures of us that had been showing on news stations across the country for a week now had the word "Innocent" over them. The screen flashed to a mug shot of Daisy and had information about her arrest playing. But we turned to each other instead of watching. Tears fell freely from my eyes as I reached up to them. They enclosed me in their arms, and we all embraced while laughing and crying our relief. They smelled like unwashed boys and nervous sweat, but I breathed them in, nonetheless.

"Fucking hell, that was the scariest thing to ever happen to me," Nate said, while kissing the top of my head.

"No kidding," Everett scoffed and was the first to break away.

"Let's get out of here," I said, and looked at the doors. I could hear the din of reporters outside the doors, but I wanted to leave more than anything.

"Yes, ma'am," Everett said, and we headed towards the doors as a unit. We opened the doors, and a blast of cold air and noise met us as people started shouting to us. Reporters and cameras crowded us, but we clutched each other's hands and pushed to the street where a few cabs were slowly driving by. Nate waved one down and we quickly got in and shut the door.

The driver looked at us with a furrowed brow, like he was wary of picking us up outside the police station. He must have recognized us. "We're innocent. It's all over the news," I said.

Nate squeezed my knee.

The cab driver's brow relaxed, and he nodded in understanding. "Alright, so where are you headed?"

I paused. Where *were* we going? I looked to Nate, whose open mouth and raised eyebrows told me he also didn't know.

"Airport, please," Everett told the driver.

"Airport? Why?" Nate asked.

Everett smirked at us with his signature cool smirk. "I'm taking you both home."

"Breaking News on the Truman College attack in Cleveland. Three previous suspects have been cleared of charges. New York City police and federal investigators on the case report Evangeline Reid, Nathaniel Gibson, and Everett Monroe are not guilty of the suspected act of terrorism. Francesca Rossi, who Reid identified as Daisy in her speech to Cleveland Police dash cam, has been arrested for possession of the illness-causing bacteria. A Gerald Hoffman remains at large...."

"... Real culprit was apprehended with aid from the trio of college students previously suspected of the crime...."

"... No harm has come of the fire in Cleveland and the college dropped their charge against Monroe...."

We booked the first available flight out of New York to Tennessee. During our wait for the flight, we paid for a lounge pass to use a shower and eat at a buffet. We had been fed at the jail, but it hadn't been good food. I was starving for our first meal as free people. We were each freshly showered and wearing clothes we had bought in the shops at the airport. I couldn't stand another day in the same clothes. Everett and I were getting started on the buffet we had splurged for when Nate joined us. His wet hair was slicked back into a bun, and he was wearing a t-shirt boasting "I love New York."

I laughed and Everett tsked.

"What? I've never been here before," Nate defended, rubbing his belly and looking over my head at the food on the buffet.

"We didn't tour the place, we were fucking locked up," Everett scolded.

"Yeah, well, I'm never coming back here so I grabbed a souvenir," Nate said and grabbed a plate and started filling it high with food. "'I got arrested in New York and all I got was this t-shirt' was sold out."

"That's so... I don't know, tacky or something," Everett said and joined him in line.

I giggled again. They looked at me with eyebrows raised. I laughed now.

"What?" Everett asked me. "What's so funny?"

I looked around to see nobody looking at us and lowered the waistband of my new black sweatpants to show the thick white waistband of a pair of panties. "I *heart* NYC" printed on the waistband in the iconic font of all the tourist merchandise. Nate howled in laughter as he continued down the buffet. Everett shook his head, but a smile played on his lips.

Once we had landed in Tennessee, it was late in the evening, but we headed to Everett's family farm. We still had no phones, so we hadn't called ahead. Everett insisted they knew we were coming. We pulled up in a rented car to see a few cars in the driveway. One of which was Easton's truck. Someone must have driven it back to him after we left it on our way to New York. I couldn't even remember the name of the place we'd been before the helicopter ride. I had completely forgotten about the abandoned car. "No way," Everett chuckled as he threw the car into park. I smiled as we got out of the car. Lights were on inside the farmhouse despite the late hour.

A woman burst out of the front door and barreled towards us. I assumed this to be Everett's mom, and I choked on the breath I was taking. Nate put an arm around me as if he knew what I was feeling, seeing Ev and his mom reunite. The woman was shorter than Ev, but not short by any means. She was tall and strong and had his piercing blue eyes. He held on to her and buried his nose in her neck while she sobbed and prayed. It was minutes before she pulled away, wiped Everett's eyes and her own, and then turned to us.

"Oh, sweethearts," she said and ran to us, enveloping us in her arms. Her embrace with Nate and me was no less tight or heartwarming than the one she shared with Everett. I hugged her in return, and she smelled of warm hay and crisp apples. Before she left, I breathed her in. I looked up to see Everett shaking his dad's hand and hugging Easton on the big porch. "Come inside. I've got a room ready for you."

I looked at Nate, who shrugged in return.

"Yes, I know about you three. I won't pretend to understand, but I'll love you like my own anyway," Mrs. Monroe said after seeing our exchange.

Everett heard her and came over to stand between Nate and me, his arms around us both. "Mama, Dad, this is Eva and Nate."

"Welcome, home," Mr. Monroe said. His gruff voice sounded sincere, and I saw where Everett got his voice.

We were ushered into the house, given glasses of iced tea, and offered supper. We had eaten our fair share at the buffet, so we declined the food to the frowned disappointment of Mrs. Monroe. She put out a tin of cookies and we each took one to make her happy.

"What are you doing here?" Everett asked Easton.

Easton smiled. "Mom and Dad deserve to know the truth about what I've been doing," he explained. Mr. and Mrs. Monroe looked proudly at Easton. "And I couldn't have my little brother being the only hero around here."

"I don't know about 'hero,'" Everett scoffed. "I think we're just labeled as 'Not Guilty.'"

Easton shrugged like he knew something.

Mr. Monroe asked about what happened and we took turns telling the story. While it had taken me hours in the interrogation room with Agent Allen, it took all of fifteen minutes for us to tell the Monroes. They listened intently, asked only a few questions, then expressed their thankfulness for our being safe. It was a new feeling, to be listened to and respected, and one that I thoroughly enjoyed.

Mrs. Monroe showed us to Everett's old bedroom, where she had made up the bed and left towels and toiletries on the old desk. We stood in the bedroom after she left, alone for the first time since before we'd been arrested. Everett pulled us into a hug and kissed us both. Nate kissed me after.

"We're free," Nate said, closing his eyes.

"Do you guys still want… this? I would understand if you didn't," Everett asked, his voice hesitant. He backed away from us and sat on the edge of the full-sized bed, not making eye contact.

"What do you mean?" Nate asked, suspicious.

"I mean, did you two still want to be together, all three of us?" Everett clarified and swallowed.

"You're a dumbass," I said, my hands on my hips.

Ev's head shot up and he looked at me with wide eyes.

"What she said," Nate agreed and crossed his arms over his chest.

Ev rubbed the back of his neck. "I want you both to be sure."

"I stand by my original statement: you're a dumbass," I repeated and pushed at his shoulder.

Nate chuckled.

"Alright, since that's out of the way," Everett said. His tone lightened, and he smiled at us. "What are we going to do now?"

"I don't care. We're staying together and that's all I need to know," Nate said and sat next to Everett on the blue quilt.

"I was hoping we could stay here and think about it before we decide to go anywhere," Everett said, and pulled me onto his lap.

"I think that's a great idea," I agreed and snuggled into Ev's chest.

We spent most of the next few days in bed. We slept, we had sex, and we avoided contact with everyone. Mrs. Monroe delivered food and water to us and often found us asleep or quietly reading. She knew we needed time to rest and delivered blankets, cookies, library books, and chamomile tea regularly. We came out of our hibernation after the new year and started interacting with the Monroes again. Easton had stayed for the New Year and to visit with his parents more.

New Year's Eve celebrations all over the country were canceled or had increased security. We opted not to watch any of the holiday shows, not wanting to see the New Year's merchandise be used. We knew the authorities had cleaned or replaced the merchandise and decorations, but we still felt anxious. No incidents occurred like Daisy and Hoffmann had planned, and everyone was safe.

A few news stations reached out to us for interviews, and we agreed to a few of them. We filmed them in the Monroe's living room, with the large fireplace in the background and family portraits on the hearth. We knew closure was needed and our names needed to be cleared if we ever wanted to have a life after this. Closure for us meant telling our story and maintaining our honor. It meant standing tall, speaking out, and knowing our merit.

29

TWO YEARS LATER

My phone was ringing on the table near where I had been sitting for lunch. I stopped pouring my coffee and went to it when I saw Nate's name. He rarely called during the day, seeing as he often spent his lunch helping his students with their homework. Nate had turned his love of science and cheerful personality into a career of teaching middle schoolers basic biology.

"Mr. Gibson, to what do I owe this pleasure?" I teased as I answered.

"They got him," Nate said breathlessly on the other end.

"Who?" I asked, dropping my teasing tone.

I heard the crunch of gravel as he jogged, and then the beeping sound of his car unlocking as he approached it. "Hoffmann!"

"Holy shit, you're kidding!" I said and rushed to the break room TV and turned it on. The scrolling text on the news channel confirmed what he was saying. "Did you tell Ev?"

"No, I called you first. You're the furthest from home," Nate said, and I heard him driving out of the parking lot.

I worked in the lab Everett and I started eighteen months ago. He had continued working on the family farm, but we had opened a lab and hired a great team to work on creating safer pesticides and antibiotics for animals. It had been Everett's dream from the start, and I found purpose, comfort, and pride in my work. Today, Ev was working with a few local farmers who had agreed to trial some of our products.

"Okay, I'll be home in thirty," I said and hung up.

I let my team know I was leaving and quickly packed up. I had learned to drive in the few weeks after we'd gotten to Tennessee, and was now comfortable, and licensed, behind the wheel. Driving home, I thought back to Daisy's trial. It happened quickly, as investigators had hoped to find information about her radical group in her testimony, but she betrayed nothing. She was found guilty and our testimonies aided in her conviction. It hadn't felt like closure knowing Hoffmann and other members of the group were out there, but it had felt good seeing the progress.

I tuned my radio to a local station, and I heard the news reporter come on. "News out of Los Angeles this morning where a Gerald Hoffmann has been apprehended. Hoffmann is believed to be a member of a radical group responsible for the planned biological attacks on New York City two years ago. Francesca Rossi was apprehended in New York at the time of the planned attack after three college students were set to take the blame. Hoffmann was reported to be apprehended with the same biological weapon Rossi had been in possession of at the time of her arrest. Officials say the weapon has not been activated, and the city remains safe."

I pulled into the driveway of the house that had once been the "Old Barn" on the Monroe's property before we had it renovated to be our home. Everett wanted to stay near his parents and the farm since he was set to inherit it when they retired, and Nate and I felt no ties to our home states. Nate's parents visited in the summer for a week, and he kept a positive relationship with his mom. His relationship with his dad remained tense, though less combative than Nate had described in the past. My dad called occasionally, and my relationship with him had continued to wane. His grief over losing my mom had been so ingrained in his daily life that moving forward seemed impossible, so he never changed his ways. I knew he felt relief knowing I was safe and settled, but he didn't know how to express it other than letting go.

I jumped out of the car and met both Nate and Everett on our front porch, where they were waiting for me. We embraced before settling on the front steps in the warm sun. Nate grabbed us a few bottles of beer from the fridge and returned to us to celebrate. Nate was wearing his teacher's uniform of khaki pants, a pale blue button down, and his school's lanyard ID. A few binder clips lined the cuff of his right sleeve, and a pencil was still behind his left ear. He had cut his hair and still wore it long but cleanly styled. Everett was wearing a pair of dirty jeans and a fitted and worn dark gray t-shirt. His short hair was flattened where his hat had smashed it down, and he had mud on one knee. He knocked his boots together to get some of the caked-on mud off as he snapped open his beer. I was wearing my black slacks, pale pink button-down blouse, and my stark white lab coat. My last name was embroidered on the pocket of my lab coat, and I tied my hair back in a slick ponytail. I was looking at us with admiration of our achievements over the past two years, comparing our appearances and demeanors to the ones we'd worn when we limped home to Tennessee.

"It's over now, right?" Nate asked us.

"For us it is," Everett answered, and sipped from his beer.

"Finally," I said, my voice choked with emotion.

"Technically, there could be more of them out there," Nate said, apprehension in his voice.

Everett squeezed Nate's knee comfortingly. "Those others don't know us. They don't care about us. And coming after us would only get them caught. We're safe."

Nate swallowed a large gulp of his beer.

"Let's celebrate," I said, my heart beating hard in my chest. My tone was light but higher in pitch than usual as I stood. Both guys turned to look at me. Nate's expression was one of confusion, and Everett's was wary. "Wait here." I turned and went into the house, the screen door shutting behind me.

"Think it's lingerie?" I heard Nate ask Everett.

I giggled as I went up to our master bathroom and rummaged under the sink for the tampon box in the back. I grinned as I pulled out two ring boxes. It had been with my first paycheck that I'd gone out and bought the guys' rings. It was silly and a little unorthodox, but so was our entire life. I sat on my haunches before the sink cabinet and thought back to the terribly anxious, silent, and unsure person I was when I walked into the house at Truman College. I owed everything I had the courage to be to these men. And I wanted to show them how much they meant to me. I slipped the boxes into my deep lab coat pocket and hurried back outside. They were still on the front steps and my heart beat wildly when I saw them.

I didn't have a speech planned. No grand declarations. No balloons, no roses, no secret camera to catch their reactions. It was us, on the porch, with a few beers, and the sound of tractors and birds in the distance. I hopped down the steps and turned to face them in front of where their legs were outstretched in the dry dirt. I couldn't look at their faces yet, so I reached into my pocket and pulled out both boxes. Everett's cowboy boot dragged backwards and clunked against the wooden step as he sat up suddenly from his relaxed sprawl, seeing what I was holding. I got down on one knee and, with shaking and fumbling fingers, opened each box and held them out. I almost tipped over in my nervousness and contemplated getting on both knees rather than one.

"W- will you guys marry me?" I rasped out. My voice had become stronger in my time with them, but the nerves in proposing nearly erased all my progress and I fought a cough. I looked up to see them both, slack jawed and frozen.

Neither one said anything. Neither one moved.

"Is that a no?" I asked and did cough this time. I suddenly understood why people got frustrated with my lack of speech as I was growing up.

They both startled out of their stares at the same time.

"It's a yes, baby girl."

"Fuck yeah."

And I was promptly tackled to our river stone and gravel path. Hoffmann being arrested was the end of an era for us. The end of a nightmare. Two years ago, we thought it was going to be *our* end-*our* demise. But we stood up for ourselves and found honor in doing what was right, even if we were risking ourselves in the process. So, this was only our beginning.

Cat Austen is a romance author based in Ohio. She lives with her husband and their two boys. She enjoys gardening and baking and is a voracious reader of romance novels. Convergence is her first novel.

Connect with her on TikTok and Instagram @CatAustenAuthor . Her newsletter is available at catausten.com/subscribe . Subscribe for ARC opportunities and new books!

Printed in the USA
CPSIA information can be obtained
at www.ICGtesting.com
JSHW022350071123
51398JS00005B/121

9 798989 387311